NICE GIRLS FINISH FIRST

(SOMETIMES)

MEGAN WARGULA

To all the invisible kids, this book is for you. Trust me when I say that life gets better after high school. I hope this book gives you the bravery and confidence I wish I had in high school. Be bold (and nice)!

To Evan, thank you for your kindness and for making me feel seen. I appreciate you more than you will ever know!

Of course this book HAD to have playlists! Back then, we called these mixtapes. ;) Here are links to 3 mixtapes you'll find in the story. I tried to name them in a way that wouldn't spoil anything should you want to listen while you read.

www.MeganWargula.com/Playlists

www.HoundAndThistle.com

Ordering Information:

Quantity sales. Special discounts are available on quantity purchases by corporations, associations, and others. For details, contact the publisher at the address above.

Printed in the United States of America

Publisher's Cataloging-in-Publication data

Wargula, Megan.

Good Girls Finish First (Sometimes) / Megan Wargula

p. cm.

ISBN 978-0-9973807-8-1

Library of Congress Control Number: TBD

First Edition

14 13 12 11 10 / 10 9 8 7 6 5 4 3 2 1

Chapter 1

Sloane

August 1992

My stomach twists with a combination of anxiety and excitement as I pull my car into my assigned parking space on the side of Dunwoody High School. Senior year; thank God I'm almost done with high school and all the exclusive cliques here at DHS. I turn up the volume on my stereo as the organ notes from R.E.M.'s "Stand" sound. I made a mixtape, "Sloane's Senior Songs Vol. 1," to pump me up for school and this upbeat tune from one of my favorite bands was a must.

As I tap my fingers on my steering wheel, gathering the courage to start my day, I watch students filing into school and note how distinct all the groups are. I'm sure every school has the jocks, cheerleaders, brainiacs, artsy kids, stoners, metalheads, the girls who probably go through cases of Aqua Net hairspray getting their huge hair just so, but I wonder if all schools have the invisible kids. The kids who don't feel like they belong anywhere, who just exist on the outskirts of all these other groups. I am one of those kids and with this being my senior year, I'd really like to feel included for a change.

I read an interview with R.E.M.'s singer, Michael Stipe, where he talked about the meaning of this song and it made me like it even more. He said, "It's about making decisions and actually living your life rather than letting it happen."

Man, that really hit me. I feel like I've just let life happen to me. Like I'm a boat just floating around wherever the water takes me, not sailing in the direction I want to go. Don't even ask me where I want to go to college because I'm not sure yet. That's something I have to figure out. One thing I would love is a boyfriend, or heck, a date to prom. I've never been asked to a school dance and I've never had a boyfriend, so that should tell you something about me. While I don't want to be picky, I'd love to date an athlete; a football or baseball player, someone tall. I've daydreamed about it and had crushes, but no one has ever been interested. I think there are a couple of reasons for that:

1. I'm six feet tall. My options are severely limited.

2. I'm built like a string bean, not a lot of curves happening over here.

3. Let's just say I have morals and self-respect.

I think I might be considered a prude because I'm not a partier. It's hard to party when you don't get invited to parties or know where the parties are. But let's be real, I'm more likely to be the designated driver and make sure everyone gets home safely than the one puking in the bushes. Maybe that should be my selling point. Who wouldn't want a responsible friend like me? Plus, I'm super shy, like introverted times a thousand. I don't have a close friend group here, just lots of acquaintances because I'm nice to everyone.

I wipe dust off the dash of my hand-me-down car, my dad's 1984 Peugeot. My older sister, Erin, drove it until I started driving, and she got a new car. My middle sister, Bryn, is only 15 months older than me, but she almost died when she was born and has some issues related to that, so she's not driving yet. I have the car now, and I love it. It has power windows and doors, heated seats, and a sunroof, but it's inoperable and has a tennis ball stuffed into it so it doesn't leak when it rains. This car gives me freedom and that's all I care about, that and a great stereo. I turn up the volume as Michael Stipe's voice whines, encouraging us to look around.

I pick up my tape case as Stipe's voice says "Stand" one last time with emphasis on the 'd' and the song ends definitively. I turn off my car before "Alison's Starting to Happen" by The Lemonheads starts because that will be a good one to hear at the end of the day.

I shoulder my backpack when I step out of the car and take a deep breath of humid Georgia air. The parking lot is a flurry of activity with younger kids being dropped off by their parents and buses dropping kids off around front. First day of school jitters are normal for everyone but add a little (or a lot) of anxiety and introversion, plus your best friend already off to college, and those jitters are multiplied by ten—or more.

I cross the parking lot, then walk down the cement steps in my white Sam & Libby ballet flats toward the lower level of school. A flannel shirt falls from the waist of the person in front of me. "Hey!" I call out as I hop down a couple steps then lean down to pick up the blue and brown plaid shirt. As I begin to stand, my head knocks into something hard. "Ouch." My free hand instinctively goes to my head, and I look up and see that the boy in front of me is also holding his head.

"Ow, sorry. Are you okay?" the boy asks.

I'm stunned, not because our heads hit that hard, but because I've just laid eyes on the most beautiful boy in the world, Tyler Finlay. I rub my head and hold out the flannel. "Uh, yeah. You dropped this."

Tyler smiles and I think I might just melt into a puddle right here on the steps. He reaches for his shirt. "Thanks." His eyes search me as his smile fades and concern knits in his brow. "Are you sure you're okay?"

Get it together, Sloane, I think to myself. I blink hard and smile, tugging self-consciously on my shirt hem. "Yeah, um, sorry. I'm fine. Are you okay?"

Tyler mimics knocking his knuckles on the side of his head as students hustle past us on my left. "Oh yeah, this thing has felt worse. Thanks again!" He holds up his shirt then turns toward the doors and his smile makes my pulse race. With that, the beautiful football/baseball player with rebel vibes walks into the building and it takes me a minute to remember to which class I'm heading.

Chapter 2

Sloane

My first class is AP French and for me, a great way to start the day. I love French class and this year, our class should be small since only two years of a foreign language are required and only the truly devoted take it after that. There aren't many of us who stuck with French for five years. I never had a desire to take home economics which most kids took in eighth grade, so me and the dozen or so other kids who started French in eighth grade have made it to AP French.

I slide into a seat in Madame Carney's class, facing the door and take the front seat in the row. This is the same seat I had last year, but I had my best friend Tameka next to me. She's a year older and graduated last year. Madame Carney's class is set up with one small section facing front and the two side sections facing each other, but angled toward the front, so we can all see each other and our teacher. I love Madame Carney. She's tall and slim like me with a gentle disposition. Her naturally curly hair is a white blonde, just a shade darker than her fair skin. Last year, I was in a class with mostly seniors. That's where I made friends with Tameka Grant, my best friend who is in college in Alabama this year. Tameka and I became fast friends and spent most of the summer together. We are complete opposites in so many ways, but maybe that's why we get along so well. I'm really tall and thin and my skin is pale, and she is really short and curvy and her skin is dark. We joke that she got all the curves and I got none. Literally, none. She also attracts a lot of attention from guys and, you guessed it, I do not.

Kurt Stone ambles in wearing baggie jeans and a white Descendents T-shirt featuring a black line drawing of a guy wearing glasses, a shirt, and tie. He slides into the seat next to mine. "Sloane!" he exclaims as he drops his navy JanSport backpack to the floor. "From French 101 in eighth grade to AP Français. Can you believe this is our last year?" When Kurt and I sat next to each other in French 101 our freshman year, he doodled band names on my yellow folder. He repeatedly asked me to come swimming at his house, but I repeatedly turned him down. Not because I didn't like him, I did, but because I was so self-conscious of my flat-chested body and didn't want to be in a swimsuit in front of him. Four years later, I'm still waiting to fill out, but Kurt and I are friends, so that's cool. Like most of my school friends, we don't hang out outside of school, but we have a good time together in class. Kurt's one of the few people in school I know who listens to good music and is goofy like me--two great qualities in a friend.

"You know I can't wait to get out of here." I smile. "I'm so glad we're in class together again. I missed you last year."

"Me, too." He smiles back. "This year is gonna rock."

"You think?" I ask.

Kurt nods. "Senior year is supposed to be way easier than junior year, and we have cool things to look forward to like dances, Spring Break, our senior prank, all the rites of passage."

I let out a breath. "I think I'm just over the people and cliques, you know?"

Kurt nods, "The cliques are definitely tight here." He jokes, "If anyone is mean to you, you let me know."

I smile at his kindness and we both know he's not going to beat anyone up. Kurt and I have known each other since his family moved here in fourth grade when we were both awkward and wore braces. Neither of us is confrontational. "It's not like anyone is outwardly mean. Sure, I've caught girls talking behind my back or judging the way I look, but generally people are okay. It's just..." I think about how to define what my experience has been at this school. "That friendliness doesn't extend to outside of school, you know?"

Kurt frowns. "Well, we'll have to change that this year."

I half-joke, "I would just love to get asked to prom. How pathetic would it be if I don't even get asked to my senior prom?"

Kurt laughs, "You'll totally get asked to prom." He pulls a notebook out of his bag, and I notice the band stickers on the front.

I'm not so sure about that but I nod at his notebook, moving the conversation to something lighter. "Did you see any good bands this summer?"

"Yeah—" he starts but is interrupted.

"*Bonjour, chats sauvages!*" Amber Gates sings the French term for our school mascot, wildcats, as she saunters into the room in her red, white, and blue cheerleading uniform, her long, jet black hair trailing down her back.

"*Bonjour*, Amber!" Madame Carney says.

"Ugh," I whisper to Kurt. "She's definitely one who is not so nice. While I missed having you in my class last year, I certainly didn't miss her."

Kurt chuckles. "I know. I did envy you for that."

"How is she so popular anyway? She's been popular since the fourth grade, and since junior high has gotten more insufferable every year."

Kurt looks at me, "Let's just say you have principles that I don't think she does."

I look at Amber. She is not someone who you would say is pretty nor is she ugly, physically anyway, though she does often wear an expression as if she's just smelled something foul. Her body on the other hand is much more like Tameka's than mine, petite with curves all over. "I may die a lonely, single woman, but at least I'll have my principles," I joke.

Kurt stifles a laugh and covers his mouth with his hand. "Dude, guys are going to be falling all over themselves to get to you in college."

I let out a jaded laugh. "We'll see." I can't imagine a world where guys would be throwing themselves at me, but I hope Kurt is right and that things are different once I'm out of here.

Derek Cone, a blond boy who was the only other junior in my French class last year walks in and sits behind me. As we exchange a greeting, Ramsey Huff and Diana "Di" Carroll walk in together and sit on the other side of Kurt, closer to Amber. Ramsey, Diana, and I went on a French immersion weekend over the summer and they were really nice to me. Ramsey is a cheerleader and part of the popular crowd, but is super sweet, unlike some in her clique, Amber being the worst. Di is nice as well, and part of the cool crowd who tend to be artsy and into music, stuff like The Who, Led Zeppelin, Jimi Hendrix, and Pink Floyd.

I turn around after talking to Derek and Ramsey says, "Hey Sloane," with a bright smile. Amber's eyes bulge momentarily, then she rolls her eyes and turns to Ramsey.

"Hey Ramsey, Hey Di," I say to them as Di smiles and waves before pulling her notebook out. I'm glad there are some friendly faces in the group, but I know that even though I had fun with Ramsey and Di on our trip, that won't translate to being friends outside of school. It never does. The cliques are so tight, and maybe I'm just not that interesting to my peers. Or, maybe I'm just too much of a goody-goody.

Madame Carney interrupts my thoughts and asks us to tell the class, *en français*, what we did over the summer. I kissed a boy for the first time, I think to myself. Yeah, I know, seventeen is a little old for a first kiss, but boys just aren't into me. Of course, I will keep that to myself. The boy I kissed goes to a different school and I think about how nice it would be if a boy from my school wanted to kiss me, but I'm not holding my breath. I think about Tyler Finlay and daydream about what it would be like to date a boy like him. I'm good at daydreaming, but my daydreams never turn into reality.

Chapter 3

Sloane

Homeroom is after French class and is organized by our last name. When I get to my room, the teacher is waiting at the door. "Welcome, I'm Mrs. Hyde." She is a petite older woman with short dark hair and a genuine smile, wearing a long navy skirt and plaid blouse with a bow tied at the neck.

"Hi," I smile back, "I'm Sloane Warren."

Mrs. Hyde scans the paper on her clipboard and makes a check by my name. "I have the seats set up alphabetically. Yours will be in the last row on the far side of the room, up against the wall as I only have the beginning of the 'W's'." She points her pen to the far side of the room.

"Thanks," I say as I enter the room and head to find my spot. My name is on a piece of paper in the middle of the row. I actually like that I'm in the last row because I can see the whole room. I sit and watch as my fellow classmates make their way to their seats before the final bell. I've grown accustomed to not having acquaintances in my homerooms over the years. I don't know why, but alphabetically they were elsewhere. At least homeroom isn't long.

After the bell rings, Mrs. Hyde closes the door and welcomes us before going over how things will work in her room. She seems nice and easy-going, so that's cool. After she's done, the morning announcements start with the Pledge of Allegiance. As we all stand at attention, reciting the Pledge, I think back to elementary school. My mind has a tendency to wander. At the very beginning of elementary school, when we had a male principal, they would play the Beach Boys' *Good Vibrations* as the theme song of the announcements. That might have been the first time I heard the Beach Boys. I loved that song so much. It's nostalgic because it reminds me of elementary school. Looking back, the song in full may not be appropriate for elementary school morning announcements, but it was pretty cool that our principal used it, and he only used the chorus. "Good, good, good, good vibrations." Gosh, those harmonies! And the instrumentation! The Beach Boys made some really beautiful music. If our principal used that song to begin our day with a good start, with good vibrations, it totally worked for me. Maybe that's where my love of music started?

After the Pledge, a familiar voice resonates through the speakers. "Welcome back, Wildcats!" The booming voice is that of our fellow senior Brian Applequist. Brian is a football and baseball player and is the "Voice of Dunwoody High." He emcees all the events at school like the Mister and Miss DHS competition, the Battle of the Bands, and the morning announcements. Brian and I always seem to be in the same math classes and English last year after I dropped down from advanced to general to have Miss Rockett again. We're not friends but friendly to each other. As I listen to Brian, I recall that he's best friends with Tyler Finlay, the boy who I bumped heads with this morning. Now I'm daydreaming about the dreamiest boy in school again.

Colt Walker, a diminutive blond guy who's on the wrestling team and can be a bit of a troublemaker turns sideways in his chair, "I heard Brian is starting his own TV show on a cable access channel."

I cock my head, snapping out of my daydream. "Really?"

Colt nods. "Yeah, he apparently interned at Channel 2 over the summer and I guess he decided to start his own show."

My eyes grow wide. "Wow, that's cool. Like his own Wayne's World?"

Colt chuckles. "Uh-huh, I guess so."

"I wonder if it'll be funny like Wayne's World." I say as I open my spiral notebook and start doodling.

"Knowing Brian, it'll probably be about baseball, football, or cars."

"That's cool," I say, still doodling.

"But I also heard something about him documenting the lives of high schoolers, so who knows what he's up to."

"Good for him." I mean it, too. People should go after what they really want. It's finding out what you really want that's the hard part, and Brian Applequist seemed to be well on his way to having that figured out at seventeen. How lucky. He's definitely not letting life happen to him.

Chapter 4

Sloane

Marine biology is after homeroom and I am so excited for this class. Science is hit or miss for me, but marine bio interests me in ways other science classes don't, like chemistry. That was a tough one. Coach Knight is the teacher and baseball coach at DHS, and he has a room full of aquariums with various critters inside. The room has two doors, one at the front of the classroom and one at the back. I walk in the back door and survey the main rows of black lab tables facing Coach K's desk and the blackboard. They are mostly full. I guess I'm not as early as I like. The main section of lab tables is flanked on each side by one long row of tables, set end to end, each facing into the room. While I prefer facing out, the long row on that side of the room is already occupied, notably by Lori Tanner who isn't friendly toward me, but I have no idea why. Lori catches my gaze and her eyes narrow. I'm definitely not heading over there. As I anxiously try to figure out where to sit, the first bell rings. I walk to the table immediately to my left, the long row that faces into the room, our back to the doors.

"Sloaner-loner! What's up?" says the boy with the flat-top haircut and Garth Brooks T-shirt.

I roll my eyes at the nickname. "Billy, how's it going?" I ask as I plop into the chair next to him, sliding off my backpack and setting it on the table in front of me.

"Good, buddy. I missed you in Mrs. Lynch's class last year," he says as he opens his notebook.

Mrs. Lynch's class was where I acquired that very appropriate-for-me nickname from Billy. "Ugh, I couldn't take that class," I say. "Beowulf was killing me. I read so many good books in Miss Rockett's class. I'm glad I made the switch." Most people would say that dropping from AP English to general is a dumb move, but I wanted to learn and be inspired, so I dropped down and loved that class. I might regret not having that credit in college, but a great teacher makes all the difference. English is one of my favorite subjects, especially since I like writing and I didn't want to waste a good class on a boring teacher.

The final bell rings, and I hear Coach K say, "Hustle, hustle!"

I look up to my left, and a boy rushes in the front door. My heart skips a beat. Coach is smiling and pats him on the shoulder before shutting the door. The boy plops down in the closest available seat—right next to me. He sets his backpack on the table and looks at me, his dark hair falling across his right eye. "Hey," his eyes alight with recognition. "How's your head?"

I reflexively touch the spot where our heads knocked together this morning. "Totally fine." I return his smile, impressed with myself for being able to speak in his presence.

"I'm Tyler." His smile practically melts me right there in my seat, for the second time this morning. This time I notice he has the most perfect teeth and his smile looks both naughty and sweet. Of course, I know who he is. Tyler Finlay started at our school last year and is, in my opinion, the hottest guy in school. He's tall, dark, and oh so handsome. He also plays both football and baseball, my favorite spectator sports. I hadn't had any classes with him...until now.

Am I the only one who can hear the angels singing? I think as I try to collect myself. I swear I can feel my heart racing. "I'm Sloane."

"Ty!" Billy says as he leans forward so Tyler can see him from behind me. "Aw, we're going to have an awesome year!"

"Hey Billy," Tyler says. "Yeah, I'm excited about this class. It should be cool." He takes off his flannel shirt revealing a Smashing Pumpkins T-shirt.

"Oh my gosh," I say. "You like the Smashing Pumpkins, too?" I hadn't noticed his shirt this morning, being blinded by his good looks and all.

Tyler pulls a notebook out of his backpack and looks at me, smiling that dang smile again. "Yeah, are you a fan?"

"I love them! I feel like no one here knows them."

"Yeah, I think most people around here listen to more mainstream stuff."

"Totally," I say softly as Coach Knight starts class.

How is a jock so cute, so nice, so darn sexy, *and* has such great taste in music? He's taller than me, which is amazing. I think there are probably less than a handful of guys in our class that are taller than me, and I think I'm being generous. I have to try really hard to focus on what Coach K is saying as I sit next to the hottest guy in school. While coach is talking about the labs we'll be doing this year, I remember something I heard about Tyler. When he started here last year, rumors were flying about why he got kicked out of the private school he attended. The school both my oldest sister and I applied for but didn't get into. A nervousness fills my belly as I think about Tyler and what he might have done. Some said he was caught in the girl's locker room, others said he beat a kid up, badly.

Could any of it be true? He seems so nice and I hope the only thing dangerous about him is that smile.

When Coach is done going over the syllabus, how class will run, and the lesson, there are ten minutes left in class. "Just talk amongst yourselves until the bell," he says. "That's all I've got for the day."

"Tyler!" Lori Tanner hollers from across the room. "Why are you sitting *there*?"

Did she just give a dirty look over to me when she said that? Ugh, just my luck. Lori is friends with Tyler, and now he's going to go sit with her. Well, it was fun while it lasted.

Tyler grins and says, "I've gotta be close to the exit in case I have to make a quick escape."

I cock my head and look at him, and he winks at me. Oh, dear God, does this guy know what he's doing to me? It's like I feel energy emanating off of him that's sending my body into a tizzy. I wonder if he's really seventeen, because he sure acts more mature than the other guys in our class, and none of them are this...alluring. It's like he's a man and they are mere boys stumbling through life.

"Earth to Sloane," he says as he waves a hand in front of my face.

I blink hard and shake my head. "Sorry, I—did you say something?" He grins. Lord help me with that smile. How can a smile have such an effect on a person?

"I asked you what your favorite Pumpkins' song is."

"Oh, right." I tuck my hair behind my right ear. "Er, I love "Crush." What about you?" Oh my gosh, I just told him I love "Crush," a song about a crush. What am I doing?

Thankfully, he doesn't seem to think a thing of it. "Hmm, probably "Siva." But it's kinda hard to pick just one."

"Great choice. I love 'Siva' and 'Rhinoceros,' too. *Gish* is such a great album," I say. "I just love their guitar sound so much, and Billy's voice is so cool. Like, it's not something you'd say is a traditionally good voice, but I love it. It's like an instrument of its own, you know?" Oh, gosh, I'm rambling.

He nods earnestly. "Totally. You really are a fan, huh?"

I smile. "They're one of my favorite bands."

He turns in his chair, facing me, and I catch Lori watching us out of the corner of my eye. "What other bands do you like?"

I mimic his posture and turn toward him. "I love The Lemonheads. Totally different from the Pumpkins, but so good. Of course, R.E.M., Nirvana, Pearl Jam, U2, INXS..."

"You have good taste in music," he says with an approving nod.

"Oh, and The Pixies and Tom Petty," I add.

"Pretty eclectic," he says.

I smile. "What about you?"

"Metallica, Nirvana, Pearl Jam, Alice in Chains, Soundgarden, Megadeath. A bit harder stuff," he says. "But the Pumpkins and Metallica are probably my favorite bands right now."

"Cool. I'm kind of surprised that a football player has such good taste in music," I joke, but as soon as the words come out of my mouth, I regret saying them. Does he know I'm joking? I do that, you know. I'll make a joke and fret about whether the recipient knows I'm joking.

"Gee, thanks!" he says with that grin appearing again.

"No, no, I'm joking—" I start and grab his upper arm. Holy cow, that felt too good. I retract my hand as if I have just touched a hot stove. "Sorry, I mean, it's just that most of those guys seem to be just like one another and you seem...different. In a good way." I add quickly. What have I done now? I put my hand on my forehead. "I just mean, you seem like a free-thinker and that's cool."

Between the way he's grinning at me while I squirm and the electricity I felt when I grabbed his arm, it's a wonder I can even continue to speak.

He laughs, "I know what you meant. And, yes, most of the guys on the team aren't listening to the music I am. Maybe with the exception of Metallica and Megadeath. I've always been a little different." He winks at me again.

I smile, sure that my pale skin is betraying me right now as heat warms my face. "Me too," I say as my insides feel full of butterflies ready to explode. "I've always felt like that Sesame Street bit about 'One of these things is not like the other' around here."

"Then we'll get along great," he says just before the bell rings.

I feel like I must look like a grinning idiot as I grab my backpack. Suddenly, I'm not so sure I want this year to fly by after all. That is, as long as Tyler Finlay decides to sit next to me the whole school year.

Chapter 5

Tyler

As I head to meet my friends for lunch, I marvel at how my first day of senior year is off to such a great start. When I was heading into school, I felt my flannel fall from my waist as I was walking down the steps. Just as I was about to pick it up, I heard a girl's voice. We both leaned down to pick it up and knocked our heads together. Okay, so that part wasn't great, but the girl was so cute and sweet. What am I saying, she is more than cute. She's beautiful. She's really tall, which is so cool, and she has these huge blue eyes and I swear I can see into her soul. Then, when I got to marine bio, late because I was hanging with my bros in the hall for too long, I slid into the first seat, right next to the girl with the big blue eyes. I couldn't believe my luck. Even better? This girl seems cool. She has awesome taste in music which isn't common at this school, and she seems really nice. Like, genuine. She's not like other girls here, that's for sure and I want to get to know her better.

"Tyler!" I hear my name being yelled across the hallway and see my friend, Brian Applequist waving me down, camcorder in hand.

I nod and head his way. "Hey, man. What's up?" I walk up to him and he raises his camera up to his face. "Are you recording right now?"

"Yeah, say hi." I wave at the camera, then flip him the bird.

"Brian lowers the camera and glares at me. "Thanks a lot, now I have to edit that."

"Or just not use it," I laugh and we start walking toward the door leading outside.

Brian punches my shoulder. "Dude, you were so out of it. I must have called your name five times," Brian says as we head outside to eat. Being football players, we're pretty used to the heat since we've been practicing over the summer and it's just nicer getting out of the school for lunch. Once the weather cools down, lots of kids will be out here, so we relish having the picnic area mostly to ourselves.

"Sorry," I tell my best friend as we sit at the end of a picnic table where some of our teammates and friends are already eating. Of course, there are several cheerleaders who sit with our group, but I'm not into them. I mean, it's cool that they cheer for us and all, but at Dunwoody, they tend to be a bit snobby, with a couple exceptions. At my last school, we had some girls like that, but the cliques seem really defined here.

"How are your classes so far?" Brian asks before he takes a bite out of his Blimpie sandwich. I swear that's all the guy eats.

"Pretty good," I say as I pull out one of two sandwiches I made last night, this one roast beef. "I'm excited about marine biology. Coach K is the teacher, too, so that's even better."

"That's rad," Brian says through a mouthful of sandwich. "I know how much you love fishing and Coach K gets how busy we are with both football and baseball."

"Yeah, he's so cool," I say then bite into my sandwich. I don't tell him about Sloane because I want to keep that to myself for now and see where it goes, but I think marine bio is going to be my favorite class for several reasons. I just wonder if Sloane Warren is out of my league.

"Have all the rumors died down?" Brian's expression grows serious.

I shrug. "I guess so. I think it would have been worse if I weren't an athlete, you know?" I take a bite of my sandwich thinking about what happened when I started here last year. "It's crazy how people think the worst and make so many assumptions."

Brian nods as he finishes chewing. "I guess when you get kicked out of private school, people are gonna talk." A wry grin appears on his face.

"Kicked out unfairly," I scoff. "But when you beat up the richest kid in school and star quarterback for his unwanted advances on a girl, you don't always get the benefit of the doubt."

"I can't believe that even though the girl corroborated your story, you still got kicked out." Brian tosses the paper wrapping from his sub sandwich onto the table in disgust.

"Money talks," I say nonchalantly. "Besides, I'm glad I'm here. My parents really liked the prestige that came with St. Christopher's, but I think our teams here are better and could help me more with my shot at going pro."

"And, you get to see me every day." Brian flashes me a Cheshire cat grin.

"And there's that," I say as my mind starts to drift. There's also the girl in marine bio who I will definitely look forward to seeing every day.

Chapter 6

Sloane

Lunch time is crucial for your social life when you're in high school and when you're an introvert without a friend group, walking into that cafeteria is intimidating to say the least. Not to mention, it's sensory overload with the bright fluorescent lights, shiny linoleum floors, and all the chatter and clattering of trays and chairs. A nervous ball forms in my stomach as I survey the room, scanning the tables for a familiar face, resisting the urge to turn around and walk outside to sit by myself on this hot, August day. I see Lori Tanner with her friends and our eyes meet. She turns to her friend, says something to her, then they start laughing as Lori looks right at me again. I inhale a deep breath and try to ignore her and her simple mind.

I feel like an anomaly here. Most people are nice to me, don't get me wrong, but I don't have a solid friend group and now I have to find someone to sit with. I had an awesome friend toward the end of elementary school, but she went to a private school. My best friend since I was five, Miranda, is a grade below me and has her circle of friends who are simply way cooler than me and I don't think she has this lunch period. Unfortunately, we don't really hang out in school, plus we've never had a class together, or even lunch for that matter. Tameka is off to college, so that leaves me with acquaintances in various groups. There are kids that I've known since kindergarten, but don't feel cool enough to hang out with, and casual friends from junior high that I'd had classes with, but no close friends.

Just as I'm about to turn to head outside, I feel a tap on my shoulder and turn around to find Maggie Woods smiling sweetly. "Hey!" I say as relief washes over me. "It's nice seeing a familiar face."

"I'm glad you have this lunch period. I'm going to sit with Beth and Annalise. Wanna join me?" she asks softly. If there could be a quieter person than me, it's Maggie. Her bangs are curled under and her brown hair hangs to her shoulders. Her blue eyes sparkle with friendliness and warmth.

"Yes, thanks!" I say as I follow her to a table where there are more familiar faces. "Hey guys," I say as I take a seat next to Maggie and across from best friends Beth and Annalise.

"Hey!" Beth says. "I'm glad you have lunch with us."

I exhale a breath I didn't know I was holding and relax. "Me, too. How are your classes so far?" I ask no one in particular.

"Pretty good," Annalise says. "The three of us have Spanish together, which is awesome."

"Oh, that's cool," I say as I unpack my lunch which consists of a turkey sandwich, banana, Cheetos, a Hostess cupcake, and a Coke.

"How about you? What's your schedule like?" Beth asks before taking a bite of her sandwich.

"Pretty good," I say. "I have French, psychology, and marine bio before lunch. Then it's art, British lit, then trig." I take a sip of my Coke then add, "I'm excited about marine bio and art." I decline to tell them why I am so excited about marine bio for the time-being.

"Do you have Mr. Fisher for trig?" Maggie asks quietly.

"Yeah, do you, too?"

She smiles, "Yeah, we'll be in class together."

"Awesome, we'll have to sit together if we can." I smile back, glad that I'll have a friend in math, my toughest subject. I have to work hard for my grades and math and science are my toughest subjects, but the social aspect of school is even worse. I don't have the confidence to just approach people and feel so uncomfortable in my own skin sometimes. With a tutor, math makes sense, I don't think there's a tutor for high school cliques, but there should be.

"I'm so excited this is our senior year!" Beth says, then sips her Diet Coke.

"One more year in this place and we're free!" Annalise says as she clinks soda cans with her bestie, Beth.

"I'm so ready," I agree and clink my can with theirs and Maggie follows suit. I think about Tyler, though and that maybe this year will be different. I've always daydreamed of dating a cute athlete. Maybe this year that dream will finally come true.

Chapter 7

Sloane

Art class is one of my favorite classes, and by the time I get there, most of the class is already seated. I say hello to Mrs. Dale and survey the room. I must have talked to Maggie too long after lunch because most of the tables are full. A group of junior cheerleaders are at the front table on the far side. The super-artsy kids are behind them and next to them, potheads and hippies. The front table closest to the door is the black kids. I notice how each group has gravitated to those similar to them and it's as if everyone has segregated themselves based on their identities here. Once again, I am trying to find my place in this school. "One of these things is not like the other," I sing to myself.

A girl with full cheeks and short dark hair wearing a flowered shirt at the table closest to the door smiles at me.

I smile back. "Can I join you?"

"Of course," she says. "What's your name?"

"Sloane," I say as I slide out the empty chair across from her and set my bag on the table.

"I'm Denine," she says, "and this is Myke." She hooks a thumb to her left, and the boy with dreadlocks wearing a Chicago Bulls T-shirt smiles brightly.

"It's Myke with a 'y'."

"Cool," I say returning his friendly smile with one of my own. "Nice to meet you." I look at the girl next to me who's wearing a Boyz II Men shirt.

"Hey Sloane," she says confidently. "I'm Dawne—with an 'e' at the end."

"Perfect, I'm Sloane with an 'e' at the end."

"What made you want to sit with us?" Dawne asks frankly, her eyes sizing me up.

"Well, this looked like the cool table, obviously." I love it when I think fast and come up with a good answer.

"Yesss," Myke says then softly punches Denine's shoulder. "See, she knows."

Denine laughs at him then looks at me. "You're not wrong. We're gonna have fun at this table."

Dawne looks at me suspiciously. "Why didn't you sit at that table." She nods to where the cheerleaders are sitting.

"Do I look like I fit in there?" I ask.

She looks at me then at the girls at the other table. "Nah," she says, "you look way cooler than them."

I chuckle. "Cool might be a stretch, but I'm more comfortable here."

Dawne nods approvingly as Myke says, "Stretch!" He bounces in his chair, his white teeth gleaming. "You just gave yourself a nickname!"

I laugh and shake my head. "I haven't heard that one before." My three new pals break up in laughter at this.

Yes, this class is going to be a fun one. Mrs. Dale goes over how things will run in her class and gets us started on our first project. I like the fact that in art class we can talk while we work.

"What year are you?" Dawne asks.

"Senior," I reply as I open my art supply box. "What about y'all?"

"We're juniors," Denine says.

"Yeah, we've got a whole 'nother year here," Myke says, and I feel his pain.

"I don't envy you," I reply. "Junior year was tough."

Denine sits up straight and smiles. "I'm looking forward to it."

"Of course, you are," Dawne jokes then looks at me. "She's the over-achiever in the group."

"I just like a challenge," Denine says with a satisfied grin on her face.

"Well, you're smart to have this class," I say. "It will be a nice break from all the tougher classes this year."

"I can't wait for senior year," Myke says. "Y'all get to rule the school."

"Plus, you've got Homecoming, Prom, all the fun activities for se-niors," Denine adds.

"Spring Break!" Dawne adds as she does a little dance in her seat.

"I'll be lucky if I get asked to any dance," I say as I tuck a strand of hair behind my right ear.

Myke scrunches up his face as he looks at me. "What?" His voice rises an octave when he says this. "Why's that?"

I shrug my shoulders as Denine looks at me with concern in her brown eyes. "I've never been asked to a dance, so I don't really expect this year to be any different."

Dawne makes a smacking noise with her mouth. "That's just crazy. Boys are whack."

"Hey!" Myke says feigning hurt feelings.

"Well, look at her." Dawne hooks a thumb at me. "Why wouldn't anyone ask her?"

"Well for one, I'm taller than most guys," I say in a joking manner even though it's one possible reason. "Who wants to take a girl to a dance who towers over you?"

"Would you consider asking someone?" Denine asks.

"Oh, no," I say quickly as I shake my head. "I could never do that. I don't think I have the gumption."

"What about the dance where the girls ask the guys?" Myke asks.

"Yeah, Snowball," Denine says. "You can ask someone to that."

I shake my head again. "I don't know, I'd have to be pretty confident he would say yes. Besides, it would feel nice to have someone ask me to a dance, you know?"

"I totally get it," Dawne says. "You want to feel special, like someone wants to take you."

I smile, "Yeah, exactly."

"Don't you worry," Denine says, "you'll go to prom and will be the belle of the ball!"

I love how confident and positive Denine is. I think I can learn a lot from her.

Chapter 8

Sloane

September 1992

The first four weeks of senior year are off to a decent start, and I am settling into my classes well. Of course, marine bio is my favorite, and I head there with a hop in my step. I sit down next to Billy, who is seated between me and his friend, Dustin. There aren't a lot of kids into country music at our school, and those two seem to talk about Garth Brooks and George Strait like Tyler and I talk about Smashing Pumpkins and Nirvana.

Tyler slides into his chair before the bell for once. "Hey, you gotta hear this," he says as he holds up a pair of headphones.

I turn to face him. Wow, he looks dreamy when he's wearing his football jersey on game day. He puts the headphones over my ears, and I hear Kurt Cobain's voice screaming, "Yeah-aaa-aaa-aaa-yeah, yeah-aaa-aaa-aaa-yeah-aaah..." I look up at Tyler and nod, partially slipping the headphones off. "Did I tell you Lithium is one of my favorite Nirvana songs?"

Tyler smiles. "I think so, but that's not the point." He holds up a small square box. "This isn't a tape player. This is on the radio!"

I let the headphones fall to my neck. "What?" I say as I grab the device from him and inspect it. It's just a radio. I look back up with my eyes wide. "Who's playing this?"

"99X," he says with a grin.

"You mean Power 99?" I ask, shocked that the Top 40 station is playing Nirvana.

He shakes his head, still smiling. "They changed formats. It's an alternative station now."

"No way!" I say a little too loud, then lower my voice. "Oh my gosh, this is awesome." I hold the right headphone speaker up to my ear and listen as Tyler watches me with a smile. "It's almost over." I say as I wait for Nirvana's "Lithium" to end and hear what comes on next.

Through the speaker, I hear funny, kitschy music and then, "This is 99X, WNNX Atlanta. 99X, it's where music is going."

"Oh my gosh, I wanna hear what they play next!"

"Me, too!" Tyler scoots his chair right against mine and says, "Let me see those." He motions for the headphones. After I give them to him, he snaps off the right speaker and hands it to me, then holds the left speaker up to his ear.

We huddle together and listen to a few commercials and my pulse races being this close to Tyler Finlay. I look up at him, "I'm glad you got here early for once," I joke as the first bell rings.

He winks at me and gives me that smile. You know the one. I feel myself getting warm as I'm no longer focused on this exciting news. Just then, the soft notes of a guitar sound, and I recognize the band right away. I look up at Tyler, "Pearl Jam."

He nods just as Eddie Vedder's voice sounds, "Black."

"I can't believe this is on the radio!" I say quietly.

"I've been listening most of the day, at least when I can," he says. "It's like they came into my room and took my CD collection."

"I love it," I say just as the final bell rings. I hand him back the right speaker which he presses back into the clip on the headphone band. "My sister is going to be mad, though. She loved Power99, and I had to suffer through it blaring from across the hall."

His smile grows mischievous which makes him every dreamier. "I guess it's payback time, then."

I laugh as I take my notebook out of my backpack. "Totally."

The front door closes, and Coach K announces, "Partner up, we're doing a lab today."

I hadn't noticed silver trays lined up on the large table that spans the back of the room. I look at Tyler. "Will you be my partner and be in charge of cutting things open?"

"Absolutely," he says. "Cutting stuff open is the fun part."

I shudder as Coach says, "We're dissecting sharks today and each of you is going to have to do some of the work."

"I guess you get to join in on the fun, partner," Tyler says as he elbows my left arm and wiggles his eyebrows.

I laugh at him and try to quell the butterflies that awaken in my stomach. If I have to cut open a shark, or anything else for that matter, there's no one I'd rather do it with.

Chapter 9

Tyler

When I leave marine bio to meet Brian outside for lunch, I can't contain my smile. I got to be the first one to tell Sloane about 99X and we huddled together to listen through my headphones. I can still smell the soft floral scent she wears. It smelled like my mom's prized rose bushes. Whatever it is, it smells so good and it just makes me want to be closer to her. This girl is so cool and sweet. I'm going to have to play this right to see if I have a shot with her.

As I near the picnic table, I see Brian grinning at me and he quickly picks up his video camera, facing it at me. "Hey, man, what's up?" I say as I sit across from him. We are the first ones out here for a change.

"Why don't you tell me what's up with you?" Brian says as he looks around his camera with a glint in his eye.

I narrow my eyes and cock my head. "What do you mean?"

"You've got the goofiest grin on your face," Brian goes back to looking through the viewfinder behind the camera.

I still don't think I'm ready to let him know about Sloane so I say, "I'm just so excited about our football team this year."

"For real?"

"Yeah, don't you feel it during practice?" I ask and hope I can play this off smoothly so he thinks I really was thinking about the team. I'm not lying, though, the team is tight this year.

"Yeah, totally," Brian says. "But are you sure that's why you're grinning like that?"

I huff out a laugh. This dude knows me too well. "Yeah, I'm sure." I open my lunch and pull out the contents. Two sandwiches, per usual, some chips, chocolate chip cookies, an apple, a granola bar, and two juice boxes. I've got the best mom. She knows how hungry I get during football season and is always putting extra food in my lunch. "Our team seems to be firing on all cylinders, you know?"

"Oh my gosh, totally!" A screechy, kind of nasally voice says as Amber Gates bounces her way to our table and Brian turns the camera on her. "Our Wildcats rock!" She looks up at our teammates Max, Adam, and Josh, who grin proudly as the group, including a few of her fellow cheerleaders, arrives at our lunch spot. I don't know why they all seem to think that cheerleaders and jocks have to do everything together. I guess it's because we spend a decent amount of time together outside of school. I like my teammates, but I'm also fine just hanging out with Brian. I don't have to be surrounded by people all the time.

Thankfully, Max sits next to me and Adam next to Brian. Amber squeezes in next to Adam, leaving Josh to her left and the rest of the cheerleaders at the end. She perfectly situates herself in the center of the group so she can talk to the boys and girls. Amber always looks like she's holding court and I wonder how she ever got so popular. I've only been in this school for one full school year and so far, I haven't seen much appeal in Amber. To say she's not my type is an understatement. She's too short, too full of herself, and I'm not physically attracted to her. Sloane on the other hand? Man, she's beautiful, inside and out. Plus, she's cool and has great taste in music. I just hope she isn't one of those cool chicks who wants someone way cooler than a jock who was kicked out of private school. I wonder what she heard about that and what she thinks of me.

"Yo, Tyler!"

I snap out of my own thoughts as I hear Brian's voice. I focus on his face. "Sorry. What?"

"Adam asked how long we've known each other," Brian says, his camera focused back on me. "Was it first grade when we started Little League?"

"No, I think kindergarten," I take a sip of my juice, then look at Adam. "This kid was a madman even back then."

Brian laughs. "What can I say. I've always been high energy."

"And y'all stayed friends all this time?" Adam asks.

"Yeah," I laugh. "We got along from the start and always kept ending up on the same teams." Truth be told, Brian has always challenged authority. I think we were put on the same teams on purpose all those years because, for some reason, I have a calming effect on the dude.

"My mom says she thinks we were related in a past life." Brian says then pushes a button on his camera and sets it on the table. I'm glad he's done documenting us for now. I think his hunger trumps his desire to capture every moment.

Adam looks at me. "Can you believe we're playing your old team on homecoming?"

Nerves zap my stomach. "I know, it's crazy."

"You're going to have to give us all the intel you can," Adam says. "We can't lose on homecoming."

I nod. Homecoming is one of the biggest games of the year for everyone, especially the fans. You don't want to go to your dance the next night as a loser. "Absolutely. I know we've got the better team. Their studs graduated last year."

"That's right, didn't they make it to the semis last year?" Brian asks before biting into an apple.

I nod. "They did, but they've lost some key players. Only a few from that team are still there and they've got nothing on us." I say with more confidence than is warranted, then take a sip of juice, practically draining the whole box. I think of the one guy who is still a threat on that team. The quarterback, the guy I beat up because he was harassing a girl. I try to quell the anger rising in me just thinking about it.

Chapter 10

Sloane

I meet up with Maggie, Beth, and Annalise for our first pep rally of the season in the gym. We are all wearing our class of '93 T-shirts designed by our classmate, Andrea, who is a huge fan of the Grateful Dead, so they have a 60's hippie vibe. We take our position in the upper-middle section of the bleachers surrounded by our fellow seniors. During each pep rally the seniors, juniors, and sophomores all vie for the spirit stick which is basically won by the class that screams the loudest. While I'm an introvert, I am super competitive, and my family is big into football. I'm also excited to cheer for my favorite wildcat. The band is playing, the cheerleaders are cheering, and the wildcat mascot is jumping around working up the crowd.

My ears have a way of tuning into music, even music I don't like. Especially music I don't like. If I didn't know better, I'd think I was cursed. I turn to Maggie. "Is the band seriously playing *Achy Breaky Heart?*"

Maggie giggles. "Yep, they sure are." She starts to dance a little in her seat which causes me to roll my eyes and shake my head in jest.

Principal Buckley takes to the microphone to welcome us and start the festivities. After she's done, she introduces the football coach. Coach Harbin is a former college football defensive standout who is building a strong team at Dunwoody High. He further pumps up the crowd, telling us that this year's theme for the team is 'Relentless' before introducing the football team to wild cheers. The cheerleaders are assembled by the doors and hold a painted paper banner which reads, "Wildcats 'R Relentless!" and features a roaring wildcat with front claws extended in the center. As the team breaks through the banner and jogs out to the center of the gym, I look for number 44, Tyler's number.

"You know who's really cool?" I lean over close to Maggie's ear.

"Who?" she replies, as Coach talks some more.

"Tyler Finlay," I quietly divulge to the girl who's becoming my closest friend at school.

"Really?' she asks. "I thought he was just a hot jock and a bit of a rebel based on all the gossip about why he was kicked out of St. Christopher's."

I laugh, "Yeah, me, too. I've gotten to know him in marine bio. He's nice and has great taste in music. The rebel part is still to be determined."

"That's cool," she says. "He's certainly not hard to look at."

"Not at all," I say as my eyes are fixed on him. "His smile will melt you if you're not careful."

Her blue eyes sparkle from beneath her bangs and her dimple appears on her cheek. "Uh-oh. I guess I know who your favorite Wildcat is."

I feel my cheeks flush. "Yeah, but it's not like anything will come of it," I say as my eyes fix on him. "Why would a guy that hot, that cool, and that talented go for a girl like me?"

Maggie looks at me with sympathy like I'm a homeless cat. "Well, he should, but I get it. I'm so ready to graduate. All these cliques are so annoying. It's as if guys like him feel like they have to date a cheerleader, or at least someone in the popular crowd."

I nod my head as the football team takes their seats on the front row of the bleachers for their class. "It's so weird because I've gone seventeen years without anyone asking me to a dance or asking me out, yet I went down to Jacksonville over the summer with my friend Tameka, and I actually got interest from boys."

"That's because you are beautiful and sweet" she says as she gives my arm a squeeze.

"I'm so glad you didn't say 'nice.' That's like the kiss of death adjective," I joke.

Maggie laughs. "I know! When people call me nice, I'm like can't you call me interesting or sweet, or I don't know, maybe even creative."

"Yes!" I say a little too loud. "I certainly don't want to be called mean or rude, but nice just feels so...boring."

"Totally," she says.

"Also, I think because we're shy, we got lumped into some kind of classification from the time we were in elementary school, and it just stuck."

"Yeah, I think you're right," she says. "Plus, we're not partiers, and we don't sleep around."

"Exactly." I think about the friends I've lost because of my morals.

"The boys in Jacksonville met you as who you are now, which I'm sure is at least a tad more outgoing than you were in elementary school or junior high. And you were new to them. Plus, you're pretty, have legs for days, and of course, you're extremely *nice*." She giggles as she says that last word.

I have to stifle a laugh which almost bursts right out of my mouth. "I do have an easier time meeting new people than I used to. I think I finally started coming out of my shell in tenth grade," I say quietly as Principal Buckley takes the stage before the spirit stick competition starts. "I always was a late bloomer," I joke and make Maggie laugh.

"At least Tyler is friendly. Do you talk much?"

"Oh yeah. We talk a lot about music and paired up on a lab together today."

"Well, that's something!" Maggie says optimistically. "Who knows, one of us nice girls may finish first for a change."

I smile. "Well, I'm not going to get my hopes up, but that would be a fabulous way to end my time in this place," I say as I look around at my fellow seniors. It's a weird thing to go through your entire school life with some of these people yet feel so detached from them. Maybe my standards are too high, but I'm certainly not going to change who I am to have more friends. I've seen other friends go the drinking, partying, and chasing guys route, but that's just not me. I've gotten used to being a loner, maybe college will be different.

"Honestly," I turn to Maggie, "I'd just really like someone to ask me to a dance this year. Preferably prom since it's practically a rite of passage, but I'd take homecoming."

Maggie's eyes get all sympathetic again, and she cocks her head. "Oh, Sloane, you'll totally have a date for prom. Any guy would be lucky to take you."

I can see in her eyes that she means it. "Thanks. Is it too much to ask for a tall guy to take me?" I half-joke. "I'd feel really awkward with someone shorter than me."

Maggie laughs as she waves her pom-pom. "Of course not!" She pauses to holler and cheer, and I join her as the spirit stick comes to the senior section. After that dies down, she says, "That will drastically reduce your options, but I bet one of the handful of tall guys will ask you. Who knows, maybe it will be Tyler Finlay."

I smile and feel myself blush. "Well, that would be amazing. It would be right out of a Hollywood movie, and I'd have the hottest date at prom." We laugh, but I start daydreaming about what it would be like to go to prom with Tyler. He's so handsome and tall, we have great conversations about music, and I can talk about football and baseball with him. Mental note, talk sports with Tyler so he knows I can talk about more than just music with him. But, he does scare me in a way. Not like he would hurt me, but he just seems way more experienced than me and most of the boys in our grade for that matter. As each of the classes yell and scream, my mind drifts to what it would be like to be on Tyler's arm. I've always wanted to date an athlete. Maybe this will be my year?

Chapter 11

Sloane

November 1992

It feels like school just started and already the halls are being decorated for Homecoming. While I knew Maggie and I would go to the game together, I assumed I wouldn't be going to the dance, but I held out hope that I might get invited. Even if it wasn't Tyler but someone who just wanted to go as friends, it would be cool since this is my senior year and all. I get to marine bio early, as usual, and Billy is just sitting down.

"Sloaner, what's up?" He greets me with the irritating, yet funny term of endearment derived from his earlier, "Sloaner-loner" nickname.

I've come up with a nickname of my own for my country-loving classmate and can't wait to use it. "Hill-Billy!" I say as I set my backpack on the lab table and pull out my chair to sit. "You know, if you're not careful, I'm gonna start calling you Billy the Kid." I smile at him as his eyes light up.

"I'd take that as a compliment," Billy says while taking his seat next to me.

I laugh. "Of course, you would." I lean forward to look at his black T-shirt. "Who are you wearing today?"

He turns toward me in his seat and pulls at his shirt so I can see it. "George Strait."

"It's funny," I tell him, "On my right side is a guy whose music I've never listened to, and on my left is a guy who shares the same taste in music as me. It's kind of crazy when you think about it."

Billy says, "Well, you know Judas sat on Jesus' left, so..."

I laugh. "You think Tyler is going to betray me on our next lab or something?"

"You never know with Tyler," Billy jokes.

"Never know what?" Tyler's voice sounds behind me.

I turn to see Tyler standing by his chair, grinning that Sloane-melting grin and the butterflies awaken in my belly. Feeling playful, I say, "Oh, Billy was just comparing you to Judas, that's all."

Tyler cocks his head and gives Billy a questioning glance. Billy explains our conversation, and Tyler walks next to me, leans down, and puts his arm around my shoulders so we are both facing Billy. Our heads separated by mere inches and his touch sets my shoulders on fire. Man, he smells so good, and the butterflies in my stomach are practically moshing in there now. "I would never betray Sloane," he says, then gives my shoulders a squeeze and stands up straight. Tyler walks back to his seat and sits while I try to catch my breath. My face grows hot, and I can tell Billy notices my current state of discombobulation by his raised eyebrows and amused appearance.

Just then, Lori Tanner strides up and stands in front of our table. "Hey, Tyler!" Her smile is so huge it makes her eyes squinty. I look down and inhale to settle myself, then busy myself with getting my book and notebook out of my backpack.

"Hey, what's up?" Tyler holds his book in one hand and drops his backpack on the floor to his left.

"I was just wondering who you're taking to Homecoming," she asks, and my heart speeds up.

I'd like to know, too, I think to myself as I look up. Lori catches my eye and glares at me like I'm a cockroach on her kitchen floor before returning her attention to Tyler.

"Oh, um, I'm not. My cousin is getting married in Tennessee, so we're leaving early Saturday morning."

While that confirmed I had no shot at him asking me, it wouldn't be because he was taking someone else. It would also mean he wasn't going with Lori, either, and that's great news. Don't get me wrong, it's not that I dislike Lori. She seems to dislike me, and I have no idea why. Honestly, there aren't many people I dislike in my grade, with the exception of Amber, and this guy who wrote racist stuff in my yearbook in ninth grade. Yeah, he literally wrote it right next to where one of my black classmates had signed it. He wrote it in pencil, and I was going to erase it because I was so disgusted, but I decided to leave it there so I could remember how awful some people are. Anyway, with Lori, she acts like I'm lame, and she's so much better than me. I've honestly never even had much contact with her, so I don't know what her issue with me is.

"Oh, cool," Lori says, her voice no longer chipper and bubbly. "It's a shame you'll miss the Homecoming dance, though."

Tyler lets out a puff of air through his nose. "Yeah, I think I'll survive." Sarcasm coats his words making Lori's smile disappear. "I'm psyched for my cousin's wedding. We're super close. I'm not gonna miss being here."

Lori tries to play it off and forces a tight smile. "Yeah, I bet that will be way more fun." She's literally saved by the bell. "Gotta go!" She glares at me and tosses her long hair over her shoulder and turns her chin up before quickly returning to the other side of the room and takes her seat facing us.

Tyler looks at me. "Are you going to Homecoming?"

I tuck my hair behind my right ear. "Uh, no. Just the game, probably."

"Oh." Tyler's face shows an expression I can't quite decipher. "Do you watch the games or just go for the social aspect?"

I cock my head and feel my eyes narrow. "I go to watch the games. I love football. And baseball," I add for good measure.

"Rad," Tyler's eyes shine as if he's pleased to hear this. "I think we have a strong team this year."

"I do, too," I say as I feel excitement course through my veins. "Our defense is amazing and as they say, defenses win championships. I think we could make a run at the state title."

"As a linebacker, I can't argue with that." Tyler smiles proudly. "You really do like football, huh?"

"Oh yeah, we're huge football fans in my household. My mom may even be the biggest fan I know." I smile proudly because I think I've pleasantly surprised Tyler. It always seems to surprise guys when a girl actually knows football.

"Why aren't you going to the dance?" Tyler asks as his face grows serious.

I shrug. "Because no one asked me." I state plainly.

Tyler nods as Coach walks in from the hallway having closed both doors and starts our lesson. I knew I didn't have a shot with Tyler, but at least I could still hope he might have asked me if he didn't have that wedding to attend. A girl can dream, right? I'm pretty good at dreaming. It's the dream turning into reality that I'm waiting for.

Chapter 12

Tyler

As we break for halftime, I wish I was going into the locker room with my team, but I have to stay out on the field because I was nominated for homecoming king. I should be in the locker room helping pump up my team to beat St. Christopher's. The game is closer than I thought it would be and I was able to tell coach some stuff I've been seeing that might help us. Having played for the Lions, I know some of their weaknesses and it looks like they haven't corrected them since I was kicked off the team and out of the school.

A couple of my teammates are out here with me, including Brian, having been nominated as well. At least we're in our uniforms. I feel for the guys who have to wear suits. This kind of thing is silly to me and I hope I don't win. The only thing that makes it better is the pride on my parents' faces as they join me out here.

"Don't expect me to call you 'Your Highness' if you win this thing," my dad jokes as we stand on the field waiting for all the all the names to be called.

This makes me laugh as I scan the crowd.

"Oh, Tom, don't be a spoil sport," my mom squeezes my hand. "You would make the best Homecoming King, Tyler."

A smile spreads across my face at my mom's sweetness. "Thanks, mom, but you know all I care about this year is getting a scholarship to play ball."

"And you will, Sport," my dad calls me his nickname for me. "You're too talented a player not to get one."

"Thanks, dad."

My parents are so supportive of my athletics, but were disappointed in how I handled the situation with Chad Childers, the QB for the Lions. I explained why I did what I did and while they were proud of me for standing up for the girl, they weren't proud of the beating I put on Chad, especially my mom. St. Christopher's is a prestigious school and I think she felt it made her look bad that her son was expelled. Of course, no one wants to hear why, they all assume the worst.

As we're standing there, listening to the remaining names of nominees being announced, somehow, my eyes fall on Sloane Warren in the stands. How is it that I was able to pick her out of this crowd? Of course, she's too far for me to see if she's looking at me, but I hope she is. I can't believe no one asked her to Homecoming. If I were going to be in town, I would have asked her right there in marine bio. She looked sad that she wasn't going, but acted like it was no big deal. A girl like her deserves better than that.

The last guy to be announced is Brian and I nod to my best friend as he smiles like a kid then waves to the crowd like he's already king. I chuckle as they announce the last girl, Amber Gates. She struts proudly in her red, white, and blue cheerleading uniform.

The announcer's voice booms over the stadium. "Ladies and gentlemen, your DHS Homecoming King is..." He pauses for effect. "Brian

Applequist!" A cheer erupts and Brian looks as proud as a peacock as he is crowned. Good for him. I'm glad someone who wants this got it. "And, your DHS Homecoming Queen is...Lavonda Washington!" The crowd roars and I'm pleasantly surprised. I don't know Lavonda well, but she's smart, quiet, and if I'm being honest, a little nerdy. A few of the popular girls on the Homecoming Court look shocked, but quickly cover up their emotions and clap for Lavonda who looks genuinely surprised. I glance up at Sloane and see that she and her friends are on their feet clapping and hollering and my heart squeezes. Everyone loves an underdog.

***

After halftime, we dominate the game, but in the fourth quarter, it's gotten close again. This game has been a back and forth and it feels like whoever has the ball last is going to win. I can tell the Lions are getting tired, their offensive line isn't as quick as they were earlier in the game. Coach Harbin makes sure conditioning is a big part of our training and so far this season, it has helped us stay strong while our opponents have tired out. I've been able to put pressure on Chad, but I haven't gotten a sack yet. I'm hungry for a sack. It would feel good to tackle that guy out here on the field. I've caused him to have to throw the ball away a few times which is good, but I want that sack.

There are two minutes left in the game and the Lions are driving. I focus on Chad as we line up for the next play. I shift my focus to the Lions' snapper and as soon as he lifts the ball, I'm off. I break through the tired linemen and have a clear shot at Chad. I feel adrenaline coursing through my veins as I close in on him and see his eyes go wide. He throws the ball just before I can get to him and I know better than to follow through with the tackle. I pull up and turn to watch the play. Our safety, Andre Southerland flies in front of the receiver and snatches the ball out of the air as the Wildcats fans roar. I run toward the other side of the field to block for Andre, but he is ultimately tackled at the 47 yard line. My teammates and I celebrate Andre's interception as we jog to the sidelines.

"Nice job, Finlay, Dre." Coach pats Andre's shoulder pads, then mine, stopping me. "Great pressure. Way to hold up. Keep it up. You're rattling him. You'll get him." Coach pats my back releasing me to the sidelines where I grab a paper Gatorade cup and drink down the cool liquid. Coach knows I play hard and, of course, he knows all about my situation with Chad. He understands that I want this sack on Chad more than I would any other QB.

I sit on the bench and watch our offense put together a great drive while our defensive coordinator goes over our plays. The score is 20-24 with the Lions currently in the lead. When we're at the 21-yard line, our quarterback, Sam Nash, throws a tight spiral to Brian in the end zone. I stand up to see the play and Brian catches the ball in the back corner of the end zone. We erupt on the sideline as our fans go crazy in the stands. Our kicker, Adam, nails the point-after, right through the middle of the uprights. Nerves fill my stomach as I look at the clock which reads 1:17. There's still enough time for the Lions to score and we're only up by 3 points. If they get close enough, a field goal could tie the game. A touchdown wins it, so our defense has to give it all we've got.

Our special teams go out onto the field as our defensive coordinator tells us what to look out for and pumps us up for one last stand. The kick is returned ten yards and the Lions are at the 19-yard line. I put my helmet on, secure the strap, and jog out onto the field with my teammates. The Lions' O-line seem to have gotten an adrenaline boost because they're stronger than when they had the ball last and I'm getting blocked. I can't break off my blocks and am frustrated that I can't get to Chad. Even more frustrating, the Lions are putting a drive together and get two first downs.

On the first play of the next down, I'm practically tackled, but no flag is thrown. Frustration boils inside me. "Hey, Ref!" I holler at the closest referee. "They're holding all over the place. Sixty-six practically tackled me!"

"All right, forty-four. Line back up."

I don't know whether that means he's going to look out for it, or if he's just telling me to move along, but now I'm angry. On the next play, I'm able to get off my block, but it was a running play, opposite from where I am. "Look for the pass," I tell my teammates as we line back up for third down. There are thirty-two seconds on the clock. Still enough time for them to score.

Chad releases the ball quickly this time, so I have no shot at him, and it's a good pass. Andre is playing the receiver tight, but misjudges his jump and is unable to fend off the pass. The Lions have another first down and are close to field goal range now. Twenty-nine seconds on the clock.

I gather my team as the Lions are in their huddle. "We will not let them win this game. Play your positions and don't let anyone by you. I'm getting off these blocks and will get to Childers. I don't want to go into overtime."

As we line up, my former teammate, Jay Peterson sneers at me. "I told you at the start of this game, you won't get Chad. Not again."

"You're lucky the refs are blind," I holler back. "That's the only way you can stop me."

The Lions throw a quick screen pass to the sideline and gain five yards, stopping the clock at twenty-six seconds. They line up quickly and gain another two as their running back is chased out of bounds, stopping the clock at twenty-three seconds. They are definitely in field goal range now and only need three yards for a first down. As I survey the offense, I realize they are going to go for a pass play. I holler to my teammates. "Pass, pass!" Our coverage is tight and the receivers aren't open. Nineteen seconds. I break off my block and tear toward Chad. Fifteen seconds. His feet are dancing and he looks for a passing option. I see his eyes lock in and know he's found a target, even though I can't see what's happening behind me. Twelve seconds. Chad sees me coming his way and drops back. Three yards, then two more. I have him on the run. He hastily plants his feet and brings his right arm back. Eight seconds. Just before he releases the ball, I crash into him, slamming him to the ground.

"Ball, ball, ball!" I hear the shouts and jump up, looking for the ball. I see it bouncing behind where Chad fell and dive for it, capturing it in my arms, protecting it as if it were my child. The clock runs down and our sideline and stands go wild. I jump up and hold the ball high over my head as I run to the sideline, my team cheering me as I run. I hand the ball to Coach Harbin as my teammates encircle me with shouts of victory.

Chapter 13

Sloane

"Hey buddy, how was your weekend?" Kurt asks as he slides into his seat next to me in French class.

I shrug. "Aside from not going to Homecoming, it was pretty good. The game was amazing, I'm glad we pulled off a win." I don't dare mention how cool it is that Tyler Finlay secured the win for us in the last seconds.

Just then, Amber Gates saunters into the room. She looks right at me and says, "I think we really helped our team get that win." She points to herself and her fellow cheerleader, Ramsey Huff.

Ramsey is so unlike Amber that I'm not surprised when she smiles tightly and shifts uncomfortably in her seat. "We have a great team this year," Ramsey says diplomatically, then smiles kindly at me.

"We sure do," I say to Ramsey, not even looking at Amber. "I think we have a shot at going to State."

"I don't think I saw you at the dance, Sloane. Did you not attend?" Amber jabs at me while pretending to stifle a laugh.

My pulse races as anger starts to boil inside me. "No, Amber, I did not." I turn to Kurt, and thankfully, he starts talking so fast that Amber can't get a word in edgewise.

"Hey, have you heard that Dinosaur Jr. song on 99X? It's so good!"

I'm so grateful for his quick thinking. My pulse starts to slow back down. "Yes, I love it! I bought the album, it's so good." The anger that boiled inside me reduces to a simmer.

"They're coming to town in a couple of months, you know."

"Yeah, Tameka and I have tickets, and she's bringing her friend, Ray. Are you going?" I ask.

"Nah," he says as he pulls his spiral notebook out of his backpack. "Shelly has a big recital that night, so that's where I'll be."

Shelly is Kurt's girlfriend, and a sweet, smart girl. She is also a talented dancer. "You're such a great boyfriend," I say, thinking about the opportunity I might have missed back in eighth grade when he kept trying to get me to come swimming at his house. At least I have a sweet, quirky friend who loves some of the same music as I do, which is rare in this school. Besides, Kurt is total friend material; there aren't the feelings for him like there are when I see Tyler.

"Oh, Jesse Thatcher is having people over on Saturday," Kurt says. "You should come."

Jesse lives next door to Kurt and went to elementary school with us. Once we started junior high, Jesse's dad decided private school was the better environment for his son, and I can't say that I blame him. Our junior high school was a bit rough compared to Vanderlyn Elementary. I don't know if all those ruffians dropped out of school or what, but the atmosphere is different here at Dunwoody High. Instead of druggies and fights in the halls, it's just really cliquey.

"Earth to Sloane." Kurt waves a hand in front of my face.

I shake my head and refocus my eyes on him. "Sorry, um, I dunno. You know I'm not really a party person." Just thinking of going to a party makes me feel unsettled, let alone, a party that's bound to have people I don't know. I get uncomfortable in social situations and haven't really been to any parties, so it's intimidating.

"Aw, come on, you should go." Kurt encourages me. "I told you this year would be different. You said you've never been included and I'm your friend, so I'm including you. Plus, I'm sure Jesse would love to see you."

I cock my head. "You think?"

"Yeah, he always tells me how much he loved Vanderlyn and the kids we graduated with."

I look across the room, "Including Amber?" I ask softly.

Kurt huffs out a laugh. "Who knows."

"Do you think she'll be there?" I ask as I fidget with my pen cap.

Kurt shrugs. "Maybe, but don't let that stop you from coming. Shelly and I will be there, so you can hang with us."

"I'll think about it," I say. "Maybe I can convince Maggie to come with me." The thought of showing up to a party by myself makes me nervous in the present. I'd rather get a tooth filled.

Chapter 14

Sloane

Even though Maggie is as shy as me, if not more so, she's game to go to Jesse's party with me. She went to a different elementary school, so she doesn't know Jesse, but her rationale makes sense. "The way I look at it," she says as we walk up the steep street in my neighborhood where Kurt and Jesse live, "is this guy goes to a different school, so most of the people there won't know us and they won't have any preconceived ideas about us."

I nod my head as I think this over. "You're right. Kind of like when I went to Jacksonville with Tameka and met all her friends. When I met those kids, I was immediately accepted into their world because I was a friend of a friend." I'm getting more optimistic about this party with each step. I smile and face Maggie. "Maybe this will turn out to be a really good night for both of us for a change!"

Maggie smiles sweetly. "Let's hope so." We pick up our pace and are at Jesse's front door in no time.

I'm facing Maggie on the front porch. "How does this work? Do we ring the doorbell?"

Maggie frowns as she shrugs. "I dunno."

I decide to knock as I can't imagine how embarrassing it would be to just open someone's front door. We wait a few moments, but no one comes to the door. I can hear music inside, so I'm sure no one heard my knock.

"Should we just go in?" Maggie asks as she fidgets with her cross necklace.

This time, I shrug. "I guess we could." I really don't want to be the one to open the door.

As we debate this, three cute guys who I don't recognize walk up to the front porch. A tall, fit, blond guy wearing a burgundy and forest green rugby shirt says, "Ladies."

"Hi," Maggie says softly as her eyes light up. "We knocked but we're not sure anyone heard it."

The blond boy looks at her and smiles. "Let me help." He opens the front door and "Baby Got Back" by Sir Mix-a-Lot pumps through the air. He extends his hand with a flourish. "Ladies first!"

We walk into the foyer, making room for the boys to join us. "Are you friends of Jesse?" the blond boy asks.

I nod. "I went to elementary school with him and live in the neighborhood. We go to Dunwoody High."

"Nice," the blond boy says as he extends his hand. "I'm Scott." He points to the boy on his left wearing a long-sleeved Duck Head T-shirt. "This is Pete." He then points to the guy on his right wearing a hunter green button down, "this is Steve." He looks out the still open front door. After a few seconds, a fourth boy jogs through the door. "And this is-"

"Dave," I say as my stomach drops. The last time I saw him was when he invited me over a couple of weeks after our first kiss and he had another girl at his house who he was flirting with right in front of me.

"You two know each other?" Scott asks.

"We hung out over the summer," Dave says as he gives me a one shoulder hug, his heather gray St. Christopher's wrestling sweatshirt hanging loosely on his frame. "How's it going?"

"Awesome," I say with sarcasm. Unsure what else to say to my first kiss who basically told me that he was the type of guy who wanted to play the field after we made out.

Scott seems to notice the awkwardness between us and says, "Let's go check out this party."

I'm more than happy to follow Scott through the house so we can go find Kurt and Shelly. We make our way to the kitchen and great room area and Scott and his buddies head straight out the back door. I see a pool glowing blue out back, but I want to find Kurt and Shelly, so I scan the kitchen and great room first. There are lots of kids in the great room, out on the patio, and around the pool. I pull Maggie to me and clutch her bicep. "That's the Dave I met this summer."

Maggie's blue eyes go wide and her mouth forms a circle. "Oh, wow. Your first kiss."

I nod. "Yeah, my first kiss who then told me he saw girls like shoes. He couldn't have just one pair."

"He said that to you?" Maggie's eyebrows arch high on her forehead.

I roll my eyes. "Yep. Can you believe that?"

Maggie shakes her head. "That's so lame."

"Totally," I say as I scan the great room for Kurt, but not seeing him. "Let's go outside and see if Kurt and Shelly are out there."

Maggie follows me outside, and as we stop on the patio to survey the back yard, she says quietly, "At least you've had your first kiss." She fiddles with her necklace, and I follow her gaze to the boys we just met as they grab drinks.

"Yeah," I agree. "At least I got it out of the way, even though there was nothing special about it." I stop scanning. "Ah! There they are." I point to the left side and the diving board where Kurt and Shelly are seated. "Come on, let's go."

"Sloane!" Kurt says as he and Shelly stand to greet us. Kurt wobbles a little, then pulls me into a hug. "I'm so glad you came." He looks at Shelly. "Isn't it great that they came?"

Shelly smiles sweetly and gives me and Maggie hugs. "Yes, it's nice to have some friendly faces here."

Kurt nods to the other side of the pool. "Your favorite person is here."

I recognize the sarcasm my friend is known for and look to the other side of the pool. "Ugh, why the heck does she have to be here?" Amber Gates and her crew of cheerleader friends are sitting around the hot tub's edge, dangling their legs into the hot, steamy water. Since it's too cold for the pool, no one is swimming, but the hot tub is full of jocks. "Of course, the football players are with them. Do they go everywhere together?"

I make my friends laugh as Jesse walks up with a red plastic cup in his hand, his eyes are a bit glassy. "Sloane! Oh my gosh, I'm so glad to see you!"

I hug Jesse and smell the alcohol on him. "How's Saint Christopher's?" I ask, referring to the private, Catholic school he went to after seventh grade.

"It's cool," he says. "I miss a lot of the kids we went to Vanderwood with, though. Those were great times."

"Yeah," I say. "I get that, but there are a few I wouldn't miss." I look over at Amber and her friends.

Jesse follows my gaze. "Oh yeah? Does Amber give you a hard time?"

I scoff. "She's pretty much insufferable. I guess when you're shy, everything's just harder."

"You're like the nicest person in the world!" Jesse says. "No one should give you trouble."

"Thanks, Jess," I smile at his exuberance that is definitely a result of his beverage of choice. There's that adjective again. Nice. Ugh. "Oh, sorry, this is my friend, Maggie."

"Hey, nice to meet you," Jesse says.

"You, too. Thanks for having us," Maggie replies softly.

"I'll go grab you some drinks," Jesse smiles. "You've gotta try my punch."

"Oh, um. Do you have a Coke or something?" I ask. "I don't really drink."

"Yeah, sure," Jesse says then looks at Maggie. "What about you?"

Maggie thinks for a second. "A Coke would be great, thanks."

"Awesome, be right back!" Jesse says as he heads back inside.

He returns shortly with two red cups. "Here you go." He hands us each a red cup filled with ice and brown liquid. "There's more in the fridge, and if you want to try my punch," he holds up his own cup, "it's spiked, so go slow." He winks at us then notices a group of people walking out the back door. "Oh, I've gotta go say hi. It's so good to see you. And meet you," he looks at Maggie. "I'm glad y'all came," he says sincerely before rushing off.

"I kinda wish he would have stayed in school with us." I say to Kurt. "It's so cool that you two have stayed friends."

Kurt nods. "When you live next door to your best friend since fourth grade, it's hard not to."

I think about Miranda who moved to my street when I was five, and she was four. I hate that we don't hang out a ton anymore. We get together from time to time, but it's not like it used to be. Her parents got divorced when we were in junior high and that really affected her a lot. Plus, she had to move which sucked. We kind of drifted after that. I feel a tugging at my elbow and snap out of my thoughts.

"Look who just got here," Maggie whispers as she nods over to where the cheerleaders and jocks are.

I look that way and see the most beautiful boy in school. Tyler Finlay is here. My pulse quickens as I watch him greet his fellow football players. I take a sip of soda out of nervousness. My eyes are fixed on Tyler and that darn smile.

"I didn't even think he would be here," I say to Maggie, "But, I guess it makes sense since he went to St. Christopher's." I watch as Tyler laughs at something his best friend, Brian, says. His smile makes my heart flutter. "At least I'll get to admire him from afar."

"Hey guys," Kurt says, "We're gonna go inside for a bit. Wanna come?"

Of course, I don't want to leave the area where I can ogle Tyler from a distance. "Um, I think we'll stay out here a little longer. We'll come find you in a bit."

After Kurt and Shelly amble off toward the house, Maggie offers a knowing smile. She turns to face me so I can adjust my position and have a clear view of Tyler and his friends, without being totally conspicuous. With her back to the hot tub, I can talk to her and steal glances at Tyler.

"He's so gorgeous. It should be criminal to be that good looking," I tell Maggie as I unconsciously sip from my red plastic cup.

"You should go say hi," she suggests.

"No way! In front of all those people? Forget it." It makes me uneasy just thinking about that. Everyone would be staring at me, and I hate that feeling.

"I get it," Maggie says.

I raise my cup to my mouth, then stop abruptly. "Oh my gosh, I think he's about to take his shirt off." Maggie turns to look.

Tyler pulls his T-shirt over his head exposing his abs and chest. "Oh, dear God," I swoon. "It's like I've died and gone to heaven."

As we watch, Tyler tosses his shirt onto a nearby lounge chair and adjusts his swim trunks before stepping down into the hot tub. As he braces his hand on the edge, he looks right at us and grins. Maggie turns, quickly facing me and trying to play it cool, but probably not succeeding.

"Oh my gosh, do you think he saw us?" I ask, raising my cup to my mouth.

"I hope not," Maggie says, fingering her cross necklace and looking serious. "But we did look totally obvious."

"Did you see those abs?" I ask her quietly.

Maggie nods quickly, her eyes bright. "How does he not have a girl-friend?"

"I have no idea, but I'm not complaining." I take another sip of my Coke.

"I guess he knew there would be a hot tub and came prepared," Maggie says.

"Yeah," I reply as I realize that some of the kids here were prepared for a pool party even though it's cool out. "I'm so glad he did." Maggie and I giggle.

I glance back and see Tyler chatting with a few of the football players in the hot tub. "I swear the number of cheerleaders around the hot tub just doubled," I lament. "I'm sure any one of them would love to date him."

Maggie says, "Maybe he wants a nice girl?"

"If he wants a nice girl, sign me up!" I joke, but we both know it's not a joke at all. However, in my experience, the nice girl doesn't get the guy, ever. But I hold out hope that maybe Tyler is different. Maybe he wants someone who isn't just a popular cheerleader.

"Okay," I say to Maggie, "we can't stand here and ogle Tyler all night. Let's go inside for a bit."

As we walk beside the pool, I keep glancing over to the hot tub. Tyler is smiling as he talks with his buddies, and I'm surprised I haven't turned into a puddle next to the pool. His smile lights up his whole face and my insides. Suddenly, I feel arms wrap around my shoulders, and I let out an involuntary squeal. My body is swung over the edge of the pool. My legs swing out over the water. The remaining Coke from my cup, which was at least half full, is now all over the front of my sweater. Mercifully, I'm set down on the pool deck and not thrown into the water. I whirl around to see who the culprit is and find Dave grinning at me.

"I thought you might want to go for a swim," he says as he chomps on a piece of gum.

I swat his arm. "Oh my gosh, you're crazy!" My back is to the pool, and he pushes me back then grabs my forearm so I can't fall. I move away from the side of the pool with my back to the house and some distance between me and Dave. He's still grinning at me like this is fun, and still annoyingly chomping his gum. I pull at my sweater as the cold fabric sticks to me and glance around and see that everyone is staring at us, including Tyler and his friends. I feel my face heat up. While the jocks and cheerleaders are laughing, and Brian Applequist is capturing this on his camcorder, Tyler's captivating grin is gone, and there's a hint of concern in his eyes.

"I'm just playing with you," Dave says. "You're lucky it's not warm out, because if it was, you would be in that pool."

"Ha-ha," I say. "It's a good thing it's cold, then." Speaking of cold, I shiver as my soda-soaked sweater clings to my chest. I look at the dark stain on my pretty sweater. "I can't believe you spilled my drink all over me."

"Here," Dave says with a grin, holding out his hand, "take it off, I'll go wash it for you."

"Ugh," I groan. "You're so gross." Dave laughs and luckily heads back over to his friends.

I look around and thankfully, everyone has gone back to whatever else they were doing and not watching me and Dave, everyone except Tyler. Is he worried about me? I think to myself, wishfully.

Maggie's hand wraps around my wrist. "Come on, let's go inside."

Chapter 15

Sloane

Maggie and I go into the kitchen and find Kurt, Shelly, and Jesse talking.

"What happened to you?" Jesse asks.

"Oh, Dave Flemming grabbed me and pretended he was going to throw me into the pool," I say. "Spilled my Coke all over me." I shudder as a chill runs through me.

Jesse shakes his head and chuckles. "Of course it was Dave." He sets his cup down and says, "I'll go grab one of my shirts for you. Be right back."

"Do you know that guy?" Kurt asks.

I nod my head. "Yeah, we hung out a couple of times over the summer. He goes to Saint Christopher's." I say as I feel my cheeks grow warm.

"Aww, he's flirting with you!" Shelly says, her green eyes sparkling. "That's cute."

I groan. "He was kind of a jerk this summer, and that's why we stopped hanging out."

"Oh," Shelly says. "Well, clearly he realized he let a good thing go."

I smile at her. "Thanks."

Jesse returns grinning with an armful of clothes. "Okay, Sloane, you're going to kill me, but your choices are limited because I need to do laundry." He sets the small pile on the counter and picks up a black T-shirt. "You've got a choice between this one which I got at a school assembly." He shows me the front of the shirt which says "D.A.R.E" in a red brush font and below it, "KEEPING KIDS OFF DRUGS" in smaller white text. He sets the shirt on the counter and picks up another black T-shirt, this one with long sleeves. "Or this one." Jesse is smiling as he holds up the second shirt which has "Pantera" in bold white letters across the top and shows a fist punching a guy in the face.

I groan again. "Ugh, really. Those are my choices?"

Jesse shrugs. "Beggars can't be choosers!" He smiles and says, "I brought a flannel, too, because neither shirt will be as warm as your sweater."

Kurt chimes in. "Dude, you've gotta go with the Pantera shirt. No contest."

"Dude. I hate Pantera, remember? They're like one of my least favorite bands."

"At least the D.A.R.E. one could be seen as funny," Maggie suggests. "But if you want to hang out outside, you'll be cold."

I totally catch her drift because the one place I want to be is outside, even if I'm just stealing glances at Tyler. "Maggie's right, the Pantera shirt will be warmer." I grab it from Jesse, then he picks up the brown and white flannel shirt and tosses it to me.

Jesse leads me down a narrow hallway off the kitchen to the bathroom so I can change. I attempt to wash the stain out of my sweater, without much luck. I look at myself in the mirror. While I'm comfortable, I look like the biggest tomboy ever in Jesse's Pantera shirt and flannel. Don't get me wrong, I *am* a complete tomboy, but I do make an effort to look cute at school and events like this one. Plus, with my crush here, being cute is kind of a top priority. I open the bathroom door and as I'm looking at my stained sweater, I turn and walk right into a wall.

"Oof," I say as I look up and see a shirtless Tyler Finlay grinning at me. My face flushes and the butterflies wake up in my belly. "Oh, um, sorry Tyler." I realize my hand is on his bare chest which is still damp from the hot tub, and I immediately snatch it away like I've just touched hot coals. "Er, sorry."

He chuckles as electricity hums through my body. "No problem." His gaze drops to my non-existent chest, and his eyebrows squish together. "I didn't peg you for a Pantera fan."

I let out a laugh. "Yeah, definitely not." I tuck my hair behind my right ear. "My drink spilled all over my sweater, so Jesse gave me something to wear." Tyler's grin is killing me over here, and we're so close to each other in this tiny hallway that I'm starting to feel out of breath. Seriously, how can one person have this much of an effect on another?

"Jesse's awesome. How do you know him?"

Being this close to a half-dressed Tyler Finlay has seriously limited my ability to think. "Oh, uh, we went to elementary school together."

"Cool. Well, I'm glad you've got something warm and dry to wear." His smile fades. "I saw what that guy did and was afraid he was going to throw you in the pool."

The butterflies have sped up in my stomach, and my nerve endings tingle. "Yeah, me too." I move to the side to let Tyler pass. "I'll, um, get out of your way." Uncertain about what to do, I turn toward the kitchen.

"Hey Sloane?" Tyler calls after me.

I turn back, my breath leaving me for a moment. "Yeah?"

His dark hair has fallen over his right eye, and he pushes it out of the way. "I was wondering-"

"Oh *my gosh*, there you *are*," squeals a voice from behind me which I immediately recognize as Amber Gates. I turn to see her pulling Lori Tanner along behind her. "We've been looking all over for you!" It's evident that they've both had a lot of punch. They're looking past me, at Tyler, of course.

"We're going to get beer pong set-up," Lori exclaims. Her eyes squint from the huge grin on her face.

The two girls have practically squished me up against the wall, and Amber finally acknowledges my presence. "Did you need something?" She sneers as her eyes cut to me and look at me up and down.

"Uh, no," I say quietly as I turn and squeeze out of the hallway and back to the kitchen.

"What's with that outfit?" I hear Lori say under her breath.

"Seriously," Amber cuts back. "I guess she thinks she's all grunge or something."

Mocking laughter fills my ears, then tears prick the back of my eyes. I take a deep breath, willing myself not to cry, at a party of all places. I enter the kitchen and see my friends smiling and chatting right where I left them. I put on a smile, determined not to get upset.

"Rock on," Kurt exclaims, then his eyes search my face. "Hey, what's wrong? It's not that bad, Sloane."

I take a deep breath. "No, it's cool." I try to mentally shake off my mean-girl encounter. "I just had a run-in with Amber and Lori."

"What happened?" Shelly asks.

I shake my head. "You know, just making fun of the way I look and acting like I don't belong anywhere near them."

Maggie puts a hand on my shoulder. "I'm sorry, Sloane. They're probably just irritated that you can pull off this look."

"Hey, Bleacher Buddy!" I hear as a friend from elementary school barrels into me and wraps me in a bear hug. Tameka and I went to most of the DHS baseball games last year and Sara was there quite a bit, too.

"Sara!" I hug her back, then she releases her embrace and holds me by the shoulders taking in my outfit.

"Girl, I love this." She gestures to my T-shirt and flannel. Sara's long brown hair is naturally curly. The kind of loose curls you'd kill for, and she always seems to have a smile on her face. Tonight is no different.

I laugh and fill her in on what happened.

"You could wear a sack and still look cute," she tells me, but I wave her off.

"See?" Maggie says with a smile.

Sara's best friend and soccer teammate, Wendy, walks up with two plastic cups, handing one to Sara.

Wendy joined me and Miranda for an INXS concert at the Omni last year that my dad got tickets to from his job. The company he works for sponsors events around Atlanta, and one of the perks is free tickets to a lot of good shows.

"I didn't know you were a Pantera fan," Wendy says gesturing to my shirt.

We all laugh, and I fill her in on the debacle with Dave.

"Phew," she jokes, "For a minute I started to worry about you."

We hear the jangly intro to Cyndi Lauper's, *Girls Just Wanna Have Fun*, and Sara drags us into the great room. I'm not a dancer, in the least, but I hop around with my friends. When you're six feet tall and as thin as a rail, you kind of just look like knees and elbows and feel like you stick out like a sore thumb. At least that's how I imagine I look when I'm dancing. I'm a good five inches taller than my friends, but I try not to feel self-conscious. Maggie looks like she's trying hard not to be self-conscious either, but Sara and Wendy move with ease and don't look like they have a care in the world. That must be such a great feeling.

When the song is over, I can tell Maggie needs to make a quick escape, so we go back outside and let Sara and Wendy tear it up on the dance floor. We grab a seat on a lounge chair where we have a view of most of the pool area.

"You know what I love about Sara?" I say to Maggie. "She became kinda popular this year, but she's still nice to her old friends."

"That is cool. It's not common for one of us nice girls to be embraced by the popular girls."

I laugh. "Right? I guess when she became a cheerleader for the basketball team last year, that elevated her status."

"For sure," Maggie agreed. "Something you and I could never do."

"Totally. I can scream from the stands, but cheering while everyone is looking at you? No thanks."

"I'm glad we have classes together and became friends," Maggie says. "I've never really felt like I've had a place here."

"Same here," I agree. "It's like, I have acquaintances in lots of groups but don't feel like I fit into any of them." I hug Jesse's flannel shirt around my torso. "And people like Amber and Lori just make everything so much harder. Like, just leave me alone, do your thing, and I'll do mine."

"Exactly. I know I should be excited for our senior year, but I'm just so ready to graduate and move on from these people."

"Yes!" I bump her with my shoulder. "That's why I'm glad I have you. You love football, you don't want to party and chase boys, and you're...*so nice*." I say that last two words with emphasis, and we giggle. "Now, if I could just get you interested in my music."

"Nah, I'm not that cool," Maggie says. "Thankfully you have Miranda and Kurt to talk to about music...oh, and Tyler."

She winks at me as the dimple in her cheek reappears. I scan the area looking for Tyler, remembering what he started to say to me in the hallway when Amber and Lori interrupted us.

I grab Maggie's knee and sit up straight. "Oh my gosh! I almost forgot. Before Amber and Lori stumbled into the hallway, I ran into Tyler. Like, literally ran into his bare chest." Thinking about it makes my pulse race.

"What?" Maggie exclaims as she turns toward me. "What happened?"

I fill her in and say, "Just before Amber interrupted us, he said, 'Hey, Sloane, I was wondering-'"

"Wondering what?" Maggie asks as she sits on the edge of her seat with wide eyes.

I shrug my shoulders. "I have no idea. That's when stupid Amber and stupid Lori interrupted."

Maggie slouches down, and her shoulders roll forward. "No," she pouts.

I nod, "Yep. Talk about the worst timing ever."

Maggie sits straight up, faces me, and grabs my hand. "Let's go inside and find him. You've gotta find out what he was going to ask you."

I mull this over in my head then let out a breath. "Alright, but you're coming with me."

Chapter 16

Tyler

I look at myself in the bathroom mirror as I wash my hands. I can't believe that random dude grabbed Sloane like that and acted like he was going to throw her in the pool. Anger surfaces inside me just thinking of the way he had his hands on her, then spilled her drink all over her. I had a feeling she might be inside cleaning up and I was so glad when she bumped into me. Just thinking about her hands on my chest sends my pulse racing. She nearly took my breath away. She's so beautiful, but I don't think she knows it. She carries herself in a way that is shy, like she's trying not to stand out, trying to make herself unnoticeable for some reason. She's definitely not unnoticeable to me. Whenever I'm in the same room with her, it's like my eyes know exactly where to find her, even if it's in a crowded gymnasium during a pep rally. Aside from her physical beauty, there's this happiness that just exudes from her. Like pure goodness. Add to that, her awesome taste in music and sense of humor and she's the total package. I just wonder if I'm good enough for her. Does she believe the rumors about me? Even though she said she likes football and baseball, I wonder if she would ever date a jock who was kicked out of private school. She seems like she would want a musician or artsy type, not me.

Knocking on the door brings me back to reality. "Tyler!" Amber's nasally voice squeals.

When I open the door, Lori says, "Come play with us!"

Just as I'm about to decline, Brian pipes up from further down the hall. "Yeah, man, come on, let's play some beer pong!" I step into the hallway and see him grinning from behind his camera. I can't turn down my best friend. He's the only reason I'm at this party, plus, in the distance, I see Sloane dancing with her friends. Of course, I want to be wherever she is.

I smile at my friend. "Alright, dude, let's go," I say to Brian, not wanting to give Amber or Lori any encouragement.

As we walk into the kitchen, I see Sloane, but she doesn't see me. Although she still looks uncomfortable in her own skin, her smile makes my heart flutter. What is it about this girl that has made me so smitten?

"Hey, man, can you and Brian help me with something?" I feel a hand on my shoulder and force my eyes from the makeshift dance floor and Sloane's magnetic pull. Jesse looks at me expectantly.

"Sure, of course," I say as Brian stops recording and sets his camera down. We follow Jesse out into the garage.

"My mom will kill me if we play beer pong on her dining room table," Jesse says as he shifts aside a kayak and some boxes to get to a large plastic table. "Heck. my parents will totally kill me if they find out about the party, but ruining her table would do me in."

"Dude, what about the neighbors?" Brian asks.

Jesse grins. "They went to the mountains *with* the neighbors. Kurt Stone lives next door and our parents are really close."

"Smart," I say as Brian and I extract the heavy, six-foot long table from behind a bunch of boxes. Brian and I carry the table toward the door that leads into the kitchen while Jesse puts everything back in the garage. When we enter the kitchen with the table, Brian heads straight for the makeshift dance floor and everyone moves out of the way.

Brian shouts, "It's time for beer pong!" A loud cheer erupts as I look around, trying to find Sloane. But she's nowhere to be found. My heart sinks a little.

Amber and Lori enter the room clutching plastic cups and start arranging them on the table. "I'll be right back," I say to Brian.

"Oh, no you don't, mister!" Amber slurs. "You and Brian against me and Lori. Come on!"

I groan internally. At least I'm on Brian's team and didn't get paired with one of them. Brian grabs my shoulder, "This should be easy."

The next thing I know, I'm wrapped up in a game of beer pong, hoping that Sloane hasn't left the party yet. I really want to talk to her before the end of the night.

Chapter 17

Sloane

Maggie and I head inside and I figure I have a bit of courage since Tyler did sound like he was going to ask me something. I'm already rehearsing in my head what I should say to him to make it sound natural. The kitchen and great room are now pretty packed, and it appears the beer pong game was set-up in the great room, although it's hard to see the table through all the spectators. *Jump Around* by House of Pain is pounding through the speakers and there are more kids jumping and dancing around every inch of the great room. It's easy to find Tyler, though, since he's one of the tallest guys here. Plus, I swear my eyes are naturally drawn to him. He's at the far side of the beer pong table, facing out and oh my gosh, he just saw me staring at him and I look away as soon as I'm caught.

"Ugh, he totally just caught me staring at him," I tell Maggie as my nerves start to work overtime. "No way am I going to interrupt him while he's playing," I lean up against the case opening and fold my arms over my chest. "Plus, it's too loud to talk."

"Why can't we be like Sara and Wendy?" Maggie asks me, nodding to them. "Looks like they had no fear joining in."

I look at Sara and Wendy as they play with Amber and Lori, against Tyler, Brian, Jesse, and a guy I don't recognize. I wonder what it would be like to have the kind of confidence they have. I'm simultaneously jealous of them for a split second and mad at myself. Maybe that's why so many of my classmates drink? I think to myself. It probably makes socializing way easier than when you're sober.

"Yeah, but we'd have to drink beer with that game." I say as I watch two nice girls holding their own amongst the popular crowd. "I wish I didn't have a paralyzing fear of social situations. If I could catch Tyler one-on-one, it wouldn't be as hard to talk to him." I think back to running into him in the hallway. "Ugh, if Amber and Lori hadn't interrupted..."

We hang out in the kitchen, talking with Kurt and Shelly some more, but since it would take the entire bowl of Jesse's punch to give me the nerve I need to go up to Tyler in this setting, we decide to call it a night after a while and head to my house. Tyler is still wrapped up in the game and I can't stand watching Amber and Lori flirt with him any longer. Maybe on Monday, he'll ask me whatever it was he was going to ask me in the hallway?

As Maggie and I descend the steep hill and walk back toward my house, she says, "Snowball is coming up. Do you think you might ask Tyler?" Snowball is DHS's version of the Sadie Hawkins dance where the girls ask the boys.

"I don't know," I sigh. "I would have to be pretty sure he'd say yes to ask him. Not only would I be mortified if he said no, but then, I'd have to sit next to him for the rest of the year and that would be so uncomfortable." I squeeze Jesse's flannel tight against me as my still-damp sweater is tucked under my right arm.

"Yeah, I get that," Maggie says. "Just think about it. I can tell how much you like him and it sounds like you have a lot in common with your love of music and sports. Plus, from what you've told me, he kinda seems like you in that he's a free-thinker and doesn't just follow the crowd."

I inhale deeply and the cold air makes my nose tingle. "I know, he's like, so perfect." I toss my head back and see the pinpricks of tiny light against the dark sky. "I'll think about it, but I just don't know if I'm willing to gamble making things awkward between us, you know?"

"I totally do," Maggie says.

"Are you going to ask anyone?" I look at her and think that maybe if she can ask someone, it might give me the motivation to ask Tyler.

"Nah, there's no one I want to take."

"Not even a friend?" I ask as we turn the corner onto my street.

"Not really. Plus, my brother is going to the lake for the weekend and I don't want my mom to be alone."

"I'm sure she would be cool with you going to the dance for a few hours," I suggest. I don't know what's going on with her mom since her dad left, but it's not my place to say anything and I don't want to pry.

"If there was someone like Tyler who I liked, I might ask him," she says then looks at me with a smile. "Might."

"Yeah, it's so intimidating. I would be crushed if he said no. Besides, he probably already has a date."

"Well, I know it's easy for me to say, but you should totally think about it," Maggie says encouragingly.

"Says the girl who isn't going," I joke. "But yeah, I'll think about it." Just thinking about asking Tyler to the dance makes my stomach turn. I know I'll be thinking about it all night until I can fall asleep. That and standing so close to him in the hallway tonight. Maybe I'll work on Sloane's Senior Songs, Volume 2. I can put songs on it that remind me of

Tyler, that'll help pass the time. I really wish I knew what he was going to ask me tonight and I wish I was brave enough to approach him to find out. I really have to stop letting life happen to me.

Chapter 18

Sloane

"Hey buddy," Kurt says as he takes his seat next to me in French class Monday morning. "Did you have fun at Jesse's party?"

I smile at Kurt, "I did, thanks for encouraging me to go." I pull Jesse's shirts out of my backpack. "Can you give these back to him?"

"Are you sure you don't want to keep the Pantera shirt?" Kurt jokes.

I laugh. "Positive, but thanks for thinking of me."

Kurt takes the clothes and stuffs them into his backpack. "Snowball is coming up. Who are you going to ask?"

My stomach grows nervous just thinking about asking a boy to a dance. "Uh, I don't think I'll ask anyone."

"Aww, come on, Sloane, it's our senior year. You should ask someone. Even if it's just a friend."

I fidget with the cap on my pen. "You're my only guy friend, and you've got Shelly." I can't believe how nervous I am just talking about this.

"You could bring someone from another school. What about the guy from the party?"

I look at Kurt with my eyebrows raised. "The guy who pretended like he was going to throw me in the pool and spilled my Coke all over me?"

Kurt nods. "I think Shelly was right. I think he was flirting with you."

I shake my head. "He might have been, but he was a jerk over the summer. I don't want to hang out with him."

"Oh," Kurt says. "Right." He rests his chin in his hand, and I can see the wheels turning in his head. "Isn't there anyone in any of your classes who might be fun to go with?" He grins. "Besides me, of course."

I smile at him. "There's one guy for sure, but I could never ask him."

Kurt bolts upright, his eyes wide and bright with excitement. "Who?"

"It doesn't matter. He would never want to go with me."

"Oh, come on, you totally underestimate yourself. Is this someone you actually talk to in class?"

My shoulders drop, and I glare at him teasingly. "Yes, I actually talk to him."

"Do you have stuff in common?" Kurt asks.

"I guess so," I say as I think about it. "I mean, we definitely talk music and have similar taste, and he's nice."

"See, there you go. Ask him!" Kurt says a little too loud.

"Ooh, ask who and what?" Amber slides into her desk and perches her chin on her hand.

"Nothing," I say as I open my French book and try to busy myself with my notebook.

Amber pops up, her large eyes bugging out of her skull. "Are you talking about Snowball?" She singsongs like she's talking to a child.

My stomach is in knots, and Kurt looks at me sympathetically. "No," I tell her. "I'm not going to Snowball."

"Why not?" she asks with fake concern. "Afraid you'll get turned down?"

My eyes burn, and I start doodling in my notebook willing myself not to cry.

"Amber, lay off," Kurt says in a loud voice. "Why do you have to be so mean?"

At almost the same time, Ramsey says, "Amber, come on."

A look of surprise washes over Amber's face. "What? I was just joking." Now she's the one busying herself with her books because she can tell that no one in this small class is on her side.

Kurt puts his hand on my desk to get my attention. "Hey, sorry," he whispers.

I give him a weary smile. "It's okay."

"You should seriously ask him," he whispers so only I can hear him. "He'd be lucky to take you."

Again, I wish my lack of self-confidence hadn't caused me to turn Kurt down in junior high, even though I've never felt butterflies around him like I do with Tyler. Thankfully, Madame Carney walks into the room and starts class. I have never been so grateful to immerse myself in the French language than today. I just wish Amber's desk didn't face mine. I can't even stand to look at her. I wish I had the guts to stand up to her like Kurt did.

After class, Kurt walks with me. "I was thinking about how you're nervous to ask this guy to the dance."

"Kurt, I appreciate it, I really do, but this guy is out of my league. I have no business asking him to go with me."

Kurt grabs my bicep, and we stop. "Seriously, Sloane? You're pretty, funny, smart, and you have great taste in music. Any guy would be lucky to go with you."

I huff out a sigh. "Kurt-"

"Just hear me out," he says as we continue walking. "I know what it's like to be nervous to ask someone out, and I've become a pro at asking in a way that won't make things awkward if I get turned down."

I think about our friendship and nod for him to continue.

"Just do it in a real casual way, like, 'Do you have a date for Snowball, because I'm gonna need someone to join me in making fun of the music they play.' You know, something like that."

"I don't know..." I twist the strap of my backpack as my heart rate increases.

Kurt stops me again and looks at me earnestly. "Look, I don't want you to miss out on what could be an amazing experience. Be bold. Go for what you want, you totally deserve it."

My shoulders relax. "Thanks, I'll think about it."

"Hey," he says quietly. "If I swear to keep it a secret, will you tell me who it is."

I think for a moment looking at Kurt's eager expression. "You have to promise not to tell anyone. Like, I won't talk to you ever again and you'll be forced to talk to Amber in French class instead."

Kurt chuckles and his grin is goofy. "I promise, Sloane. Scout's honor." He holds up three fingers.

"Okay." I lean toward Kurt's ear and feel my cheeks start to burn as I whisper the name of my crush to him.

His eyes go wide, and he smiles broadly. "Nice choice! I figured it had to be a tall guy."

"I'm way out of my league, aren't I?"

Kurt shakes his head. "Not at all," he says earnestly. "I hear he's a decent dude. You should totally do it." He pats me on the shoulder as the warning bell sounds, and the kids in the hallway start picking up their pace. Kurt has to double back to his homeroom which we've already passed. He starts walking backwards and calls out, "Be bold!"

I laugh at him, thankful that he's made me feel better and head to my homeroom.

Chapter 19

Sloane

As I listen to the morning announcements in homeroom, I think about what Kurt said. He's right, I should be bold. Why not me? I am so nervous just thinking about asking Tyler to the dance that my pulse races as I stare at the back of Colt's head. I can't even imagine how I'll feel if I do get up the gumption to ask Tyler to the dance. By the time the bell rings releasing us from homeroom, I can't even remember anything I heard in there. All I can think about is whether or not I should ask Tyler and coming up with the right words. I rehearse most everything I say, especially when I'm nervous. I like Kurt's idea but am so scared to get a "no," that I try to think of other ways to ask. How do boys do this? It's completely nerve-wracking.

I'm in my own head while I trudge through the crowded halls on my way to marine bio. I can feel my heart pounding in my chest. I inhale a deep breath as I turn the corner and make my way to my classroom. As usual, Billy is there but no sign of Tyler.

"Sloaner, how was your weekend?" Billy asks with a genuine smile.

I return his smile and feel better for the distraction. "Good, thanks." I pat the top of his newly cut flat-top hair style. "Looks like you got a haircut over the weekend."

"Yes ma'am," he drawls. "I was starting to look like a hippie."

I laugh at him. "What? Your hair was only about a half inch longer on Friday."

"I know, wasn't it awful? All long like that..." He fake shudders then leans back in his chair patting his chest. "I've got the legend on today."

I sit down and toss my backpack on the lab table and look at his chest. "Johnny Cash, huh?"

Billy gives me a look like I'm an alien. "Uh, yeah, and you say it like the man is just some average street musician."

I take my book and notebook out of my bag. "Of course, I know he's important. I just don't know if I could tell you what he sings."

Billy clutches his chest, "Dear God, who raised you?"

I laugh at him. "Ha, two people from Buffalo, New York."

"That's right, I forgot you're a Yankee," Billy says with a smile.

"Hey!" I feign taking offense. "I was born and raised here."

"By Yankees," he says, his face looking like he just took a gulp of sour milk, though I know he's joking.

Billy leans forward, looking past me and says, "Ty, can you believe this one can't name a Johnny Cash song?"

I freeze, Tyler must have sat down while I was facing Billy. I turn in my chair, feeling flushed.

Tyler looks at me and grins. Danggit! I'm nervous enough today, and now he's got to go and smile at me like that. I can't even think straight. "Really?" he asks as he cocks his head, still grinning as he takes off his letterman's jacket.

I shake my head tentatively and think about how proud I would be to wear that jacket of his. "I don't think so." Great, now I'm too scared to even look at Tyler because I know what I want to ask him.

"Ring of Fire? I Walk the Line? Do those ring a bell?" Tyler asks, leaning his head down, trying to catch my eyes.

I look at him. "I think so?" I answer it like a question because I have no idea, then busy myself with my backpack.

"What are we going to do with this one?" Billy jokes as he hooks his thumb toward me.

I scoot my chair back so they can see each other. Tyler grows serious. "We'll educate her, of course. We can't in good conscious let her continue on like this."

I laugh as they pretend like this is really important to my development as a human being.

"Oh, this isn't funny, missy," Billy jokes. "You listen to all that," he waves his hand in disgust, "grunge stuff, but you wouldn't have that if not for the work of the legend." He pats his chest and smiles.

Billy makes me smile and I turn to Tyler. "Is he pulling my leg?"

Tyler shakes his head, his expression as serious as a heart attack. "No, ma'am, he is not." He points to Billy's chest. "That man right there is the original rebel."

My eyes grow wide. "Really?"

"Oh, yes," Tyler says. "Would I deceive you?"

I look at Billy for confirmation, and he nods. "Seriously, he is known as the Original Rebel."

I can tell that Billy isn't joking. "Okay, it looks like I've got some homework to do, then." I feel a little more comfortable, and we're joking around, so now might be the time to ask Tyler. Oh gosh, just thinking that makes my stomach nervous. I take a deep breath.

Billy and Tyler exchange satisfied grins as the bell rings. "I mean, he's no Pantera, that's for sure," Tyler jokes, and winks at me which almost makes me forget who I am.

"Ha-ha," I say, then gather myself together. "Just for the record, I don't think I could name a Pantera song, either. I just know I've heard them, and they kinda scared me."

Now Tyler laughs out loud and this eases my nerves a smidge. "That was a pretty fun party, huh?"

I manage a smile even though I'm nervous right now. "Yeah, it was." I'm so glad he opened the door to this conversation, but my stomach is literally starting to hurt from nerves. "Oh, I meant to ask you-"

Coach K slams the back door hard and is in a flurry searching the back counter for something. "I'll be right with you," he snaps. "Start reading the next chapter."

"Yikes," Billy says quietly. "It looks like something's got Coach upset." All of our eyes are focused on our affable teacher who has one of the most easy-going dispositions in the school.

Clearly Coach K has something he has to say because we barely crack our books open when he turns around and addresses the class. "One of my students was in here this morning and was playing with my tarantula." He rakes his hand through his thick dark brown hair and grimaces. "It appears as if she didn't put the lid on tightly, and my rare red Chilean tarantula is missing."

My fellow students and I gasp, then Coach continues. "It's okay, it's okay, they are very docile." He waves his hands in a downward motion to settle us. "It's probably hiding, but just keep an eye out, okay?"

"Keep an eye out?" I gasp to Billy and Tyler and feel like my own eyes are going to pop out of my head. "You mean, that thing can be anywhere?" I pull my legs up off the floor and onto my chair. "Will you guys look under the table?" All my nervousness is now directed at the thought that a giant spider is loose in our classroom.

Billy and Tyler look underneath our table as other students do the same around their space. Tyler extracts his long frame from underneath his side of the table, his hair falling into his eyes. "All clear on my end."

Billy does the same, though his face is red from exertion. "Same here." He pats his hair. "You made me mess up my hair," he jokes. "Let's go help Coach look," he says to Tyler.

After several minutes, they return, telling me that they couldn't find it. If I was nervous before, I'm even more nervous now. Holy cow, there's a tarantula loose in our classroom! I'm acting like a scaredy-cat, and I'm not ashamed.

"If that thing appears, I will jump right out of this chair," I warn my classmates as I try to focus on my textbook. My skin feels all itchy, like there's something there when there's not, but I rub my arms, nonetheless.

Tyler looks at me and grins. "Don't worry, it's not on you. I would tell you if it was." He winks at me. Well, that's one way to get my mind off of a tarantula on the loose.

"Gee, thanks," I say as I continue to scratch my phantom itches. "If you see it on me, please don't tell me, just get it off, thank you very much."

Tyler laughs as his smile grows deeper, and he turns back to his book. As we're reading, Tyler whispers, "Hey Sloane?"

I turn to look at him, my eyebrows arched, my heart speeding up. "Yeah?" Maybe he's going to ask me the question he had on Saturday night? Or, maybe the spider is on my back...

"You were about to ask me something right before Coach came in."

"Oh, yeah." Great, now I have to remember how the heck I was going to ask him to the dance. "I wondered if-"

"Doggonit!" Coach K huffs. Okay, that's not the word he said, but let's just pretend he said something PG in front of his entire class. "It's dead." He is holding his rare spider and examining it. "Looks like it cracked its exoskeleton. Dang it!" He walks to the front of the room and tosses the spider onto the top of his trash can which is full of papers. There's literally a dead tarantula sitting right there on top of the trash pile. I can tell he's really upset and sad, and I bet he would cry if we weren't all in here staring at him.

"That was one of just five left in the world," he laments as my heart breaks for him. He runs his hand through his hair again. "It must have crawled out and fallen off the table."

I feel so bad for Coach and for the student who was careless with the tank lid. I bet they are going to feel horrible when they find out. Coach dives into the lesson, and now I'll have to wait even longer to ask Tyler to the dance.

As the clock ticks away, I'm half-listening to Coach, half-preparing what I'll say to Tyler, running scenarios through my head. When the bell finally rings, the butterflies wake up. I inhale deeply, mentally preparing myself when I hear Coach K say, "Finlay, I need to see you."

Seriously? I think to myself. You've got to be kidding me. By the way Coach called Tyler by his last name, I suspect this must have something to do with baseball, even though we're still in football season. I shoulder my backpack and see the poor tarantula still sitting on top of the trash. I hope this isn't some kind of omen.

Chapter 20

Sloane

By the end of the day, I am absolutely exhausted, but told myself I would find Tyler before football practice and ask him to the dance. This is getting ridiculous. Kurt is right, I have to be bold and honestly, I don't want to wait another day. The dance is still a month away, but I don't want to miss my opportunity. I didn't tell Maggie or my lunch crew that I was going to ask Tyler to Snowball, because let's face it, I could still chicken out. The day is still young.

Normally, Maggie and I leave Trig together, but I make up an excuse that I have to go see my French teacher. Obviously, I know where Tyler's locker is, and I have to get there before he goes to practice. My stomach is in knots as I pass kids at their lockers preparing to head home for the day. I'm practicing what I'm going to say in my head as I walk.

I get to Tyler's locker, but there's no sign of him. Luckily, Billy has a locker nearby so I go say hi. "Hey Billy!"

"Sloaner! What brings you to these parts?" Billy asks as he stuffs books into his backpack. His belly strains against his Johnny Cash T-shirt.

"Oh, um, I had to go see my French teacher," I lie and immediately feel bad about it. "That was awful what happened in marine bio, huh?"

Billy winces. "Yeah, I've never seen Coach so upset."

I nod, scanning the area. Tyler is nowhere to be seen. "I know, I felt so bad for him because he seemed so sad but couldn't really show it in front of all of us."

With every second that passes, I worry that I've already missed Tyler. Billy notices me looking around. "Looking for someone?" he asks as he slams his locker shut.

"Yeah," I say as I keep scanning the area and fidget with my backpack strap. "Have you seen Tyler? I wanted to ask him about this band." Why am I continuing to lie to poor Billy? It's like someone else has taken over my brain.

Billy smirks. "I think he's at practice. He grabbed his stuff and took off when I got here."

My eyes go wide. "Oh, okay, thanks!" I hurry off, then turn. "Thanks, Billy, see you tomorrow."

I walk so quickly down the hall, I must look like one of those stupid speed-walkers. I look at my watch and groan. I'm pretty sure football practice starts at 3:30, and it's already 3:21. I run down the staircase leading to the gym, and when I open the door, I see a few of the younger players milling about.

"Hey," I ask as I'm trying to catch my breath, "have you seen Tyler Finlay?"

A boy who I recognize as being a junior says, "Yeah, he just went out that way." He points to the doors leading to the parking lot.

I smile. "Thanks!" I head out the doors hopeful Tyler has gone to his car and not down to the practice field yet.

I search in front of the doors and scan the parking lot, but don't see any sign of him. I take the path that goes around the back of the school where stairs lead down to the field. As I walk briskly, I scan the parking lot over my right shoulder to see if Tyler might be at his car. As I'm walking, I collide with something. "Oof!" I say as my shoulder takes the brunt of it.

"Careful!" I hear as a hand grabs my shoulder.

I look up and see Tyler and that darn grin that melts me. Plus, he's in his practice uniform- pads and all. "Oh my gosh. I'm so sorry." I feel hot all of a sudden, even though we're well into Fall. Again, my hand reflexively braces his chest, and again I snatch it away as if I just touched something hot. Well, I kind of did. I step back and notice how good he looks in his uniform up close. Good lord. His helmet hangs in his right hand by his side.

"Being chased by a big hairy spider?" He jokes.

I laugh, grateful that he's so nice and has a good sense of humor. I huff out a laugh and smile. "Yeah, didn't you see it?" I joke as I motion behind me. "It's like we're in a horror movie around here."

I make Tyler laugh and that sends warmth through my belly. "Are you looking for someone?" he asks.

"Yeah," I say a little breathless from racing down here and being in Tyler's presence. "I was looking for-"

"SLOOOOOANE!" a male voice bellows from behind me.

Oh, for crying out loud! I whip around to find its source and see Kurt jogging toward me with Shelly trailing behind him. I feel my eyebrows move together. How many times have I been on the verge of asking Tyler to go to this stupid dance and been interrupted? This time, by the one and only friend who suggested I do this no less.

"Sloane!" He hollers again as he picks up his pace and closes in on us.

As he reaches us, I say, "Is everything okay?"

He's panting hard and is bent forward with his hands on his knees. "Yeah-" he gasps for air. "I just-" Still trying to catch his breath. "Really need to-" More gasping. "Talk to you."

"Okaaay," I say as I tilt my head at my wheezing friend. Tyler and I are looking at him, waiting to hear what he has to say.

Kurt is still panting, leaning forward, and holds up a finger. I cross my arms over my chest and Tyler's cleats scrape on the cement as he adjusts his weight to one side.

"Forty-four!" calls a voice from the field below. "Stop flirting and get your pretty face down here!"

Tyler and I turn toward the source and see Coach Harbin on the field with his hands on his hips. Tyler looks at me and Kurt. "Sorry, gotta go!" He turns and dashes down the cement stairs toward his teammates, and I can't believe I missed yet another opportunity to be bold and ask Tyler to the dance.

Kurt comes to my side and puts a hand on my left shoulder. "Sloane, I'm so sorry," he says still panting, but not as bad and by now, Shelly has joined us. "Did you ask him yet?"

I turn to look at my friend, his eyes eager for the answer. I shake my head, "No. Every time I've had an opportunity, I've been interrupted." I give him an accusatory glare then smile. "Why?"

Relief floods Kurt's eyes, and his shoulders noticeably relax. "Good." He wipes his brow. "Because Sara asked him at lunch today." He pants. "I found out this afternoon and wanted to find you as soon as I could."

And just like that, my smile fades, and my heart breaks into a million pieces.

Chapter 21

Tyler

"Man, Coach Harbin was tough on us today," I say to Brian as we head to my truck after practice.

"I know. I can't believe he made us run gassers just because some of the guys were goofing off," Brian says as he throws his gym bag onto the floorboard of my truck then sits in the passenger seat.

I sit down heavily behind the steering wheel and let out a sigh. I am so glad to be off my feet. "How many times did we run the width of the field and back? I lost count."

"I think I counted five, maybe six." Brian leans his head back and stretches his legs out in front of him.

My stomach growls. "I think we need protein. Wanna get a burger and a shake?"

"Yes!" Brian pumps his fist. "I'm starving."

I drive us over to Riley's Diner and when we walk in, my stomach growls again upon smelling the place. The scent of burgers grilling and coffee brewing double the hunger I was feeling before we walked in. A waitress takes us to a booth and we give her our order since I'm so hungry. I feel like I could eat my own hand right now.

"So, you're going to Snowball with Sara. That's cool," Brian says.

I nod. "Yeah, she's really sweet. It should be fun." I take a sugar packet out of the holder and fidget with it.

"But..." Brian says, looking at me with raised brows, prompting me for more.

"But what?" I say as the waitress brings us each a water and a chocolate shake.

"Dude, I know you, you're holding something back," Brian says as he pushes his straw into his thick shake.

I tear the paper off my straw and do the same, then take a long sip, giving myself brain freeze. I wince. Brian is still looking at me expecting a response. "I was kinda hoping that Sloane Warren would ask me."

"Really?" Brian's eyes go wide with surprise. "She's pretty and all, but she's so quiet and seems like a goody-goody. I think you'll have more fun with Sara."

"Actually, she's really cool. I sit next to her in marine bio. She has great taste in music and is pretty funny." Just thinking about her makes me smile.

"Huh." Brian says. "I had Pre-Algebra with her in ninth grade. Sat right behind her. She was nice, but super quiet. Like didn't say much at all."

"What do you think of her?" I ask as our waitress arrives with our burgers and fries.

"I don't, actually." When I cock my head Brian explains, "I mean, she's kind of like anonymous or something. Like you don't know she's there. But Sara...she's bubbly and bright. I think she'd be more fun at the dance."

Brian takes a bite of his burger. "Maybe," I say, then take a bite of my own.

"Besides, I don't think Sloane is into dances and stuff. I don't think I've ever seen her at one."

"Really?" I'm surprised to hear this, but Brian's been in school with her much longer than I have.

"Yeah, but, if you wanted to go with Sloane, why didn't you just ask her?" Brian says between chewing. "Just because it's Snowball, doesn't mean a guy *can't* ask a girl."

"I almost did. Well, I almost asked her at the party if she was going. You know, to open the door, feel things out, but we got interrupted." Brian has another mouthful, so I continue. "Then, when I saw her a little later, she totally looked away like, not even interested. And, she was kind of weird in class today."

"How do you mean?" Brian takes another bite of his burger.

"I don't know. She seemed happier talking to Billy than me. She normally seems happy to see me and she wasn't like that at all today." I chomp on a fry.

"Maybe she asked someone else?"

I think about Sloane asking someone else to the dance and my heart sinks a little.

"You didn't have to say yes to Sara," Brian says.

"I know." I toss my napkin on the table. "I guess it felt like Sloane wasn't going to ask me. I like Sara, too, and want to go to the dance, so..." I take a long sip of my milkshake, then lean forward and say, "Repeat this and I'll kill you, but—I don't think I'm cool enough for Sloane."

"What? That's crazy." Brian looks at me like I have three heads. "If that's so, it's her loss, Homes. She'd be lucky to take you to Snowball." Brian shoves a few fries in his mouth.

"She's not like other girls, and it's cool," I dunk a fry into some ketchup. "She doesn't seem to be into all the cliques and stuff, like she's a free-thinker and I love that."

"Yeah, well, you are that way yourself, so I could see why that appeals to you." Brian has finished off his burger and wipes his hands on a paper napkin, tossing it on the table when he's done. "I hate to say it, but maybe she's not into jocks. If she's super into music, she may be the artsy type who wants some brooding artist or musician who's pale and skinny."

I laugh. "I can be brooding."

Now it's Brian's turn to laugh. "Tell me about it." He stretches his legs under the table. "Man, I swear Coach is trying to kick our butts before the playoffs."

I'm grateful for the change of subject. "I know, I'm starting to feel it now."

"Dude, I think we're good enough to make it to State," Brian says, his eyes serious.

I nod, then have déja vu. "Wait. Sloane said that to me months ago."

"That we could go to State?" Brian cocks his head.

"Yeah, I almost forgot that we talked about football. She's really into it. Apparently, her whole family is. Baseball too." The conversation is flooding back from the recesses of my brain.

"Huh," Brian says. "And you're sure she's not into you?"

I shrug. "Man, I don't know. Normally, it's so easy to tell if a girl is into me. Like with Sara. There's this excitement in their eyes and, I don't know, I can just tell. With Sloane, sometimes I think she might be into me, but other times, I'm not so sure."

Brian leans back against the booth. "Like I said, maybe you're just not her type. She is really nice and friendly to everyone, maybe that's all it is?"

"Maybe you're right. Maybe she doesn't want to date a jock." I think for a moment as I sip my shake.

"That's got to be it," Brian says. "You're a stud, man. I see the way girls look at you. You could have any of them."

Yeah, but the one I want doesn't want me, I think to myself.

Chapter 22

Sloane

While I'm crushed to hear that I missed my opportunity with Tyler, I am happy that it was Sara who asked him to Snowball. If it couldn't be me, I'm glad it's her because she is a genuinely sweet person. Even after getting in with the popular crowd, she's remained friends with her friends from elementary school--girls who are more shy and nerdy than bubbly and popular. Of course, I've thought a million times about what would have happened if I hadn't felt so out of place at Jesse's party. What if I had stayed longer? What if I had joined in on the game? Would *I* have had a shot with Tyler? I may never know, but at least I have a cool person who I can talk music with in marine bio.

As the days turn into weeks, Tyler and Sara have become an official couple at Dunwoody High. I can't help but feel pangs of envy when I see Sara wearing Tyler's letterman's jacket as they hang out in front of our marine bio class daily or see them walking down the hallway with their arms wrapped around each other, but such is life when you're a shy, introverted, outsider at DHS. I can't help but wonder what things would be like if I weren't so scared, if I was bold like Kurt suggested.

While I may not have a tight group of friends at Dunwoody who share my interests, I am so grateful that my friend Tameka goes to college a short drive away and loves to come back to Atlanta for concerts. Tonight is the Dinosaur Jr. show at the Masquerade and I can't wait.

I pick up Tameka and Ray, her friend from college, at her house, and we head down to the Masquerade for the show.

"I'm so glad that 99X started playing Dinosaur Jr.," I say as we exit the highway and get closer to the venue, "otherwise, I don't think I would have found out about them."

"I know," Tameka says from the passenger seat next to me. "Their sound is so cool and different."

Ray chimes in from the back seat. "Have you seen them live before?"

I look in the rear-view mirror and can see his eyes, "No, have you?"

Ray nods. "Yeah, I saw them with Babes in Toyland and My Bloody Valentine. It was awesome!"

My eyes grow wide. "Wow, I bet that was a great show." I pull my car into the parking lot as anticipation for the show builds. "I'm so glad y'all wanted to go to this show. I wouldn't have had anyone to go with if you didn't, and there's no way my parents would have allowed me to go by myself."

"You don't have any friends that are into this music?" Ray asks.

Tameka turns toward him. "Dunwoody doesn't have the hippest kids," she jokes. "And, one person who might have been interested in going is spoken for." She rubs my shoulder. "Poor Sloane found the perfect guy but someone else snatched him up before she could."

I swat the air between us with my hand. "Ah, it's okay, he picked a good girl and at least I get to talk music with him in class."

"Girl, we've gotta get you from friends to lovers with these guys. You are way too cute and cool to be single," Tameka says as I pull into a parking space.

"'Tameka!" I squeal as I feel myself blush. Tameka is way more experienced than I am and her use of the word, "lovers" freaks me out a bit. I am not ready for that. "Please tell me the options are better in college," I say as we unfasten our seatbelts and get out of the car. "There are like three guys in my grade who are taller than me *and* cute." We make our way to the front of the club, our sneakers crunching on the gravel parking lot. "And only one of them has good taste in music."

"You won't have a hard time finding someone in college," Ray says as he sweeps his long blond hair off his face. "High school is just weird. Once you get classified into a group, that's it, your fate is pretty much sealed."

I turn to him and grab his shoulder. "Exactly!" I fling my head back. "Someone who understands me."

Once inside the club, we head to the merch table where we each buy a T-shirt, and then grab a decent spot in the middle of the room, center stage. "I love seeing shows here," I say to Tameka and Ray who are on my left.

After the opening band, the club is packed and as I'm talking to Tameka and Ray, Tameka leans toward my ear and whispers, "Don't look now, but a total hottie is standing next to you."

I play it cool and chat with my friends for a moment and then casually turn to my right, pretending to look back toward the merch table to look for someone. "I don't see them," I say so the dreamy guy next to me can hear, then turn back to my friends.

I look at Tameka with wide eyes and my eyebrows crawl up my forehead. I mouth to her, "Oh, my gosh!"

Tameka winks at me and Ray chuckles shaking his head at us. Tameka leans over again and says, "You should totally talk to him."

I face the stage as we wait for Dinosaur Jr. to start, so my back isn't to the tall, dark-haired boy standing next to me and contemplate it. After what happened with Tyler, I figure now is as good a time as any to start being bold. I turn to my right and catch the cute boy looking at me. He smiles, and his brown eyes light up. I return his smile, and he leans down toward my ear. "Have you seen them before?"

A shiver runs through me as I feel his breath on my ear. I shake my head. "No, but I can't wait. I love their music." Wow, this guy has a sweet smile, and he's just awoken the butterflies that have been dormant in my belly for a while.

"Me, too," he says raising his voice over the house music. "I'm Ky, by the way." He turns to his right, "And this is my friend Joey."

"Nice to meet you," I say and nod to Joey. "Ky, that's an interesting name."

He laughs and looks at the ground, then back at me. "It's short for Kyle, so not that interesting. It's also my dad's name, so Ky is easier."

"Gotcha," I say and can't help but grin at this cute guy. He's no Tyler Finlay, but he seems sweet, and I lost my chance with Tyler. I introduce Ky and Joey to my friends just as the house music cuts off and the lights dim.

The crowd starts to cheer as Dinosaur Jr. takes the stage. The jangly, fuzzy, distorted chords ring from J Mascis's guitar as the band plays a song I don't recognize, but I love it. It's hard, fast, and distorted. The crowd is energized, and we're all bouncing and nodding along to the fast beat. I'm lost in a haze of music, lights, and the energy of my fellow humans enjoying an amazing sonic experience together. I look at Tameka and Ray and smile as the multi-colored lights dance across their faces. Tameka sees me and returns my smile.

When the song ends, Ky leans down and says, "Pretty good, huh?" The way he leans into me is almost intimate, and I shiver again.

I clap and nod, smiling at him. "Amazing!" He's pretty sexy when his chin-length brown hair falls across his face.

Dinosaur Jr. continues with an awesome set list, including a cover of The Cure's, "Just Like Heaven". Seeing a band live is such a cool experience. It's like you forget everything that's on your mind and share an incredible experience with complete strangers. A little over halfway through the show, as I'm lost in a song, I feel Ky's hand take mine. As his fingers weave with mine, my body feels as electric as the guitars ringing out. I can't believe this cute stranger just took my hand at a concert! I look up at him and smile, and he flashes his sweet, wide smile with perfect teeth.

When the song is over, he releases my hand as we clap for the band. When they break into the next song, I grab his hand, letting him know I like him too.

Ky and I watch the rest of the show, hand-in-hand, and I can't believe a tall, handsome boy is interested in me! And, clearly, he likes good music. When the band finishes their encore and the house lights turn on, Tameka and Ray see that Ky and I have made a connection.

"Wanna go to the bar for a bit so we can talk?" Ky asks us.

I look to my friends for their input. "What do you think?"

"Absolutely," Tameka says, and her smile tells me she's happy for me. When Ky turns and leads me toward the room with a separate bar, I turn to Tameka and give her a huge smile. She wiggles her eyebrows at me, and her brown eyes sparkle.

Ky and I sit at the bar together and order sodas while Tameka, Ray, and Joey sit at a table behind us. I'm grateful that they have given us some time to get to know each other.

"We can't stay long because we have a bit of a drive," Ky says, "but I wanted to get a chance to talk to you without shouting over the music." His hair falls across his face as he smiles shyly.

I feel my cheeks heat up, and I smile. "Where are you from?"

"South Georgia, near Valdosta," he tells me. "Thomasville."

"Oh, wow," I say, and disappointment dulls my happiness upon learning that he's not local. "That is a bit of a haul. Are you in school down there?" I can't tell how old Ky is, so I figure this is a good way to figure it out.

"Yeah, I'm going to the community college until I figure out what I want to do."

"How old are you?" I hold my breath.

"Nineteen," he replies.

"Oh," I say as I search his face. "So, totally out of high school."

"Yeah," he says as he dips his head. "Is that a problem?" His eyes make him look like a puppy trying hopefully to get some table scraps.

"No," I tuck my hair behind my ear. "But I'm still in high school. Senior year. Is that a problem for you?"

He shakes his head and smiles. "Not at all."

I add, "I'm seventeen."

He grabs my hand. "Seriously, it's cool." He pauses, then looks all bashful again and says, "I really like you."

Oh my gosh, the butterflies have started moshing in my stomach. How is it that a tall, cute boy likes *me*? I smile as my cheeks grow hot. "I like you, too."

We sit closely, drink our sodas, and learn about each other before exchanging phone numbers. I'm totally smitten with this boy, and I'm sure it shows all over my face. Ky takes my hand and his eyes search mine. "Can I kiss you?"

I bite my bottom lip as my body tingles and nod my head. "Yes," I practically whisper.

Ky leans forward, and when his lips touch mine, my stomach does a somersault as if it is celebrating. I place my hand on his chest as we share a brief but sweet kiss, and I don't want this night to end. He leans back and smiles then brushes a strand of hair off my face. "I'll call you tomorrow."

I clutch his hand and say, "Promise?"

"Promise," he says with a smile.

We hug when we stand up from the bar stools, and I feel so good in his arms. His tall frame makes me feel delicate and safe. Saying goodbye to Ky is hard, but I'm so happy. I don't have time to dwell on the fact that the boy who likes me lives almost four hours away.

Chapter 23

Sloane

Ky kept his promise and called me on Sunday and we talked for over an hour. By the time Monday arrives, I feel like I'm floating and am so happy. Finally, things are going my way!

"Hey Buddy," Kurt says as he tosses his backpack on his desk and slides into his seat. "How was the Dinosaur Jr. concert?"

I can't contain my smile. "Oh my gosh," I say as my cheeks grow warm. "It was amazing!"

"That good, huh?"

"It wasn't just the concert, which was so good, by the way." Excitement floods my veins and I feel my smile grow. "I met a guy there." I practically bounce in my seat.

Kurt's eyes soften and he smiles back. "Wow, that's cool."

"He's tall, cute, has chin-length brown hair, and of course he likes good music."

"Ooh, who are you talking about?" Amber asks as she slides into her seat.

I wave my hand, "Oh, uh, no one you'd know." I turn back to Kurt and speak quietly. "He is so nice. We talked on the phone for over an hour yesterday."

"Where does he go to school?" Kurt asks.

"Um, right now he's going to community college in South Georgia. He's nineteen."

Kurt's eyes go wide. "Oh, dang. So, it's a long-distance thing?"

I can feel my smile fade as I nod. "Yeah, that's the only crummy part." I grab Kurt's forearm. "It was so cool, Dinosaur Jr. was like halfway through their set, and he just held my hand."

"Wow, that's gutsy."

My smile is back in full force. "I know! We talked a little before the band played, but like, wow, I couldn't believe it. It was so cool." I glance up and see Amber trying to eavesdrop but playing it off like she's not. I smile to myself.

"That's rad, Sloane, I'm happy for you."

"Thanks," I say and then raise my voice a little louder. "He's gorgeous and sweet and way more mature than the guys around here. Except for you, of course." Yeah, I totally said that for Amber's benefit. Just to make her squirm.

***

By the time I head to marine bio, I can't wait to share my news with Billy, and if I'm being honest, I want Tyler to hear it to show that I am, in fact, a desirable girl. As I turn the corner to walk down the hall to class, I see Tyler and Sara in the hallway by the front door of our class sharing an intimate conversation as usual. Seeing them almost daily hanging out by our classroom has been hard, but today I only feel my heart sink a tad.

"Sloaner-loner," Billy says as I toss my backpack on the lab table. "What's shakin'?"

"Hey Hill-Billy!" I joke. "Did you have a good weekend?"

"Actually, I did," Billy is all smiles. "I went fishing with my granddad."

"Aw, sweet," I say as I sit in my chair and take out my book and notebook. "Isn't it a little cold for fishing, though?"

Billy gives me a look like I have horns growing out of my head. "It ain't ever too cold for fishin' with your granddad."

I smile thinking of my own grandpa. "I guess you're right. Did y'all catch anything?"

Billy nods, "We sure did. My granddaddy taught me to fish, but more than the fishin', it's spending time on the water together, you know?"

"I've never fished, but I could see where just hanging out in nature with your grandpa would make for a really nice weekend."

"You've never fished?" Billy asks.

"Who's never fished?" Tyler's voice sounds behind me, and I turn in my chair to address him as he slides into his chair.

"I've never fished." I look at Tyler and am surprised he's in here so early, versus with Sara in the hallway, since there's still plenty of time before the final bell. That smile still melts me, but not as much as it did before this weekend. I turn back to Billy. "My parents are Yankees, remember?"

Billy laughs, and Tyler leans forward to see Billy, "Did you go fishing this weekend?"

"Yeah, with my granddad on Lake Burton."

"Nice," Tyler says. "Did you catch anything?"

After Billy details exactly what they caught, the type of fish, size, and what bait he used, Tyler turns to me. "I know you didn't go fishing, but did you do anything nearly as cool?"

I laugh. "As a matter of fact, I did." I'm wearing a proud smile as I sit up in my chair. "I saw Dinosaur Jr. at the Masquerade." I pull at the shirt I'm wearing that I got at the concert, showing it to Tyler.

"Oh, cool," Tyler says.

"Who?" Billy asks as he leans forward and squints at my T-shirt, then flinches at the slightly macabre-looking art on my black shirt.

I laugh at Billy. "They're an alternative band. I don't think you'd like them very much."

"How was the show?" Tyler asks before Billy can respond.

I'm beaming at this point. "The show was amazing, *and* I met the cutest boy," I say as I look at Tyler, and did his smile falter just a smidge?

"Who's the lucky guy?" Billy asks.

My eyes go skyward, and my smile spreads as far across my face as it can go. "His name is Ky, and he's really nice, so cute, has chin-length brown hair, and he's tall!" I continue, "We talked a bit before the show, and mid-way through it, he just held my hand. It was the sweetest thing." My eyes go upward again as the memory warms my insides.

"Wow, bold move," Tyler says, and I smile and nod.

"What kind of name is Ky?" Billy asks, his face wrinkling up like he just smelled a skunk spray our classroom.

My face goes from blissful to shocked as I playfully swat Billy on the arm. "It's short for Kyle." Billy snorts a laugh, and Tyler chuckles as well. "No, wait, it's not pretentious or anything. It's his dad's name, too, so he goes by Ky for short."

"Hmph," Billy grunts, "Why not go by Junior?"

I roll my eyes. "Be nice. I finally found a tall, cute boy who likes me back. Let me bask in this moment." I grin at him.

Tyler seems to be thinking then says, "Where does he go to school?"

My smile fades. "That's the thing, he lives all the way down in Thomasville. He's nineteen and goes to the community college down there."

"An older man." Billy feigns surprise and clutches his chest, laughing. "That sucks that it's long-distance, though."

"I know," I pout just a little. "He's so sweet and cool. Hopefully we'll get to see each other when he comes to town for shows."

"So, he's into that," Billy waves his hand at me and Tyler, "alternative music you two like?"

"Yeah, he's definitely into some of the harder stuff that Tyler likes, and not as into the poppy stuff I like, but his taste in music is pretty good."

"It's too bad you couldn't find a tall, handsome guy with your taste in music around here," Billy says as he rolls his eyes toward Tyler, and I try hard not to react.

I don't know what to say so I busy myself by searching for my Chapstick in my backpack, trying not to look at Tyler. "Boys at this school just aren't interested in me, so I had to look elsewhere." I didn't plan on saying that, but I'm glad I did. "Maybe an older guy is able to appreciate me more," I say with a joking smile then uncap my Chapstick and swipe it across my lips, tasting the sweet cherry flavor.

"Now, Sloaner, I'm sure that's not the case," Billy says.

"I do," I say confidently, then snap the cap back on my Chapstick with a pop as I roll my lips together. "My friends and I have concluded that we're all categorized into groups by middle school, if not sooner, and that's it. Our fate in school is sealed."

Billy squints his eyes as he contemplates this. "I mean, I guess you're right. We kinda are." He looks at Tyler. "What do you think?"

Tyler has been uncharacteristically quiet and appears to mull this over. "I don't ascribe to the established groups."

"I don't either," I say, "but they are pretty distinct. Besides, you're lucky. You only came here last year so you were an unknown. Plus, you're an athlete, football *and* baseball, so that's an automatic in." I put my Chapstick back in the front pocket of my backpack and drop it to the floor. "I've been with the same people since kindergarten for the most part, so I was classified a long time ago."

"Do you think you can change your classification?" Tyler asks with genuine interest.

I nod. "Yeah, I mean Sara did," I say, referring to his girlfriend. "She was always a nice girl who didn't have the most popular friends, but she was able to start hanging out with the right people when she cheered last year, and they embraced her. I mean, how can you not like Sara? She's so sweet and fun." He smiles as I say this.

Billy says, "So why don't you give it a shot?"

I think about this before answering. "Because if these people don't care enough to involve me in their world, then why would I want to hang out with them? I'm friendly with some of the popular kids here, but I've never been invited to hang out with them. Many of them I've known since elementary school and we were cool then, but I guess things changed for them. Besides," I say, "I'm not a partier. I'm extremely introverted, and I guess I have high standards for my friends."

"I respect that," Tyler says.

I smile, "Thanks. I guess by now I'm just ready to graduate and move on. If people wanted to invite me to their parties, hang out, or get to know me outside of school, they would have by now."

"Have you tried reaching out to them?" Billy asks.

I shake my head. "The cliques here are pretty well-defined. You don't just invite yourself in, you know?" I look at Billy and he nods. "I'm nice to everyone, so I figure that's my way of reaching out."

"Do you think other kids feel the way you do?" Tyler asks.

"For sure. See, the weird thing is that your social life in school is kind of dictated by your schedule, who you're in classes with, who you have lunch with. I bet there are some awesome people who I don't really know because I've simply never ended up in a class with them, and that's kind of a shame."

"That's a good point," Billy says.

I smile. "If I didn't sit here," I point to my spot at the table, "next to you, I wouldn't have gotten to know you so well. I probably would have figured we didn't have much in common since you're basically a cowboy." We all laugh. "But we have a great time together--in school. The three of us don't hang out outside of school, much like my relationships with most people here." I look at Tyler and continue. "And if you didn't squeak in right before the bell and take the first available seat, I doubt we would have gotten to know each other."

Tyler smiles and yes, I melt but try to fight it. "Is it because I'm basically a cowboy, too?"

I chuckle. "No, but you're this good-looking football-slash-baseball player who seems so confident and a bit mysterious, so maybe that would make someone like me think you're unapproachable, you know?"

"Wait, I didn't hear anything after you said I was good-looking." Tyler jokes, and I must be turning red based on the heat I feel in my cheeks.

"How do you think people look at you?" Billy asks, and I'm happy for the redirection because I almost can't believe I just told Tyler he's good-looking.

I think for a moment. "I don't know. Most often I hear the adjectives *tall* and *nice,* but neither of those qualities has people wanting to be my friend." I pause as I consider this more. "I'm shy and uncomfortable in new situations. I wouldn't approach an established group of friends on my own. That would be terrifying. When I don't know someone well, my goofy side doesn't come out right away, so maybe that, plus my shyness, makes me seem...unapproachable?"

"I think you're right," Tyler says.

"About my shyness making me seem unapproachable?" I ask.

He shakes his head. "No, I mean, maybe, but I think that we probably miss out on meeting some cool people based on our class schedules. I am glad I sat next to you two and wish we'd had a class together last year."

My butterflies take this as a cue to flutter awake for a split second. Did Tyler Finlay just call me cool and say that he wishes we had met sooner? Well, it doesn't matter now because he has Sara, and I have Ky. At least I hope we can make this long-distance thing work. As happy as I am that I met someone, I sure would have loved it if he went to my school. It's clear that I'm still affected by Tyler and that darn grin. Dang it!

Chapter 24

Tyler

I head to gym class, glad that Brian and I have it together because I'm so conflicted right now. Sloane Warren said I was good-looking in class today, right after she told me and Billy about the hot, cool guy she met at a Dinosaur Jr. concert. This shouldn't even bother me because I'm dating Sara and she's great. So why am I even thinking about this?

After we change, Brian and I head to the track because we're not allowed to risk an injury while we're still in football season, the state championship being our next and final game of the season. I should be thinking about that, but instead, I'm thinking about Sloane. My hands are tucked deep in my sweatshirt pocket as we walk the track on this cold afternoon.

"So, tell me what's up now that we're out here by ourselves," Brian says as we jog down the cement steps that lead to the track around the football field. "Is it the game? Because we're as ready as we're ever going to be and lucky that our team isn't beat up."

I inhale a deep breath and let it out before replying. "No, it's not the game." I pause. "This shouldn't even be on my mind and I don't know why I'm thinking about it." I say as we reach the track and start walking. "But, Sloane told me I was good looking today in marine bio."

Brian's face looks all screwed up. "She just flat out said that?"

I shake my head. "No, she had just told us about this guy she met at a concert at the Masquerade over the weekend and she, Billy, and I got into this whole conversation about cliques here. She said no guys at school have ever been interested in her and was pretty happy about this guy she met. Ky." I say his name like it tastes bad.

"Ky? What kind of name is that?" Brian scoffs.

I huff out a laugh. "Yeah, so she was saying that she thinks we're all classified into groups at an early age and since she's been around most of these kids for her whole life, it's hard to change that classification. She told me that I was lucky because I've only been here since last year and I'm a good-looking jock, so it's easier for me."

Brian nods his head as if this makes sense. "So, maybe she is into jocks after all." He grins at me.

"That's the thing, and I feel bad that I'm even thinking about this because Sara is so sweet."

"It's not like you two are engaged," Brian says. "And she's fun, right?"

"Yeah," I nod. "I mean, it's still new, but why am I jealous about this Ky guy?"

"What do you know about him?" Brian asks.

"He's tall, has chin-length brown hair, nineteen, good taste in music, lives in Thomasville, and is apparently *so* cute." I feel my eyes roll involuntarily at the last part.

"Yeah, but is he pale and skinny?" Brian jokes making me laugh.

"He sounds cool and ballsy because apparently they talked for a minute before the show and he just held her hand midway through."

"Geez, that is ballsy," Brian says as we complete our first lap. "Well, you and Sara are dating and now she's got this Ky guy, so..."

"I know," I run my hand through my hair. "I think it's because she called me good-looking that has me even thinking about all this. Maybe I shouldn't have been so quick to assume that she wasn't into me."

"Well, buddy," Brian pats me on the back, "there's not much you can do about it now. Just see where it goes with Sara and see what happens with this dude. Long distance relationships never work out."

"Yeah," I reply.

"But if you're not into Sara, don't string her along," Brian says.

"I really do like her...I just...like Sloane, too. They're different, you know?" I feel bad even saying this, but it's true.

"Yeah. You'll figure it out, just don't let it get in the way of football, please." Brian grins and elbows me in the side.

I laugh. "No way. Football is the most important thing right now." I'll focus on football and see where all this goes. There's not much else I can do, and hopefully, I won't have to hear about Ky every day.

Chapter 25

Tyler

December 1992

We roll into Valdosta, a town in South Georgia, and the support for their high school football team has my mouth hanging open as I look out the window of our cushy chartered bus. Valdosta High School is known statewide as a powerhouse and there are messages of support for the team all over town. Their mascot is the wildcat, too, so I just pretend that the paw prints painted all over town, leading to the stadium are for us.

When we pull up to the stadium, Brian's focus is outside. "Geez, look at this place. It's huge."

"Seriously," I reply as I stare at the stadium that could be that of a junior college. "Ours only has seating on one side, they have three sides of bleachers."

"That's all they've got in this town," Adam says from across the aisle. "High school football is practically a religion down here."

Coach Harbin stands up from his seat behind the bus driver. "Welcome to Valdosta where the players are big, but the mosquitos are bigger." Coach makes us all chuckle which helps all of our nerves, I'm sure. "We'll head into the locker room and get settled. Just remember, you deserve to be here as much as they do. Let's do our thing and play this game like we have all the others. One play at a time."

Assistant Coach Beecham gets up. "I would say Wildcats on three, but since that's their mascot, how 'bout Dunwoody on three. One, two, three!"

"Dunwoody!" We all scream and clap, then start standing up and gathering our stuff.

Brian looks at me. "Still feelin' good about this?"

I nod. "Absolutely. Coach is right, we earned our place here. Besides, our defense is so strong."

"Defenses win championships, baby!" Travis Suggs, our massive D-lineman hollers from behind me, causing the rest of the defense to roar.

I smile because I love my teammates, but also because Sloane uttered that same phrase when she said that she thought our team could go all the way to State. She was right about that, now we just have to bring home that W.

***

If you had listened to the pundits, they would have told you that a school in the suburbs of Atlanta didn't have a shot against a powerhouse team from South Georgia where football is second only to God. Coach was right, they do breed guys big down here, but we have some huge guys ourselves and some real competitors. We've held Valdosta to a field goal, but they've held us to a goose egg. We haven't been able to score and it's starting to get under my skin. I missed one tackle when the guy stiff-armed me in my face mask, and even then, I got up and assisted in the tackle. Other than that, I've been on fire. It's like I can see the ball tonight and am so fast upon the snap. I'm staying in my zone and taking care of business.

I look at the scoreboard. The clock reads 2:43 in the second quarter and Valdosta is driving. When the ball is snapped, I can see that it's a pass play. Their quarterback drops back and throws a quick pass down field about twenty yards. I watch as the ball is caught on the opposite side of the field. I run in the direction of the play, even though I'm the farthest defender. He runs five, ten, fifteen...crap, twenty yards and is approaching the goal line. I hustle and watch as one of our fastest guys, a safety named James, catches up to him and tackles him at the three-yard line.

As Valdosta huddles up, I tell my teammates, "We're only down by three, we can't let them score before halftime."

We line up and stand firm as they try a run play in my direction, but I'm ready for them and so is Travis. No gain. We line back up. Second down. They try another run play, this time to the other side, but we stop them again. Third down. They run again, this time, back towards me. Travis lunges at the runner and misses, but makes him stumble. I manage to do the same, but merely trip him up. I land flat on the turf but jump up to continue after him. Thankfully, Andre and Justin take him down on the two yard line. Fourth down. "Yeah!" I holler as we line back up.

"They're going for it!" Travis hollers and we line back up.

This gives me an adrenaline rush. They think they can score off of us. We stopped them from getting in the end zone three times and instead of kicking a field goal for three points, they're going for it. They think they can get past our defense! I know my guys are as pumped as I am to stop them from the two-yard line. They snap the ball quickly and try to run up the middle, but before I know it, I see #74 charge through and wrap up their running back, driving him back three yards while we swarm them to assist with the tackle. But we don't need to. Little 74, a sophomore handles the tackle on his own.

"Woo!" I holler and grab him by his shoulder pads. "Way to go, Andy! Good job!" My fellow players congratulate Andy as we head to the sideline and the clock ticks down ending the half, sending us to the locker room.

***

During halftime, Coach Harbin reviews the plays that are working and those that are not while Coach Beecham pumps us up to go out and finish strong.

"We can do this!" I tell Brian as we jog back out onto the field.

"Totally," Brian says as he runs next to me. "I want a reception."

"I know. Their defense hasn't given Sam much of a chance."

"They're covering me tight, too." Brian puts his helmet on and snaps the buckles in place. "I have to get open." He walks with purpose over to the offensive players to listen to coach before kickoff. We get the ball first which is awesome.

For the next seventeen minutes and change, it's a slog. This is one of those games that announcers hate because it's a defensive battle. No flashy scores, no long runs, or punt returns. While I'm glad we've been able to defend well, I'm frustrated that we haven't been able to score. With every tackle, I try to cause a fumble, but can't make it happen.

With just under seven minutes left in the game, the score is still 3-0 Valdosta. We've just forced them to punt again, and I head over to the offensive bench. "We just need a score. Just one score. Come on, we can do this!" I try to pump up our offense, but they look pretty tired. We're able to get a couple first downs, but are ultimately stopped again. I look at the scoreboard. 3:48 is left on the clock and Valdosta has the ball.

We kick-off and Valdosta runs the ball up to the thirty-eight-yard line. I'm on special teams, but the runner is on the opposite side of the field. Valdosta has adjusted their plays and they try not to run where I am. I'm flattered, but chomping at the bit to make a play.

On first and ten, they make it across the fifty-yard line, ending up at the forty-six-yard line. Again, I'm on the other side of the field and can't make a play. Their next play is a running play and they try to go up the middle. I'm off my block and on their running back fast as Travis and I make the tackle. Second and eight. Their next play is a pass and all I can do is watch the ball sail to the twenty-yard line, right into the hands of their wide-open receiver. "Crap!" Our coverage was off and our defender threw himself at the receiver, just missing him. There's no one else even close on our side and their receiver runs into the end zone, scoring a touchdown. Their stands erupt in glee and I head to the line to defend the point-after. The snap is good, the kick is good and now we're down by ten with just two minutes and thirty seconds left in the game. The State Championship.

Our offense gives it a valiant effort, but ultimately, we're only able to get two first downs but can't score. Even if we did, we'd have to score twice and against this defense, we'd need a miracle to pull that off. Their team runs onto the field to celebrate their win as I watch from the sideline. A group of their players dances on the far side of the field and I can only watch and wish it was us who were celebrating. I turn my back on the celebration and look up at our fans who traveled all the way down here for this. I wish we could have given them something to cheer about. I know my parents will meet me by the bus after we meet with coach. I look up in the stands and see Sara chatting with some of the popular girls she's become friends with recently. I continue to scan the stands and see Sloane walking down the steps with her best friend, her big blue eyes meet mine. She gives me a sympathetic smile and I hold up my hand in a wave. Her smile brightens and she heads toward me, and I walk to where the bleachers meet the field.

"You okay?"

I nod. "Yeah, just bummed we couldn't get that win. They were tough."

"You should really be proud of yourself," she says encouragingly. "You were all over that field tonight and holding them to two scores is pretty impressive."

I huff out a laugh. "You sound like Coach." I smile up at her and her face brightens more.

"Y'all really played well," her friend Maggie says softly.

I smile at her. "Thanks." I look back at Sloane. "Thanks for coming all the way down here. Having all our fans here was great." I make sure to look at Maggie, too.

"We wouldn't miss it," Sloane says.

I look up into the stands and Sara is still chatting with her friends and I try not to show the disappointment on my face. "Well, I should get going for our meeting with Coach before we get on the buses."

"See you back in Dunwoody," Sloane says with a sweet smile taking some of the gloominess away from my current state of mind.

"Bye," I smile at Sloane and Maggie then jog over to Brian who is coming from the field. "Socializing with the enemy?" I joke with Brian who seems to know someone everywhere we go.

"Just congratulating a few of the guys I went to that summer skills football camp with." He gives me a look like I'm in trouble. "What about you? I could ask you the same thing."

"What do you mean?'

Brian laughs at me. "I saw who you were talking to, and it wasn't your girlfriend."

I laugh off his comment. "Come on, man. I was talking to a friend and her friend who happened to be walking my way. Besides, my girlfriend wasn't in any hurry to come talk to me." I know Sara and I had planned on meeting at the buses after the game, but the fact that she was so busy talking with her new, popular friends, not even looking for me did hurt.

Chapter 26

Sloane

December 1992

Ky tells me that he is going to come to Atlanta over Christmas break, and I cannot wait. We've been making the long-distance thing work well and have spent countless hours on the phone learning a lot about each other. Not only is it tough that we can't see each other, but our calls are often interrupted by my mom's real estate business as agents are always calling about setting up showings and seeing if properties are available.

I talk to Billy and Tyler about Ky all the time. I'm sure a part of me wants to make Tyler jealous, even though he has an amazing girlfriend. I would never do anything to jeopardize that. Plus, I have no idea if he would even like me like that. I'm just so happy that someone has finally shown interest in me. But why am I still thinking about Tyler like that when I have Ky?

Ky and I are both off from school the week between Christmas and New Year's. Although Ky has to visit me around his work schedule, he is able to come up for two days, and I've been counting the days. I'm trying to read a book in my parent's formal living room, a room we never use, but it's hard to concentrate. I spent the day cleaning and doing chores which helped the time pass. When I knew Ky should be about an hour out, I got ready and waited as the clock ticked by slowly. When I hear his noisy VW beetle ramble down the street, those butterflies wake up, and I hop off the sofa and run to the front door. I watch Ky extract his tall frame from his little car and grab his bag. My stomach is nervous with anticipation. As he heads up the driveway, I open the door. Ky hears the door and when he sees me, his face lights up.

I feel my smile spread across my face as I hop down the brick porch steps toward the cement walkway. I notice Ky's pace quicken, and I trot down the path to meet him. As I approach him, he drops his canvas duffle bag and envelops me in a huge hug, picking me up off the ground. When he sets me down, he leans down and places a sweet kiss on my lips. He leans out of the kiss, his eyes searching my face, "You're a sight for sore eyes."

I smile and kiss him again. "It's so good to see you." I wrap him in another hug, and my cheek feels right at home against his chest. I can hear his heart beating quickly and am glad he's as excited to see me as I am to see him. I release the hug and look up at him. "Was the trip okay?"

He tucks my hair behind my right ear and says, "I would have driven twice as far to see you." He kisses me on the forehead. "Let's go inside. I want to meet your family."

Obviously, I have filled him in on my family over our numerous phone calls, and of course, our parents have talked. My parents are great and will be cool, I think. My sisters are wildcards. Erin is home from college and we have a weird relationship. We bicker a lot and she finds joy in pushing my buttons which is super annoying. I have always hoped it would get better as we got older, but so far, that hasn't happened. We get along, but it can be strained depending on which way the wind blows. Bryn is my middle sister and since she almost died when she was born, she has some challenges. She can be really guarded with strangers, and at times, she can say some inappropriate stuff, so you never know what you're going to get. I love Bryn, but sometimes it's tough because my mom tries to get me to let her tag along with my friends, but let's face it, it's hard enough for me to make friends on my own. I don't think my mom realizes how hard it is for me, too. Bryn's disability is more prominent than my anxiety and shyness, so I just have to suck it up. That's pretty much how we grew up, and now that I'm older, I kind of just want something for myself.

As we walk up the front steps and stand before the front door, I look up at Ky. "You ready for this?"

He smiles, "Ready or not, here I come."

I laugh at his corny response, and he gives me one more kiss before we go inside. When I lean away, he looks up over my head with a quizzical expression on his face. "Is someone watching us?"

I turn around and follow his gaze up to the windows. "Ugh," I groan as I lean my forehead on his chest then look back up at him. "That's Bryn's room, and yes, she's probably spying on us. Probably will be all weekend."

Ky rubs his thumb across my cheek and smiles. "It's okay. Come on, let's go meet your family."

Chapter 27

Sloane

After I introduce Ky to my parents and sisters, we gather around the dining room table for dinner. My mom has cooked a delicious meal, and as we enjoy pork tenderloin with vegetables and baked apples, my parents ask Ky all sorts of questions while trying not to act like they are interviewing him.

"So," my mom says as she shakes salt on her mashed potatoes, "have you lived in Thomasville all your life?"

"Yes, ma'am," Ky says, and his use of the word ma'am makes his slight southern accent thicker. "Born and raised."

"Isn't William Andrews from there?" She asks, mentioning a player for Atlanta's football team.

"He is," Ky says as surprise lights his eyes. "Are you a football fan?"

My dad laughs before my mom can answer. "Louise is the biggest football fan I know," he says, smiling sweetly at my mom.

"Yeah," I add, "huge fan. If you don't like them, don't say anything because she will fight you," I joke, but not really.

Ky smiles, and I feel myself melting right there in my chair. He looks at my mom, "I'm a huge fan, too, and we're all pretty proud that William

Andrews is from Thomasville." Ky wipes the corner of his mouth with his napkin. "There are quite a few football players from Thomasville, but maybe even cooler is one of the founding members of The Temptations is from there."

"No way," I say. "That's so cool."

"Yeah," Ky says, "Elbridge Bryant."

"Uh-oh. Are you going to sing *My Girl* to Sloane?" Bryn asks as I try to laugh off her comment. She has an affinity for music and despite her learning challenges, she has quite a memory and knows the lyrics to practically every song. I'm sure it's because she's constantly listening to the radio. Ky takes her comment in stride which quells my embarrassment.

He chuckles. "I might just have to, Bryn." He smiles at her and she grins, pleased with herself for coming up with that idea. My heart clenches at his sweetness toward my sister.

"Isn't Thomasville the City of Roses?" Erin asks, and I'm grateful to her for moving the conversation along.

"Yeah," Ky says, "There's a rose festival every Spring. It's really pretty."

"Oh, how neat," my mom says. "I bet that's beautiful."

"So, Ky," my dad says, and I get the feeling he's about to ask something a bit more serious by his tone. "Sloane tells us you're going to a local community college back home."

"Yes, sir, I'm taking core classes while I figure out what I want to do."

"Do you have any idea what it is you'd like to do?" I'm kind of embarrassed because it's not like we're getting married or anything.

"I'm not really sure," Ky says, "but I know I don't want an office job. I don't know if I could sit at a desk all day." My pulse rate quickens as Ky pauses, then adds, "Sloane says you get to travel a lot, and I think that would be pretty cool."

"I do," my dad says with a smile, "but I also have to sit at a desk quite a bit."

"You've got time to figure it all out," my mom says, and I'm grateful for her sensitivity on this topic. My mom is so supportive, and I know she wants this visit to go off without a hitch.

Since I know I'm not going to get a moment alone with Ky for a while longer, when my mom starts collecting plates, I stand and say, "Mom, you sit, you've been cooking all day and throughout Christmas. Ky and I can clean up."

"But he's our guest," my mom says.

Ky stands. "I insist. Sloane is right, you've done enough. Let us clean up."

My mom smiles at Ky, and I can tell his good looks and charm are winning her over as her eyes sparkle. "Such a southern gentleman." She looks at me and smiles. "Thanks, sweetie. I'll just get the coffee brewing."

My sisters look elated that they don't have to help clean up and quickly head to the family room with my parents to watch television. Unfortunately, the family room has a case opening with accordion doors which are wide open and don't give us much privacy. So, as we're clearing the table, I pull Ky to the side of the dining room, away from the door to the kitchen and plant a kiss on those lush lips of his.

"I'd volunteer to clean up more often if this is my payment," Ky jokes and I feel my cheeks heat up as we move to finish our task.

I don't think I've ever had such an enjoyable time washing dishes. Ky and I steal moments together as he washes, and I dry. When we're done, we head into the family room with dark paneling on the walls and mauve carpet. Ky and I bring coffee for my parents and ourselves. My parents are on the love seat, Bryn is on the sofa, and Erin is on the floor. This leaves room for Ky and me on the sofa, and I take this opportunity to sit as close to him as possible without freaking out my parents, or Bryn. As we watch TV and chit chat, I start to grow impatient.

After a little while, my mom says, "I'm going to go get blankets for Ky. Why don't we all head upstairs and give these two time to catch up."

Wow, who knew my mom could be so cool. I smile at her. "Thanks, mom. Do you need help?"

"No, sweetheart, I'll be right back."

After my family leaves the room, I grab the remote control, and we search for something to watch on TV. "We can always put in a movie," I tell Ky. "We have a few tapes in the cabinet."

My mom returns with blankets and pillows for Ky. "Don't stay up too late," she says as she sets everything down on the love seat. "It was great getting to know you Ky. Goodnight, you two."

"Goodnight!" we say, almost in unison.

I continue to flip through the channels, buying time until the coast is clear, and Ky says, "Oh, this show is great. Have you seen it?"

I see what looks like a weird B-movie and silhouettes of a person, and two other characters that look like they are sitting in a movie theatre. "No, I don't think I have."

"It's called Mystery Science Theatre 3000," Ky says. "This guy is imprisoned on a spaceship and they force him to watch B movies as a form of torture. He builds two robots to be his friends, and they basically make fun of the movies. It's hilarious."

"Sounds interesting," I say. I set the remote down and snuggle up under Ky's arm. Honestly, I'd watch almost anything he suggested because I'm just happy he's here. The butterflies start to flutter. "I'm so glad you're here," I tell him as I place my right hand in his left hand.

He brings my hand up to his mouth and kisses it. "Me too."

I sit up and face him. Gosh, he's cute. My insides feel funny, and my pulse quickens. I smile at him, and then we kiss. As the kiss grows deeper, I pull away and whisper. "I'm going to go close the doors. Bryn has a tendency to spy." I walk over to the case opening between the kitchen and family room and try to quietly and slowly close the squeaky accordion doors without making too much noise. I grab a comforter my mom left and sit next to Ky, covering us in the blanket. I look at Ky and can't stop smiling. "I'm so glad you held my hand at the concert."

He cups my cheek with his hand and says, "Me, too." He gently kisses me. Our kisses grow more passionate and my body tingles all over. When I kissed Dave over the summer, it wasn't like this. At all. The chemistry with Ky is definitely different. Kissing Dave just felt...awkward. Ky kisses my neck and that sends an entirely new sensation through me. I run my fingers through his hair, "God, you're a great kisser," he says.

I lean back. "Really?" He nods with an eager look in his eyes as he moves toward my mouth again.

When we come up for air, I say, "I don't have a ton of experience." I look down at my lap as I feel embarrassed admitting this.

"Then you're a natural," he says with a twinkle in his eye.

We kiss some more and when footsteps sound from the kitchen, we freeze. I hear the refrigerator door open as I cuddle under Ky's arm again, and we're back to watching TV. "I bet it's Bryn," I whisper. "Sorry."

He chuckles. "It's okay." He kisses the side of my head. "We probably needed to take a break anyway." He hugs me tighter, and I feel so happy and safe. I wonder if Ky would come up here for my prom, I think to myself.

Chapter 28

Sloane

I could have laid in Ky's arms all night long, but there was no way that would fly if my parents found me on the sofa with him in the morning. I was blissfully exhausted by the time I went upstairs in the wee hours of the morning, but I couldn't stop thinking about him. That beautiful boy was downstairs, and it drove me crazy until eventually, I fell asleep.

I awake to my door opening and Ky standing there looking all gorgeous and sleepy-headed with a mug in his hand. "Morning, sunshine," he says with a sweet grin. He looks adorable in sweatpants and a long-sleeved Led Zeppelin T-shirt.

I self-consciously run a hand through my hair as I sit up, pulling the covers up to my shoulders. "Hey," I smile, trying to knock the cobwebs out of my brain.

He notices my unease and says, "You look even more beautiful first thing in the morning."

My insides turn to mush, and I can feel myself blush. I laugh. "I don't know about that-"

"I do," he says as he seems to remember he's holding a mug. "Oh, here's some hot chocolate." He brings me the mug, then sneaks a quick kiss.

I cover my mouth with my free hand. "I bet I have morning breath."

He laughs, "No, you don't." He's back in the doorway with that grin that's doing all sorts of things to my insides. "I'm going to shower downstairs. Your dad's making breakfast, but we have enough time to shower."

"Cool," I say. "I'll be down soon." I take a sip of cocoa. "Mmmm, this is so good, thanks."

He winks at me then says, "Go get ready, I only have one day with you, and I don't want to waste it."

***

After breakfast, I show Ky around Dunwoody. It's not like there's a ton to see as it's basically a small suburb of Atlanta. "It's too bad it's winter because we could go to a park or the lake," I say as I'm wrapping up the short tour. "We could go down to Little 5 Points," I suggest, "but we'd basically be shopping or eating."

"Didn't you say there's a movie theater by the mall?" he asks.

"Yeah, wanna go see a movie?"

He rubs my right leg just above the knee. "Sit with you in a dark room or go shopping? No contest," he says with a devilish grin.

I clasp his hand and smile at him as the butterflies stir. "I agree."

As I approach a stop sign Ky reaches across the car and plants his hand on my forehead. I shoot him a quizzical glance trying to hide my irritation of his erratic motion while I'm driving. "What the heck was that for?"

"The sign said, 'Stop Ahead.'" He laughs at his own joke and I politely chuckle but internally roll my eyes at his attempt at humor. *I guess girls do mature faster than boys*, I think to myself.

The movie theatre in the parking lot of Perimeter Mall is small so we only have a couple of choices. We walk up to the ticket counter and Ky checks his watch. "Hmm, so it looks like it's between Single White Female and Home Alone 2, based on the time."

"Single White Female, don't you think?" I suggest.

Ky smiles and puts his arm around my shoulder, pulling me close. He says so only I can hear, "Yeah, because it wouldn't be appropriate to make out in a kids' Christmas movie."

I feel my cheeks burn and I giggle. "Agreed."

Okay, so we only kissed a little in the theatre, but there were plenty of opportunities for me to bury my head in Ky's chest during that movie. Afterwards, we head across the street for dinner, then to my favorite place in town, a European-style café with the best desserts and coffees. We snuggle up in a corner of the small restaurant with hot drinks while we share a delicious chocolate and caramel cake.

"I never would have thought sharing a cake with someone could be this fun," Ky says as he feeds me a piece.

I smile as I savor the scrumptious dessert. "I know." I give him a sweet kiss that lingers only for a second. My face is close to his. "I'm not one for PDA, but I'll make an exception for you."

Ky smiles but then seems to realize something as his smile quickly fades. "I hate that I have to leave in the morning."

I inhale deeply. "I know," I pout. "I've been trying not to think about it and just enjoy the moment, but it's hard the later it gets."

"Do you think you'll be able to come down to Thomasville?" he asks, his eyes hopeful.

"I don't know. It's a long way for me to go by myself, but I can ask my parents and see if they'll let me." I think for a moment. "How far is Thomasville from Panama City Beach?"

"About two and a half hours. Why?" He asks, then takes a bite of cake.

"My friends and I are going there for Spring Break the first week of April. If I can't make it to Thomasville before then, maybe you could come to Florida when I'm there?" Now, I'm the one with hope in my voice.

"I could try," he says. "I'm not sure if I'd be able to get a place to stay, or the time off, but once I get back, I'll see."

I feel my shoulders slump. "I hate that you're so far away." I take his hand in mine and look down, gently rubbing the pad of my thumb along his knuckles.

He tilts my chin up with his free hand. "Don't be sad. Maybe I can come up here for another show."

I sit up straighter as hope fills my brain. "If you do and it's a weekend show, you can always stay at my house. I'm sure my parents wouldn't mind."

He smiles at me then pecks my mouth. "Don't worry, we'll figure this out."

We finish up and head back to my house, after a quick make-out session in the car, of course. I'm discovering that these teenage hormones are no joke. When we get home, we spend a little time with my family before my mom ushers everyone upstairs so Ky and I can hang out together. Just like the previous night, we cuddle up under a blanket, watch TV, and yes, make-out some more.

Being with Ky, I'm totally beginning to understand when people talk about having chemistry. At least physical chemistry. When we talk, Ky isn't as deep as I would like, and he's a bit immature, especially for a nineteen-year-old, but he's sweet, and cute...and he likes me. Granted, I don't have a lot of experience, but when I'm with Ky, it feels way more passionate and natural than it did with Dave.

We stop to catch our breath, and Ky stares deeply into my eyes. He runs his index finger across my jawline. "I love you."

I blink hard. Holy cow, did he just say that? My insides are as nervous as a long-tailed cat in a room full of rocking chairs. What do I say? Do I love him, too? Are we there yet? I have to say something. "I love you, too," my mouth decides to say, though I'm really not sure if I do. In fact, I'm pretty sure I'm not there yet. Since I know my face has a habit of betraying me, I pull him into a hug and bury my face in his neck.

Chapter 29

Sloane

Saying goodbye to Ky was really hard, but I remind myself that at least I'm not alone anymore and that makes me happy. I also have to wrap up my college applications before Christmas break is over, so as soon as he's gone, I get to work on them. After a couple of hours, I need a break, so I call Maggie.

"Hey!" I say as I hear her voice on the other end. "How was your Christmas?"

"It was pretty good, but we had to go see our dad." Maggie's parents had a rough divorce, and I know she still harbors ill feelings toward her dad. She's never really said what happened, but I think he cheated on her mom and that would make me mad at him, too.

"Ugh," I groan. "I know you didn't love that, but he is your dad."

"Yeah," she admits, then changes the subject. "Wait, did Ky come visit you yet?"

I fling myself back on my bed so that I'm staring at the ceiling. "Yeah. He only left a few hours ago and I miss him already."

"So, it was a good visit then?"

I bolt up on my bed. "Maggie, it was awesome! We have great chemistry. He's so cute, and I think he made a good impression on my parents. It just stinks that he lives so far away." I fling myself onto my back again.

"I bet," Maggie says. "Tell me all about it. What did you do while he was here?"

I fill Maggie in on every detail, and my pulse races when I tell her about our time alone together. As I'm telling her I remember what he said that freaked me out. "There are a couple of things, though," I start.

"Uh-oh," Maggie interrupts.

"The first one isn't that big of a deal. He's just kinda corny and not as mature as you would expect a nineteen-year-old to be. Like, I feel like Tyler is way more mature than him."

"You're still thinking about Tyler?"

I squirm a little. "Yeah, I guess so. I hate to compare the two, but Ky doesn't seem as...deep."

"Well, maybe he was just nervous?" Maggie suggests and I think it through. "What's the other thing?"

I inhale deeply. "So, we were making out on the sofa, and...he told me he loved me."

"What?" Maggie shouts through the phone so that I have to hold it away from my ear. "He said that so soon?"

I sit up and put the phone back to my ear and fidget with its spiral cord, wrapping it around my index finger. "Yeah, kinda weird right?"

"I mean, I don't have tons of experience in this department, but, yeah, I think it's kind of fast to be saying that." She pauses then says, "You don't think he was trying to get you to-"

"I actually thought about that," I tell her. "But, no, because he didn't push me to do anything more than kiss him. Besides, we were in my family room with my entire family right upstairs."

"What did you say?"

I inhale sharply. "I told him I love him too," I whine, my voice full of regret. I fling myself onto my back again and put my free hand on my forehead. "It's like my mouth took over, and it came flying out!"

"Sooo, you don't love him?" Maggie asks, her tone serious.

"No!" I bolt upright. "I mean, I don't think so." I pause "It's just, I really like him, and we have good chemistry, but I've spent all of, what? Maybe 48 hours total with him in person?"

"You've talked a ton on the phone, though, right?"

"Yeah, but, it's so new."

"I agree," she says. "You haven't had time to figure out if you love him or not."

"Exactly," I say, feeling better that she understands. "It's not that I don't love him. I really like him, it's just too soon to know." I hear a click on the phone. "Hello?"

"I'm still here," Maggie says.

"Did you hear a click?"

"Yeah."

"Dang it!" I say as I feel my blood pressure rise. "I bet Bryn was eavesdropping." I fling myself back again. "Ugh!" I groan as I hold the phone away from my mouth.

Maggie chuckles. "Listen, try not to sweat it about the L-word thing and just see where this goes. I can tell you really like him, and it's cool that he thinks so highly of you since he said it out of how he was feeling and not an attempt to get you to...you know."

"Yeah," I say as I sit back up. I smile as the memories of our two days together warm me from the inside-out. "I just wish he went to our school or at least lived in the area."

"When do you think you'll get to see him again?"

"I don't know. He asked if I could come down to Thomasville, but I honestly don't think my parents will allow me to drive there by myself. He said he might be coming to more concerts up here, and if he does, I'm totally going to ask my parents if he can stay here so he doesn't have to drive back the same night."

"Well, that would be cool," Maggie says encouragingly.

"And," I say, "he's only two-and-a-half hours from Panama City, so I'm hoping he can meet me when we're on Spring Break."

"Ooh, that would be awesome," she says as her voice goes up an octave. "I really want to meet him."

This has me smiling widely now. "I know! Wouldn't it be amazing if he could meet us, even if just for a few days?" My mind starts to imagine how awesome it would be to hang out with Ky during Spring Break. "We could watch the sunset together, take walks on the beach hand-in-hand. I could spend all day with him while he's wearing nothing but board shorts..."

Maggie starts laughing. "I see you already have this planned out."

I giggle. "I finally have a boy, and I want to do all the little things I've dreamed about for so long."

"So, if you're already talking to him about Spring Break, have you thought about asking him to prom? It's only, like, a month and a half later."

I get excited just thinking about it. "I totally thought about it when he was here, but it's so far off, and I didn't want to scare him. I mean, he's nineteen and is out of high school. He may not want to go to a stupid prom."

"Sloane," Maggie says, her voice serious, "the guy just told you he loves you. If he loves you and things continue to go well for the next 4 months, there's no way he's not going to take you to your prom."

"You think?" I nervously fidget with the phone cord again.

"Absolutely," she says. "If he cares that much about you, he'll take you. Why would he want to let another guy take you to your prom?"

"I guess you're right," I agree. "Mags, this means that my dream of going to a school dance might actually happen!" I squeal a little as I think about doing all the things that I've missed out on so far as a high schooler: the dress, corsage, pictures taken by my parents, a limo, dinner, pictures at the dance, the actual dance. And, I think about having that tall, cute boy with the chin-length brown hair by my side as my smile goes as far across my face as possible.

Chapter 30

Sloane

January 1993

I finish my college applications over Christmas break and after we ring in 1993, it's time to go back to school. I have a hop in my step as I make my way to marine bio, because it's always nice to see Billy and Tyler. The three of us have a good time bantering before and sometimes during class. I turn down the hallway and Tyler and Sara are in close conversation by the front door to class, again. "It must be nice to have a boyfriend that goes to your school instead of four hours away," I think to myself.

"Hey Sloaner, how was your Christmas?" Billy asks as I walk into class and toss my backpack on the lab table, pulling out the chair next to him.

"It was great, how about yours?" I ask as I sit in my chair.

"Really good. I got this beautiful new shirt." He turns so I can see his black Merle Haggard shirt. "And I got tickets to see Garth Brooks." Billy's smile is lighting up his eyes.

"I know you love Garth." I smile at him. "That's awesome. Is he going to be at the Omni?"

"I wish," Billy says. "The closest he's coming is Charlotte."

"Oh, wow," I say as I take my book and spiral notebook out of my bag before placing it on the floor to my left. "When is it?"

"Not until October," he says. "And, hopefully, I'll be in Athens for school, but I'm going to the Saturday show, so it'll work out perfectly."

"I applied to Georgia, but I don't think I want to go where everyone else from here is going, you know?"

"Gee, thanks," Billy jokes, feigning hurt feelings.

"You know I don't mean you. I'm just done with these people." I wave my hand out in front of me.

"What people?" Tyler asks as he slides into his seat and tosses his backpack on the lab table.

I turn and smile. He's still so handsome, and that grin still gets me every time and I wonder if that's a bad thing since I'm with Ky now. "I was telling Billy that I applied to Georgia, but I'm not sure if I want to go there since half our class will be there."

"I get that," Tyler says as he pulls his book and notebook out of his bag. "I want to play baseball in college, but I'm not sure I'm good enough to go there."

"Where do you want to go?" I ask.

"I'd love to go to Georgia, but I may go to a junior college first. I could transfer to a four-year school without having to sit out a year, or if I'm good enough, get drafted into the pros."

"Wow, that would be amazing," I say, not realizing just how good Tyler is at baseball.

"My SAT scores weren't great, but they should be good enough if I want to start at a four-year school," Tyler says as he pulls his books out of his backpack.

"Ugh, don't even get me started on that stupid test. I hate standardized tests and do not test well. Here's how bad I am at testing," I tell them. "I suck at math, it's my toughest subject, yet I scored higher on the math portion than verbal. Either I guessed well, or I completely stink at tests."

Tyler laughs. "Yeah, me too. Where do you want to go to school?"

"I have friends at Florida, so that's my first choice right now. I also applied to FSU and Southern."

"Southern is where I might go if I don't get an offer from Georgia, or start at a two-year college," Tyler says.

"Sloaner, you know if you go to Florida and become a Gator, I can't be your friend anymore," Billy jokes.

I playfully punch Billy in the shoulder. "You will always be my friend."

"Not if you wear that tacky orange and blue, I won't," Billy shudders in jest.

Tyler and I laugh at Billy, then Tyler says, "Did y'all have a good break?"

Billy and I nod, and I say, "Ky came to see me after Christmas. It was awesome." I feel myself blush and Billy catches it.

"Ooh, Sloane, you little devil, your face is pink!"

I put my hands on my cheeks, "No it's not." I try to convince them.

Tyler leans forward. "No, you're right, it's not pink, it's red. What did you and the infamous Ky get up to?"

"You guys, stop." I feel heat in my cheeks and know there's no hiding my embarrassment. I take a deep breath then drop my hands into my lap. I can't stop smiling though. "He was only here for, like, a day and a half, but it was so awesome." I tell them and my eyes go skyward as I think about Ky.

"You are smitten," Billy says. He looks at Tyler. "She's smitten."

"Totally smitten," Tyler says as his eyes search my face. He looks at Billy, "I think our little Sloaner is in love."

I feel my eyes go wide. "What? No! I mean, no, it's way too soon for that," I stammer.

"If this thing's getting serious," Billy looks past me to Tyler, "we're going to have to meet this guy and make sure he's good enough for our Sloaner."

Tyler nods. "I agree. We need to make sure his intentions are honorable."

I laugh at them, then think about what Ky said as I chew on my bottom lip and shift in my chair. Tyler notices my unease. "Everything okay?"

I nod and tuck my hair behind my right ear. "Yeah, it's just...He's like, my first real boyfriend. This is all new to me." No way am I going to tell Tyler and Billy what Ky said.

Tyler's eyes soften, and he bumps my shoulder reassuringly. "We're just giving you a hard time."

"I know," I say. "I just wish he lived here. Heck, I wish he lived *near* here. He's four hours away, goes to school, and works, so I'm not sure when I'll see him again."

"If he's as into you as you are into him, you'll see him again soon," Billy says then looks at Tyler for confirmation. "Don't you think, Ty?"

"Totally," Tyler says. "He'll probably make an excuse just to drive up here."

I smile. "I hope so, because talking on the phone just isn't going to cut it." I think about Spring Break and prom and all the things I've dreamed of doing with an actual boyfriend. It's my senior year, and I finally have a boyfriend. Everything is starting to come together.

Chapter 31

Sloane

January 1993

As we trudge through January, it seems everything is all about SAT scores and college admissions with my fellow graduating seniors. It all stresses me out so much and it seems it's all anyone other than my circle is talking about. In my advanced classes, my classmates are talking about going to Harvard, Stanford, Vanderbilt, Duke, MIT, the list goes on. As you might expect, some of my various acquaintances are nerds, I say that lovingly, and are much smarter than me. They are all talking about going to these amazing schools with incredible reputations, and I'm considering four state universities. I'm happy to be going to art class where almost everyone in there is younger, so there's not all the talk about colleges.

"Hey, Stretch!" Myke says as I toss my backpack onto the table. He cocks his head and looks at me questioningly. "What's the matter?"

I pull out my chair and sit down with a heavy sigh. "Ugh, it's just all this talk of colleges and where everyone is going after graduation. I'm so glad to be with y'all since you don't have to think about it for another year."

"Oh, I'm already thinking about it," Denine says.

"Oh, we know," Dawne says sarcastically. "Miss Planner over there has probably already started on her college applications."

We all laugh, including Denine. "Started?" she says with equal sass, "How about finished?"

Myke covers his mouth and laughs his funny laugh that sounds like only air is coming out of his mouth. "Girl, you did not."

"Yes, I did." She sits up straight as a rod. "I have my plan all set." It's cute how she looks so proud of herself.

"What if they change the application for next year, smarty pants?" Dawne asks.

"Well, then it will have been good practice," Denine says, still looking regal enough to be sitting on a throne.

Dawne turns to me. "Sloane, when did you do your applications?"

I smirk. "At the end of Christmas break."

Myke and Dawne laugh their heads off, and Denine looks at me like I've just told her that Santa isn't real. "What?"

I nod. "Don't worry, I got them done and mailed in time. That's all that matters."

Denine tucks her hair behind her ear. "Well, I'm applying for early admissions to Spellman."

Myke says, "She's got a plan. Had it since kindergarten, I think."

"I have no plan," I say as I pull out the drawing I've been working on. It's a portrait of Dennis Quaid. We had to find a picture in a magazine to draw, and this one was a perfect full size, black and white headshot. Mrs. Dale is only having us draw half the face, so the picture is folded in half.

It's kind of cool, one side is the magazine and the other is my drawing. It's turning out really well, better than I expected.

"You have no plan?" Denine asks again. Shock is written all over her face and her eyes open wide.

I shrug. "Not really." I start working on my drawing.

"Girl, you're about to freak her out," Dawne says, not even looking up as she works on her drawing beside me.

"What school is your first choice?" Denine asks.

I shrug again. "It's been Florida since I have friends there, but I'm not sure anymore."

Denine is now looking at me like I have three eyes, Myke starts his air-laugh again, and Dawne joins him. "Sloane, you better stop," she says between laughter. "You're going to make her head explode."

I set my pencil down and look at Denine. "Remember when I said I was glad to be here since we *wouldn't* be talking about college?"

"But this is important!" Denine exclaims.

"I know, so important that everyone is talking about it non-stop," I say. "A lot of people I know are way smarter than me and got killer SAT scores. They're all going to go to top tier schools, while I'm over here not knowing which state school I want to go to."

"Which one did you like best when you visited?" Denine asks, clearly trying to help me work through it.

I squirm in my seat. "I've only been to Athens a couple of times, most recently was two years ago. I haven't visited any of the other schools."

"Oh, no you didn't! Are you *trying* to kill her?" Dawne's voice goes up several octaves. "She's gonna lose her mind!"

"Why haven't you had your parents take you?" Denine asks as her brow furrows.

I fidget with my pencil. "I don't know. That sort of thing was really important to my older sister, but...I guess I just didn't want to burden my parents to take me to all these schools when I'm not sure where to go or what to study." I use a little self-deprecating humor and add, "They'll probably just be happy if I get into any one of those schools. Once I find out where I get accepted, then I can go visit."

Denine's shoulders sag. "Honey, you are bright, personable, and well-rounded. You're going to get into more than one school."

"Where did you apply besides Georgia and Florida?" Myke asks.

"FSU and my back-up is Southern," I say. "I'm not even sure why I applied to Georgia. So many kids from here will end up there, and I'm trying to get away from all of this." I say as I wave my hand in the air.

"That school is so big, you could go your whole four years without running into someone from Dunwoody," Dawne says.

"I bet you get into all of them," Myke says.

I huff out a laugh. "I don't know about that."

Denine says, "I know you have friends at Florida, but don't make that the only reason you want to go there. You'll make friends anywhere you go."

"I wish it were as easy as you make it sound."

"You made friends with us," Myke says. "We've all known each other since elementary school and you just sat down with us and became our friend."

It warms my heart to hear him say that I'm their friend. I smile, "Thanks, Myke. That means a lot."

Dawne looks at the table with the cheerleaders and popular girls. "Do you think any of them would have sat with us?"

"I don't know," I say.

"I don't think they would have," Dawne shakes her head. "You're cool, Sloane, and you're going to do great things."

Now I feel my cheeks get warm. That's huge coming from Dawne. "Thank you," I tell her sincerely. "That means a lot."

Denine looks at me. "Follow your heart with respect to college. You'll make the right decision."

I love that I can be honest with my art class friends in a way that I can only really be with Maggie and Ky, but he's different. He graduated two years ago and didn't have a lot of options when it came to college. Plus, college doesn't seem that important to him. The pressure is real at Dunwoody High. It's like this whole college admissions thing has become its own popularity contest. Being accepted by your peers, being accepted into college, the status that comes with where you actually go to school. It's all so stressful. I have a moment of panic when I consider what will happen if I don't get into any of the four schools I applied to, and my pulse races.

Chapter 32

Sloane

While the senior class all wait anxiously for our college letters to arrive, Ky is coming to town with two friends to see Mudhoney at the Masquerade. This will definitely take college acceptance letters off of my mind. As I wait for him to get here, I thank my mom for the tenth time for letting them stay the night.

"Mom, I really appreciate you letting Ky and his friends stay over tonight," I say as I unload the dishwasher.

"Of course," my mom says as she pulls a pot out of the cabinet under the stove. "You two hardly get to see each other and this way they don't have to drive back so late at night." She turns to look at me. "Are you sure you all don't want to join us for dinner?"

"I'm sure, but thanks. That would be four more mouths to feed. We'll grab pizza in Little Five before the show."

"Are things pretty serious with Ky?" my mom asks nonchalantly as she starts making meatballs.

"I mean, I guess as serious as they can be when you live four hours from each other." I think about Ky telling me he loved me on the phone. "Mom, when do you know if you love someone?"

My mom stops rolling the meatball in her hands and turns to me, her blue eyes wide. "Do you think you're in love with Ky?"

I shake my head. "I don't think so, but...he told me he loved me."

Now my mom's eyebrows arch high over her eyes. "Oh, well," she stammers. "What did you say?" She sets down the meatball and washes her hands, obviously realizing this conversation needs her undivided attention.

I shrug. "I was totally caught off guard and didn't know what to say." I pause. "But I told him I loved him, too. I didn't want to hurt his feelings."

My mom's eyes grow wide as she dries her hands on a towel. She walks over to me and drapes the towel over her shoulder, then puts her hand on my shoulder. "Honey, that's okay if you're not in love with him. But, you shouldn't tell him you love him if you aren't sure. That's a big step and those are powerful words."

"I know," I nod and feel bad for what I said to Ky. "It just caught me off guard and I didn't know what to say. It was almost like my brain just said it, like you say, 'God, bless you' automatically when someone sneezes."

My mom smiles and drops her hand from my shoulder. Then, her expression grows serious as her eyes bore into mine. "You don't think he said it because he wants to—"

I cut her off before she can say it. "No, gosh, no." I stammer. "Maggie asked me the same thing. I mean, I don't know if he does, but I'm not ready for that."

I see the relief wash over my mom's eyes as they soften, and her shoulders relax. "Good," she smiles. "That's very serious stuff." I can tell she wants to avoid the topic almost as much as I do. "Just have fun and see where this goes. It's hard to get too serious when you two don't get to see each other regularly."

"I know, I finally get a boyfriend and he lives on the other side of the state."

"Just take it slow," my mom says. "And if things get serious and you need to talk..."

Just then, the doorbell sounds, and Sammy, barks to alert us. My eyes grow wide as I smile at my mom, "Thanks, mom, I will, but like I said, I'm nowhere near ready for that."

I rush to the door and as I see Ky through the glass, my heart races. I open the door and he gives me a bear hug, lifting my feet off the ground. "Hey!" I smile up at him as he gives me a quick kiss.

"Hey, Babe," he whispers in my ear and that term of endearment makes me stiffen. "It's so good to see you."

"You, too," I say as I shake off my brief irritation with the term, "babe," and take him in. He's wearing a red, plaid flannel over a white thermal shirt, jeans and work boots looking like a cuter version of Judd Nelson from the movie, *The Breakfast Club*. It's easy to overlook some of the things that bother me when he looks like this and makes my pulse race. I look to his left and smile at Joey who's sporting a dark green sweater and jeans with a pair of Converse one-star sneakers. "Hey, Joey, it's great to see you, too."

"Thanks," Joey smiles, then shifts to the side. "This is our friend Kris."

I feel my mouth fall open when I see Kris, because she's a girl, and I totally assumed she was Chris with a 'Ch'. "Hey, nice to meet you," I say with a smile. Kris is wearing tight jeans and an even tighter sweater showing all her curves. I take Ky's hand and lead them inside, showing them to my dad's office where they can stow their bags until we get back.

"I'm gonna hit the bathroom," Ky says as he dashes into the bathroom across the hall.

I lead Joey and Kris into the kitchen to meet my mom where we chat until Ky joins us a moment later.

"So, how do you all know each other?" My mom asks Joey and Kris as Ky comes to my side and gives me a squeeze.

"We grew up together," Kris says. She appears older than Ky and Joey, and she definitely wears clothes that show off her curves which is a tad intimidating. "I've seen these two at their best and worst," she jokes.

She definitely seems to be a more dominant personality than Joey who is quiet and soft-spoken. I look at Ky and say, "I don't know if I want to hear about you at your worst."

He smiles and starts to say something, but Kris cuts him off. "No, you probably don't," she says, and I swear there's a tone of seduction in her voice. I notice Ky looks embarrassed, and my mom looks like she's trying to pretend like she didn't hear that comment as she stirs pasta in a pot.

Ky squeezes me around the shoulders and kisses the top of my head, trying to reassure me, I guess. "I wasn't that bad."

"Ha!" Kris says and shares a knowing look with Ky.

"Well," I say to change the subject, "do y'all want to head into town and grab some pizza before the show?" I look at Ky. "I figure we can go to Little Five, and we'll be close to the club."

"Yeah, that sounds good." He looks at his friends for confirmation, and they nod.

"Let me just go freshen up," Kris says, and I point her toward the bathroom.

"I totally thought she was a guy when you said your friend 'Chris' was coming," I say quietly to Ky and Joey.

Joey laughs shyly. "Definitely not a guy," he jokes.

I try to quell the jealousy I'm feeling toward Kris, but I can't help but feel like she knows Ky a bit more intimately than as a friend.

Chapter 33

Sloane

By the time we get back from the concert, I am so ready to spend some quality time alone with Ky, and I've thought about how to make that happen on the drive back. After we get Joey and Kris settled in the family room, I grab a blanket and take Ky out the French doors to the screened porch.

My parents have wicker outdoor furniture out there, and while it's not the most comfortable, it'll do. The wicker sofa faces the French doors, and we sit on it and cuddle under the blanket on this chilly night.

I snuggle up under Ky's arm, and it just feels so nice. "I could sit like this all night."

Ky sighs blissfully. "Me, too, Babe."

I feel myself stiffen at that last word and sit up to face Ky. "Can you call me Sweetheart or something else?" I ask nicely and feel bad when I see disappointment cloud his eyes.

"Yeah, I'm sorry, I didn't realize you didn't like it," Ky says looking like a sad puppy.

I place my hand on his chest. "It's okay," I peck his lips. "It's just not my favorite word." I give him a kiss that should erase any feelings of disappointment.

He smiles at me when I pull back. "How about Beautiful?" He runs a finger along my cheekbone that sends a shiver through me.

I return his smile. "That works." I peck him on the mouth then snuggle back under his arm, resting my head on his chest, listening to his heartbeat.

I start thinking about what Kris said at dinner, that the girls throw themselves at Ky and realize how hard it is to date someone long-distance. You miss out on truly knowing them in their day-to-day lives. Of course, I get a weird vibe from Kris and don't know if she's trying to mess with me, or what.

I sit up and look at Ky. "What's the deal with Kris?" I whisper. "I felt like she was trying to keep me out of the conversations all night by talking about people I don't know and inside jokes and stuff."

"That's just Kris," Ky says quietly.

I feel my eyes narrow. "So, she's like that with everyone?"

Ky shifts in his seat and sighs. "I mean, no." He pauses. "I think she might be intimidated by you."

"What? That's crazy."

"She knows how much I like you, and now that she's met you, she sees how beautiful you are." He clasps my hand.

"But if you two are friends, why would I intimidate her? Did you two date?" I feel uneasy now.

Ky's face grows serious, and he looks down. "No, we never dated."

"But?" I ask as dread fills my belly.

He looks at me with wide eyes. "But, nothing. We've never dated."

I can't tell if he's being defensive or just honestly surprised at the thought, either way, it unnerves me and by the look in his eyes, I think he can tell.

"Do you think she likes you more than a friend?"

Ky shakes his head. "I think she's just being protective of me." I must not look convinced because Ky lifts my chin with his fingers so I'm looking in his eyes instead of at the fingernail I'm picking. "Hey, she's my friend, you're my girlfriend. I'm crazy about you." His smile is sincere and his eyes are sparkling.

"Even if she's all curvy and I'm...not?" I'm so self-conscious about my figure and it's multiplied by a thousand when a boy is involved. I hardly feel womanly.

"Yes," He's still smiling. "You are beautiful, inside and out. Plus, you're super cool. I promise, you have nothing to worry about."

Ky's words fill me with relief and I lean in to kiss him. After a spine-tingling kiss, I lean back and the wicker sofa creaks underneath me. "I've been wanting to ask you something."

"Sure," he says with sleepy eyes and a sweet smile.

I start to fidget with my fingernail again. "So...I wondered if you want to go to my prom with me." I continue before he can answer. "I've never been asked to a school dance and decided that before I graduate, I would go to one, and well, I didn't get asked to Homecoming, didn't ask anyone to Snowball, so that leaves prom." I look at him expectantly and try to catch my breath after getting all of that out at once.

"I have two questions," Ky says with a serious look on his face.

"Okay, but first..." I lean in and kiss him. I sit back and smile, "Okay, shoot."

His eyes bore into mine. "Was that to try and butter me up?" He asks, his voice husky and a bit breathless.

I smile then shrug, "Maybe."

He chuckles at me. "What is Snowball?"

This makes me laugh. "Oh, it's like the Sadie Hawkins dance where the girls ask the boys."

"Why didn't you ask someone?"

"Is that your second question?" I smile.

Ky chuckles again. "No, my second question is," He moves closer to me, our faces nearly touching. His voice is low when he asks, "Who are these boys at your school and how has no one asked you to any dances?" He leans in and kisses me tenderly.

When he moves back, I bite my lower lip then shrug my shoulders. "I don't know. I just assume it's because I'm not the curviest girl, I'm taller than most guys, and I'm not going to put out. Since I'm not a partier, I'm sure most people think I'm a prude."

Ky laughs then cradles my face in his right hand. "You are most certainly not a prude, and not all guys want girls that look like they work at Hooters." He kisses me, then asks, "Do you think maybe these guys are intimidated by you?"

I smirk and shake my head. "No. I'm like the least intimidating person."

"With the body of a super model," Ky says as he rubs my arms. "I bet you intimidate some of them."

"Really?" I ask as I cock my head because this sounds like the last thing I would imagine. "But I didn't intimidate you."

He smiles at me. "Oh, yes you did." He brushes my hair off my shoulder, exposing my neck. "But I figured the worst thing you could do was turn me down, and I'd likely never see you again." He leans down and kisses my neck sending blissful shivers down my spine. Then, he leans up as his eyes scan my face. "I decided to take a chance," he says with a satisfied grin.

"Well, I'm glad you did," I lean in and kiss him.

After a moment, he slides back and narrows his eyes. "Seriously, though, why didn't you ask anyone to that Snowball dance?"

"The guy I was going to ask got asked by someone else first," I say as a matter of fact.

"And you didn't want to ask someone else?"

I shrug. "No. Not enough to risk embarrassment if I got turned down."

Ky smiles, "See, now you know how guys feel."

I return his smile. "Yeah, it's pretty terrifying."

"You could have asked a guy who's just a friend. You know, just gone as friends."

I think about it. "Yeah, I guess I could have, but I want to go to a dance with someone who wants to be there with me as more than just a friend." I move closely to him, inches from his face. "Someone who I can dance closely with and do this with..." I lean forward and kiss him.

He smiles as I sit back. "So, Ky Carter, will you go to prom with me?"

He pretends like he's thinking hard about this as his brow furrows. "Let's see," he says. "What day is it?"

"May 22nd," I say, and before he can answer, I add, "And, 99X has a concert at Stone Mountain that afternoon. The Lemonheads are play-ing." I say with an eager smile. "We could go to the concert, then prom." I bounce a little as I say this, making him laugh.

He chuckles at me. "Aren't you going to see them in April?"

"Yeah, but why not see them twice in two months?" I smile at him encouragingly. "Urge Overkill and Ned's Atomic Dustbin are playing too."

Ky takes my hand. "Sloane Warren, I would love to take you to your prom...after the concert, of course."

I throw my arms around him and hug him tightly. "Thank you," I whisper, then give him kisses on his ear and neck. I lean back, "So was it Urge Overkill that did it for you?" I joke.

"No, Ned's Atomic Dustbin." He laughs and wraps his arms around me. "Just kidding," he says as his face grows serious. "I want to be there for you, because you asked me."

"Really?"

He nods. "I wouldn't miss it for the world, Beautiful."

My insides warm at his sweetness and I kiss Ky. I can't believe that I'm actually going to get to go to my senior prom!

Chapter 34

Tyler

"Red ball, corner pocket," Brian says as he lines up his pool cue and shoots. "Yes!" He pumps his fist in the air, then leans over the table again to knock the eight-ball in. It's an easy shot which he sinks quickly. He's beat me yet again.

"Considering you get to practice here all the time, I can't be too mad." I put my cue back in the rack on the wall. "I'll beat you again one of these days."

Brian is pulling all the balls out of the pockets and I help him. He laughs. "I don't remember you ever beating me, buddy."

He loves to yank my chain. "Dude, you know I've beat you. Several times." I clear out the last pocket. "It's just been a while."

"I'm just messing, man." Brian grabs the triangular rack off a hook underneath the table and starts arranging the balls inside. "Isn't it nice to have off from games, even if just a little while?"

I nod. "Yeah, but we'll be back at it next month. We're lucky we're already conditioned from football."

"Seriously. I'm glad Coach K is going easy on us, especially after a long football season."

"I'm excited to get back at it. Coach thinks we'll get some visits from scouts this year."

The basement door that leads to the back yard opens. "The party's here!" Sara says as she holds up a pack of Zima's and smiles from ear to ear. I don't know how she and the girls drink that stuff. They even drop Jolly Ranchers in them to make them taste better. Trailing behind Sara are Ramsey and Kara, two popular girls who are also nice, so I'm glad Sara's been hanging out with them versus some of the snobbier girls.

There's not a ton to do in Dunwoody, especially in winter, so we usually hang out at someone's house. When it's warm, there are tons of places to hangout outside, but not in January. Brian's basement has become somewhat of our winter hangout. His parents are cool, but we also have to be careful and responsible. They're out of town this weekend so, Brian has invited a few more people than usual. I know I'm spending the night, but Sara has started getting drunk at these parties and I have to look out for her. I can't tell if she's just having fun or trying to fit in with the other girls. Either way, I've definitely seen a change in her since we started dating.

I walk toward her. "Hey." She stands on her toes and gives me a quick kiss. "Want one?" She holds up the girly malt beverage.

"No, thanks," I laugh. Zima is a hot new drink, but I think it tastes like crap. Most of the girls seem to have made the switch from wine coolers to these things, but I'll stick with beer.

Sara takes a Zima out of the cardboard box and opens it, taking a sip. She digs in her pocket and fishes out a green apple Jolly Rancher, takes off the plastic wrapper and drops it into the clear beverage. "There." She grins at me and makes me smile and shake my head.

Brian has grabbed his camcorder and is videoing everyone as the door opens again. "What's up!" Adam, Max, and Josh make their entrance with Amber and Lori bringing up the rear. Those two being of the snobby, not-so-nice variety popular girls.

"Hey!" Sara practically squeals, shoving her drink box into my chest. She turns her attention away from me and toward them. Her eyes are bright with excitement as she bounds over to two of the most popular girls in our grade.

Behind them are Travis, Andre, and Tim. Those boys and I have a good time together. We just click and cut up together. I'm happy to see them because I don't think Sara is going to be hanging with me as much as I'd like.

It's a pretty typical night in Brian's basement. Brian's music is playing through the stereo, right now "Remedy" by The Black Crows fills the air, and Goodfellas is on the TV in the background. Brian's parents have HBO, so there's always a movie on when we aren't watching MTV. Once midnight rolls around, I know Brian will be cool with me switching the TV to MTV so we can watch Headbanger's Ball. Travis, Andre, Josh, and Tim are playing pool while everyone else is lounging on the sofas and surrounding floor.

Amber hops up from her seat in the middle of the sofa. "Let's play a game!"

I groan to myself because I'd rather be chilling with a few people than have a whole crowd in here, let alone, be forced to play a game. I glance at the pool table, thinking about joining them instead, but I've got my arm around my girl and really want to spend time with her.

"Yes! What do you want to play?" Sara takes a long sip of her drink and is all too eager to join Amber in whatever she suggests.

Amber's eyes glisten with an almost evil gleam. "Truth or Dare."

"Oh my gosh, yes!" Sara says as she sits up in her seat.

"I'll sit this one out," I say as I begin to stand up. I know how this game goes and I don't want to play.

"Oh, no you don't!" Sara says and pulls me back down by my arm.

"Everyone in the circle has to play." Amber acts like she's the queen of Brian's basement.

Brian's filming again. "You've gotta stay man, this'll be fun."

I look around me, really wishing I had gotten up to play pool a minute ago. Sara's on my right, Amber's next to her, then there's Max, Brian, Ramsey, Kara, Adam, and finally, Lori's on my left. I thought Amber would start with me since I wanted out of the game, but I think she's drawn to the camera in Brian's hand.

"Brian," she purrs. "Truth or Dare?"

"Dare."

Amber smirks. "Try to lick your elbow."

Brian grins and hands the camera to Ramsey. He then proceeds to attempt to make contact with his tongue on his elbow contorting his arm this way and that, making us all laugh. "Sorry Amber, I guess I'm just not flexible enough."

"Shame," Amber says with mock disappointment.

Brian takes his camera back from Ramsey and points it at Amber. "Amber, Truth or Dare?"

"Dare."

Brian looks at the table which is full of empty cups and bowls of snacks. "Eat a snack without using your hands."

"I've got a snack you can eat without using your hands!" Josh hollers from the pool table making most of the group laugh.

"A snack from the table," Brian says over his shoulder to Josh.

Amber grins and surveys her options. Doritos, Chex Mix, potato chips, and Oreos are on the table. Amber kneels beside the table and leans over the bowl of Chex Mix. She sticks out her tongue and it lands on a square pretzel. The pretzel sticks to her tongue and she tries to look seductive as she puts the pretzel in her mouth and starts chewing. When she's finished, she licks her top lip. My stomach turns but Max's mouth is hanging open and Brian looks pleased to have caught that on camera.

I sigh and it must have been louder than I thought because Amber turns to me with a wicked grin. "Your turn, Tyler."

"Dare." I say quickly so I can get this over with.

"Whisper something seductive to the person on your left." She looks proud of herself and I catch her wink at Lori.

"Really, Amber?" I look at Sara and she swats me on the shoulder.

"It's just a game, Tyler," Sara says. "It's okay."

I am not cool with this and even though Sara is acting like she's cool with it, I could feel her stiffen under my arm when Amber gave me my dare. I sigh again and turn to Lori. I lean in and whisper, "Something seductive."

Disappointment washes over her face for the briefest moment, then she stifles a laugh and looks coyly at me. "Tyler, you're going to make me blush."

I huff out a laugh and look at Sara whose smile looks a little less bright than it had when the game started. This is why I hate stuff like this.

"Your turn to ask someone, Tyler," Amber practically sings.

"Uh, okay. I look around the circle. "Max, Truth or Dare?"

"Dare."

"Do one hundred push-ups." I know Max can handle this. He's on the football team and in great shape, so he can manage.

"Dude, no problem." Max hops up and moves to a clear space on the floor, getting down and counting off his push-ups.

"Max, pick someone while you're doing that," Amber demands.

"Okay," Max says between breaths. "Lori, Truth or Dare?"

"Truth," Lori says looking pleased with herself.

"What is something you would do if you knew there were no consequences."

Lori thinks for a moment. "Uh, probably kiss someone who isn't single."

"Lori!" Ramsey chastises.

Lori shrugs. "Well, I have to be honest, don't I?"

"Yeah, but you would know they aren't single and that's just wrong," Kara says.

"Kara," Lori says and there's an edge in her voice.

"What?"

"Truth or Dare?" Wow, the edge in Lori's voice just got sharper.

Kara sighs. "Dare."

"Kiss Tyler," Lori demands. "On the lips."

Before I can even say anything, Kara refuses. "No way. He's with Sara. That's not cool, Lori." Kara gets up and goes over to the pool table.

"Fine," Lori turns toward me and looks past me at Sara. "Sara, kiss Adam."

"Lori, come on," I start but am interrupted by my girlfriend.

"It's okay. It's just a game." Sara slurs a little when she says this. I look down and realize she's already drank three of her Zimas.

I turn to her with my mouth open and feel my eyes go wide. When I look back at Lori, she is whispering something to Adam. I turn back to Sara and say so only she can hear, "You don't have to do this. You don't have to prove anything to her or anyone."

"I know." That's all she says to me before getting up, walking past me, and over to Adam.

Sara leans down to kiss Adam on the cheek and he pulls her onto his lap, kissing square on the mouth. "Hey!" I yell as I stand up. "That's enough. This game is over."

Adam stops kissing Sara, but she stays in his lap, looking too comfortable. I hold out my hand. "Come on, I'll take you home."

Sara looks at Lori, then Amber, then back at me before standing up. "I'm not going anywhere." She plops back down on the sofa next to Amber. "Relax, Tyler, it's just a game."

Anger boils in my veins and I want to punch Adam in the face. Instead, I leave the room and walk upstairs to the kitchen to cool off. I can't believe my girlfriend just did that and acted like it wasn't a big deal. Even worse? I think she did it to impress her friends, or rather, girls who she wants to be her friends. Tipsy or not, she didn't have to do it and I'd be lying if I said it didn't bother me.

Chapter 35

Sloane

It's crazy how long each school year feels, but when you're a senior, time flies so fast after the holidays. I have so much to look forward to in the next couple of months. Next is The Lemonheads at the Masquerade, then Spring Break, followed by The Lemonheads at Stone Mountain the day of prom. All of that and I should be getting my college acceptance letters any day now.

In marine bio, I fill Tyler and Billy in on my weekend, just as I had done with Kurt in AP French. "I have good news," I practically sing to Tyler and Billy.

"Oh yeah?" Billy asks. "Did you finally listen to Johnny Cash?"

"Very funny," I say as I notice Tyler smirking. "I'll have you know I listened to Johnny Cash months ago, after our conversation." I wave my hand. "Anyway, I saw Ky this weekend."

Billy rolls his eyes and pretends like he's annoyed. "Here we go again," he says and looks at Tyler. "How could we forget?"

Before Tyler can say anything, I swat Billy on the arm. "No, it's not that Ky came for the weekend. It's that I asked him to go to prom with me, and he said yes!" I smile proudly. "I'm finally going to my first dance!"

"You've never been to a dance before?" Tyler cocks his head and I hear a hint of surprise in his voice.

I shake my head. "Not since 7th grade when everyone went, without dates, of course."

"Why not?" he asks, genuinely interested.

I shrug my shoulders. "Because no one ever asked me."

"Really?" Billy asks as his eyes squint.

I shake my head. "No, no one ever asked me to go to a dance."

"Why didn't you just go with friends?" Billy asks. "Or ask someone yourself?"

I scoff. "Well, let's see. I don't have a ton of friends, and if they go, they have dates. And, I could never ask someone myself."

"Not even to Snowball where guys would expect you to ask them?" Tyler asks.

I feel myself blush when I think about how close I was to asking him. "No, I mean, I thought about it, but I would have to be pretty confident that the guy would say yes."

"So, there was someone you wanted to go with this year." Billy says.

Oh, gosh, this is getting really uncomfortable. I shift in my seat. "Yeah," I reply, but don't know what else to say.

"You totally should have asked the guy," Tyler says. "I bet he would have said yes."

I huff out a laugh and look at Tyler. "Actually, it would have been a no because someone else asked him first." I smile trying to cover up anything that might be giving myself away. Tyler's eyebrows rise slightly above his eyes, but I don't think I gave anything away.

"Well, buddy, I'm happy for you," Billy says as he claps me on the back. "You'll have to introduce us to Ky. I mean, I feel like we practically know him." He looks at Tyler who chuckles and nods.

I feel embarrassment creeping up my face. "Do I really talk about him that much?" I look at them with wide eyes.

Tyler holds his index finger and thumb about an inch apart. "Just a little," he laughs as he says this making his eyes light up.

I put my hand to my forehead. "Oh my gosh, I'm sorry, y'all. I'll try to talk about him less--"

Billy says, "It's okay, Sloaner. We know you're just happy."

I smile. "I am. And I'm so excited that Ky's coming to prom!"

***

I head to lunch and feel like I'm floating. I'm thinking about my amazing weekend with Ky and can't wait to tell my friends all about it. I sit down next to Maggie and across from Beth and Annalise. "Hey guys!" I smile at the three girls I've become close with this year. I sit down and pull my lunch out of my backpack. "Did you have a good weekend?"

"Wait, wait, wait, *wait*!" Annalise says as she waves her hands in front of her, stopping anyone else from saying anything. "I want to hear about your weekend first."

My eyes go skyward at the memory of hanging out on the porch with Ky. "It was amazing." I tell my three eager friends. "The show was great. His friend 'Chris' was actually a girl, Kris with a 'k,' and she was kinda weird." I wave off the thought. "More on that later. When we finally got time alone, it was amazing."

"Okay, this is great and all, but we need to know," Annalise says, and I realize the three of them are all leaning forward in their seats. "Did you ask him?"

Beth adds, "Did he say yes?"

I nod my head and can't contain my smile. "Ky said he'd come up for prom!"

My friends emit squeals of joy and their eyes sparkle with excitement. "Oh my gosh, we can all go together. Steve will be so glad that he won't be the oldest guy there," Beth jokes.

Beth's long-time boyfriend, Steve, went to a neighboring school and graduated last year, so that makes Ky a year older than him. "Oh, that's right," I say. "I'm sure that will make Ky feel better, too."

Annalise adds, "We'll get a limo and go to a nice restaurant. It's going to be so much fun. I know we're all so ready to get out of here, but I'm glad we'll get to end our year doing something fun together. We deserve it!"

"Y'all have to let me know what to expect at my first dance," I tell them.

Maggie says softly, "It's more about who you're with, don't you think?" She looks across the table at Beth and Annalise.

"Totally," Annalise says. "There's usually a DJ, some lame decorations, and bland food, but it's senior prom. How can you not go?"

"Exactly," Beth agrees. "Prom is the fanciest dance of the year, so at least it will be in a hotel ballroom versus the gym. And, the decorations aren't *that* bad."

"No, you're right," Annalise agrees. "Just don't expect them to be as fancy as they are in the movies."

"I'm so excited to do the whole limo and fancy dinner thing," I say. "It's not like I've never gone to a fancy restaurant, but this is with y'all and our dates, not parents. In a limo all by ourselves!" I never knew going to a school dance could make me so giddy, but I am *finally* getting to do something that's like, a rite of passage. I finally feel included and a part of something at my school and it feels amazing.

Beth's eyes get soft. "Oh my gosh, you and Ky are going to have an amazing time. I can't wait to meet him!"

I shift a little uncomfortably in my seat, and Beth notices. "What? What's wrong?"

I sigh and glance over at Maggie who's heard this before. "No, it's just—Ky is great."

"Uh-oh," Annalise says as she bites into her apple.

"No, no," I pause. "We have good chemistry. Great, actually. But," I look at Maggie again, and she smiles encouragingly because she knows what I'm going to say. "We talk on the phone a lot since he lives so far away, and," I think about how to phrase this. "He's sweet, he's just—"

"Not the sharpest pencil in the box?" Annalise says.

I nod and feel so bad. "Yeah. At first I just thought he was quirky, but the more I talk to him, I realize that we probably aren't going to have the deepest conversations." I think back to the weekend. "But like I said, we have great chemistry when we're together. Let's just say we don't talk as much." I feel my cheeks burn as these words tumble out of my mouth.

My friends giggle with me, and Maggie speaks up. "But, he's nice, good-looking, and you have fun with him, right?"

A smile forms on my face. "Yeah."

"Then that's what matters," Maggie says and looks across at Beth and Annalise for their perspective.

Beth leans in and puts her hand in between us on the table. "Look, it's just prom. It's not like you're going to marry the guy."

Annalise chimes in. "Says the girl in the long-term relationship who will probably marry the guy she's with."

We all laugh at this. "I know," I tell them. "Just be forewarned."

"I'm sure he's fine," Annalise says. "Just enjoy the moment. He likes you. You like him."

"He's cute," Beth adds.

"Oh, so cute," I reply. "And tall." As I say that, another tall, cute boy catches my eye as he walks across the cafeteria. Even though I'm so happy to have a boyfriend, I think about the boy with the sexy smile who I have amazing conversations with in marine bio. And in an instant, I feel bad for having that thought. Tyler must have a flaw or two as well, right?

Chapter 36

Sloane

March 1993

I almost can't believe it, but I received acceptance letters from all four schools I applied to. Granted, they aren't Ivy League schools, but still. I think my parents are as surprised as I am. Not because I'm not a good student, but I have to work hard for the grades I get. I have a tutor for math, and I'm just not that involved in a lot of clubs or extracurriculars because I have to spend time on my studies.

As I'm setting the table for dinner, my mom is cooking. "Your dad and I are so proud of you," she says as she cuts broccoli. "Is Florida still your first choice?"

"I'm not sure," I tell her as I set forks next to each plate. "I mean, I have friends who go there, which is cool, but—" I shrug. "I'm not sure what to do."

"What about Georgia?"

I breathe in deeply. "I don't know. So many kids from school are going there, and I'm really trying to get away from all of that."

"I get that," my mom says as she begins to rinse the broccoli in a colander, "but it's such a big school, you'll probably never see them."

"Yeah, I guess so, but I don't know." I think for a moment. "I mean, I think I've been to Athens a couple of times, but I didn't tour the campus or anything. I've never toured any campuses."

My mom stops what she's doing and looks at me, almost surprised upon hearing this. "Why don't we go visit all four of them? Since you've been accepted to all of them, you can see which one you like best."

I think about it. "Yeah, we could do that if you think we have time."

My mom nods. "Why don't you write down each school and write a list of the positives and negatives of each one. If you want to visit all four, we can easily do that." She pours the broccoli into a pot on the stove. "We can go to Athens one weekend, then the other three are so close to each other, we can visit them another weekend. Maybe even take a day off to make it a long weekend."

"Are you sure you or dad would have time?"

"Of course, sweetie." My mom smiles and I feel happy that we'll get to do something one-on-one for a change, which doesn't happen often.

"I can't wait to tell Tameka when she comes to town for The Lemonheads' show this weekend."

My mom gives me a questioning look. "This weekend?"

"Yeah," I nod, "it's Saturday, remember?"

"Oh, honey, I completely forgot. Your dad and I have to go to Buffalo for his friend's funeral, and Erin just found out that she has some mandatory event for her sorority. I'm not sure Bryn will be comfortable being alone."

My heart starts to race. "But, mom," I feel tears prick the back of my eyes, "I've had tickets for months, and I've never seen The Lemonheads before." I'm on the brink of losing it. "Can't Bryn just stay here by herself until we get back from the show?"

Bryn hears us from the family room and walks into the kitchen. "I don't want to be all by myself."

I sigh heavily. "Bryn, it's only a few hours. We'll be back after the show." I'm so frustrated and starting to feel like Molly Ringwald in Sixteen Candles when everyone forgets about her birthday. I feel like I'm an after-thought in this family sometimes. I guess that's what happens when you don't demand attention and are easy-going.

Bryn starts to freak out and looks at our mom with pleading eyes. "Mom, no. I don't want to be here by myself." I can tell she's on the brink of losing it, or, acting like she's losing it to get her way.

"Mom," I say as I'm about to lose it myself. "I've had these tickets for months, and Tameka is coming to town for the show." My voice rises out of sheer frustration. "I've been looking so forward to it." I say a little less whiney and more measured.

Bryn starts crying now. "But, mom, no! I can't be here by myself."

"Oh my gosh!" I yell at Bryn, completely at my wit's end. "Yes, you can. Nothing's going to happen to you!"

As Bryn starts to protest, our mom steps in. "Sloane, I'm sorry, honey, but with Erin being gone and your dad and I going out of town, you'll have to stay here with Bryn." Bryn sniffles and recovers quickly. She appears consoled by this answer, but me on the other hand...

"Mom, she's a year older than me. She doesn't need a baby-sitter!"

My mom gets that look. You know the one. The look that if you push her too far, it's not going to be pretty. "Sloane," she says tersely communicating through her tone that the conversation is over and her mind is made up.

I toss the rest of the silverware onto the table with a loud clatter. "This is so unfair!" I shout as I race out of the kitchen and up the stairs to my bedroom, slamming the door for good measure. I fling myself onto my bed and bawl my eyes out. I can't believe I can't go to the concert because my sister is scared to be alone for a few hours. I get that she has special needs, but it's not like she's incapable of doing anything. She has a job bagging groceries. She is a very capable person. Besides, what am I going to do if someone breaks into the house, or a fire breaks out? Honestly, she's stronger than me so she could take on a burglar way better than I could. After I cry my frustration out, I put in my Nirvana *Nevermind* CD and crank up the volume. I'm still mad, and I want the whole house to know it.

Chapter 37

Sloane

I'm so grateful that Tameka decides to come to Atlanta anyway and brings her friend Ray with her. "Hey honey," she says as she pulls me into hug when I meet them on my driveway. "We're so sorry about tonight."

As we head inside, I say, "I sold the tickets to Miranda, so at least she'll get to enjoy the show." We walk into the family room, and I look at Tameka, then Ray. "Thanks so much for coming here anyway." My shoulders sag, and I lead them over to the sofas feeling like Eeyore from *Winnie the Pooh*.

"Of course," Tameka says, and Ray nods.

We sit down, and I tell them, "I've ordered a pizza, it should be here soon."

As we're catching up, Bryn comes downstairs and pulls out plates from a cabinet for the pizza. She knows I'm still mad at her and is trying to do nice things to make amends, but I'm still so aggravated about the whole thing. Once the pizza arrives, she joins us in the family room, and you could cut the tension with a knife.

"Evan Dando was on 99X today," I say to Tameka and Ray, referring to the lead singer and guitarist of The Lemonheads. "He sounded so sweet and even gave out his hotel and room number on the air! Can you believe that?"

"What? That's crazy," Ray says.

"I know," I agree. "He said if anyone wanted to come by and say hi, to come to his hotel. It would be so cool to go down there."

"Why don't we?" Ray says.

"Yeah, why not?" Tameka adds. "It's not like we have anything else to do."

I huff out a laugh. "Because we have to stay here with Bryn, remember. It's the reason why we're missing the concert."

Ray looks at Bryn. "Do you want to come with us?"

Bryn's eyes light up. "Sure!" she says eagerly.

"Guys that's not gonna work," I say.

"Why not?" Ray asks honestly.

"Because, I don't want her to freak out if something happens," I reply. "We could potentially meet Evan Dando. We have to be cool."

Tameka looks at Bryn. "Will you be cool?"

Bryn nods. "Yeah. I promise."

I give her a serious look.

"Sloane, I promise," she assures me.

"Let's do it," Ray says.

I inhale deeply and look to Tameka for her opinion. "Yeah, let's go. She said she'll be cool. We should go."

I feel a flutter of excitement in my chest. "Okay, let's do it!"

We eat our pizza and strategize about when to leave and what to do when we get there. We try to figure out what time the show should end and when we should head into town. I can't believe we're doing this, but we might get to meet Evan Dando!

***

We have so much time to kill after we eat, and we can only sit around the house for so long. We tried watching a movie to pass the time, but since the show won't be over for a while, we have so much time. We decide to pile into Ray's car and head to Little Five, the quirky, artsy neighborhood known for its eclectic collection of shops, restaurants, and clubs. Since it's late and the shops are closed, we don't spend long there. We make a pass by the Masquerade, and it appears the concert is still going, so we decide to go to the Hard Rock Café to get some food. We have to wait a while for a table and by the time we eat, it's after 12:30 a.m., and we head to the Masquerade again to see if the show is over. Finally, the club is emptying out, and we take the scenic drive to the hotel which is on Peachtree Street in Midtown. Ray parks his big, old, noisy car in the parking lot, and we head inside. Surprisingly, Bryn has been cool so far. I think she's enjoying this adventure like the time she snuck out with Tameka and me last summer. We rode around with two seniors from the DHS baseball team that Tameka was friends with. We listened to "The Humpty Dance" over and over and Bryn thought it was so much fun. I realize she wants to feel included just like I do.

As we walk into the lobby, I notice how tiny it is, and quickly realize there is no way we can hang around there until Evan Dando arrives. We'd surely be kicked out for loitering. So, I say, "Let's go upstairs to meet them," acting like we're supposed to be there in case the lady at the front desk can hear us.

We walk to the elevators, press the up arrow, and wait. My heart is beating fast, and I hope no one says anything to us. The elevator dings, the doors open, and we get on.

"What floor?" Ray asks.

"Ten, I guess. He said room 1018," I say, and Ray presses the button.

I look at my friends. "The lobby felt too small to wait in. Let's just go to the room and see if he's there. If not, we'll figure something out."

When the elevator arrives at the tenth floor, we walk out into the dimly lit and quiet corridor. Ray looks at the number signs and motions for us to follow him toward room 1018. When we get there, he looks at me and says quietly, "Okay, showtime."

"Me?" I whisper.

He nods. "Yeah, you're the biggest fan."

I inhale a deep breath and let it out slowly to calm my nerves. I lightly knock on the door, and we wait. And wait. I look at my friends, "I don't think he's here yet."

"Or he's already asleep," Bryn says.

Tameka laughs. "He's a rock star, I don't think he's sleeping." She moves to the door and puts her ear up to it. "It sounds like the message bell is ringing on the phone," she says as she steps back. "He probably hasn't come back yet."

"Where should we wait?" Ray asks.

"Maybe the stairwell?" Tameka suggests.

"Good idea," I say. "We can't just hang out in the hallway."

As we're walking to the stairwell to the left of the room, I see a door a few paces down on our right. "What's this?" I whisper.

We push open the door and realize that it's the service elevator bay. "Why don't we wait in here?" I suggest. "It's closer to the room, that way we can try to listen and see if anyone comes by."

My friends and sister nod in agreement. We walk into the service elevator bay and wait. There are two chairs and a large trash can. My stomach is a ball of nerves as we wait because I don't want to get caught and get in trouble. Thankfully, it's late and so far, no one is using the service elevator, so that's good. We chat in whispers while we wait.

"I wonder how long we'll have to hang out in here?" I say.

"Hopefully not too long," Bryn says. "I'm getting tired."

"Who knows," Tameka says. "At least Ray thought to drive by the club, so we know the concert is over."

After about ten to fifteen minutes, we hear voices in the hallway.

"It sounds like a man and some women," Ray says.

"I think I heard someone ask for an autograph," Bryn says.

"Maybe it's him," I whisper as I sit up straight and feel my eyes go wide. Adrenaline courses through me.

"Let's wait a minute and then go see," Tameka says. "If it's not him, we don't want to get in trouble."

Once the hallway gets quiet again, we decide to make our move. Ray opens the door and peers into the hallway. "The coast is clear." He pushes through the door, and we file out of the small service elevator room and into the quiet hallway.

Again, my friends make me knock on the door, but I make Ray stand by my side. My heart is pounding. I'm anxious enough as it is, and my nerves are humming as I'm knocking on a rock star's hotel room door. After a moment, the door opens, and my wide eyes land on the most beautiful human in the world. Evan Dando, lead singer and guitarist for The Lemonheads, swings open the door, and I swear I can hear the angels singing from the heavens.

Chapter 38

Sloane

"Hi," I say as I raise my hand in a wave. "I'm Sloane. I heard you on the radio and you said to come by and say hi. So, hi." My delivery is rapid-fire, and as soon as I get the words out, I turn on my heel to walk away.

But I hear, "Wait, what's your name?" in a soft, deep voice.

Apparently, I spoke so fast, he didn't catch it. I turn around and can't believe the rock star with the long brown hair and beautiful smile wants to talk to me. I smile. "Sloane. Nice to meet you." I turn to reveal my friends. "This is Ray, Tameka, and my sister Bryn."

"Hey," Evan says to them, then opens the door as far as it will go. "Do you want to come in?"

I look to my friends who nod and smile. "We don't want to bother you," I say respectfully.

"No, come on in," Evan says as he steps aside and waves his arm out into the room. "We're just hanging out." He has a bashful countenance and dips his head as he talks softly. His long brown hair creates a protective curtain around his handsome face. His eyes are a light, bright blue, his face is tan, and he must be about six-foot-three because he's taller than me.

I see two older girls who must be in their late teens or early twenties in the room sitting on the bed and worry that we might have just crashed their party. "Hey," I smile at them.

"Hey," the beautiful girl with the thick mane of curly, red hair says. "I'm Nikki and this is Ashley."

After introducing myself and my group, we sit on the floor at the foot of the bed as Evan perches on the end of the bed. "So, were you at the show?" he asks. His voice has a lazy, almost sleepy cadence.

"Unfortunately, not," I say. "But my friends brought me down here because I was so bummed I missed it." I wasn't going to tell all these cool adults why I missed the show.

"Well, that's a shame, but you have great friends," he says, then a knock sounds on the door. Evan hops up, ambles over to the door, and he invites two women to join us. These ladies look way older than us and are super friendly. They don't intimidate me like the younger women do. I look over at Bryn and she looks surprisingly okay. She catches my eye and smiles. I think she's actually having fun.

We chat for a bit, making introductions while Evan is rooting around in the closet. When he returns, he has his acoustic guitar with him and sits back down on the end of the bed. He starts strumming his guitar unconsciously, and I notice his gaze upon me, so I smile. Evan returns the smile and says, "What's your favorite song?" His eyes search me and my friends.

Tameka says, "My favorite is 'Bit Part.'"

I think for a moment. "Gosh, it's hard to pick just one, but I like 'Being Around,'" I reply, then add, "And I've always loved 'Mrs. Robinson.' Your cover is so good." I don't want to seem like one of those lame people who mentions a cover song, so I quickly explain why the song has so much meaning to me. "I had a teacher named Ms. Robinson in second grade and she was awesome. That song always reminds me of her."

"I had a feeling you were going to say you had a teacher with that name," Evan says as he smiles sweetly.

"Really?" I would probably believe anything he told me. He nods and I say, "She made me do the introduction to the second grade Thanksgiving Day play, and I was scared to death. I only had, like, one line, and I must have practiced it a hundred times." He smiles and chuckles at this, so I continue. "I hate getting up in front of people, and I'm really shy, so I think she was trying to break me out of that."

Evan nods. "I bet she was. That's cool." He explains, "Well, not cool that you were terrified to do it, but cool that she was trying to get you over your fear." A funny, goofy laugh escapes his mouth as he strums his guitar softly, then cocks his head. "Do you still remember what you had to say?"

I think for a moment, my eyes turning up to the ceiling. I giggle at the thought. "Yeah, I think it was, 'Welcome to Ms. Robinson's Second Grade Thanksgiving play. We hope you enjoy the show.' Or something like that." I laugh at how simple it was. "I think I was more scared of being on stage by myself and having all eyes on me."

"I can see that," Evan says. "I still get nervous sometimes, but the more you do it, the less nervous you get, usually."

"I couldn't do what you do. Getting up on stage, playing an instrument, and singing songs you wrote that mean so much to you. That would be terrifying."

Evan starts strumming, and I notice right away that he's playing 'Being Around.' It's off their most recent album and is acoustic, so it's perfect to listen to it like this. I can't believe Evan Dando is serenading us. I feel like I'm in a dream! We're all nodding along to the music with smiles on our faces, and it's the coolest moment of my life. This is way cooler than any daydream I've had.

When Evan finishes, we all clap, and he smiles at me. I can't help but think we have some kind of connection. He starts playing a second song and again, I recognize it right away. He's playing Tameka's favorite, 'Bit Part.' I look at her, her smile is wide and her eyes are shining brightly. Tameka always sings along to this when it comes on in the car, and while we've never discussed it, I can't help but think that she thinks of her dad when this song plays. The first four lines are:

I want a bit part in your life,

A walk-on would be fine.

I just want a bit part in your life,

A bit part in your life.

I've never met her dad but know that he isn't in her life because he got pretty messed up over in Vietnam. It makes me so sad for both of them. I'm glad Evan is playing this song for her.

Chapter 39

Sloane

When Evan finishes "Bit Part," he sets his guitar down as one of the older ladies holds up what looks like a cigarette. "Is it okay if we share this?" she asks, and I quickly realize it's not a hand-rolled cigarette, but a joint. I have a moment of internal panic hoping and praying that Bryn doesn't freak out. They light up the marijuana cigarette and pass it around. When it gets to Ray, he declines, so does Tameka, Bryn, and myself. I am almost in shock that Bryn just handled that like a champ. I thought for sure she would lose it, and we'd have to go right away. She played it as cool as a cucumber. I'm proud of her and grateful.

"I bet it's amazing to get to travel all over the world doing what you love," I say to Evan.

He nods lazily. "It really is. I love Spain and Italy. They are such cool places."

"Ooh, I love Italy," Nikki says. "I visited when I was studying abroad one semester. It's amazing."

"Isn't the food so good?" Evan asks her.

Nikki throws her head back, a look of ecstasy on her face. "Yes! So delicious, and how is the wine so much better over there?"

Evan laughs that cute, goofy laugh. "It really is," he agrees.

"I'd really like to go to Australia," I say thinking about the article I read where he was talking about it.

Evan's eyes light up, "That's my favorite place. It's even better!"

"I bet," I say wistfully. "I really want to see it someday."

"You'll have to come with me next time we go there," he says.

"Okay," I say, knowing full well that would never happen, but I'll play along. After all, they all just smoked something that would make one do or say silly things.

The phone rings, and Evan answers it. When he's done, he says, "I'll be right back. Will you guys let me back in?"

"Of course," I say.

"Promise?" he asks.

"Promise." I say with a smile.

When he's gone, we talk about how nice he is and how cool this is. Cheryl is the nicer of the older women, and she pulls out a disposable camera. "I'll have to see if I can get a picture with him," she says.

"Oh, can you get one of me and Evan, too?" I ask hopefully. "I'll give you my address."

"Of course," she says, and we hear a knock at the door.

I hop up to answer it, and Evan is smiling so sweetly at the door. "See, I promised." I smile.

He walks in and gives me a bear hug, then kisses me on each cheek like they do in France. I'm so giddy that I must look like a grinning idiot. We turn to walk into the room, and Evan has his hand around my waist, so I wrap mine around his. Cheryl hops up and says, "Let me get a picture!"

We smile for her and then I say, "Let me get one of you two." Mission accomplished.

Evan grabs a composition book off his nightstand and says to me, "Give me your address so I can let you know when we're going to Australia."

"Okay," I laugh.

Tameka, Ray, and Bryn are standing now, so I can tell they want to get going, even though I wish this night would never end. Or morning, as it's well into the wee hours of the morning. Evan is showing me where he writes his songs and draws while trying to find a place for me to write my address, and Tameka is at my side.

Evan turns the pages, then stops and shows the spread to Tameka. "Here's where I wrote 'Bit Part.'"

A smile spreads across her face. "That's awesome."

Finally, he finds a page with some space for me to write my address, and when I'm done, he says, "Write your phone number, too."

I almost can't believe this is happening, but this guy isn't going to call me. He probably won't even remember who I am. I write my number down and hand him the plastic pen with the hotel logo on the side. "Okay, now you better call or write," I joke.

"I will," he says with a lazy smile.

"Promise?" I say.

"Promise." Evan replies.

We say our goodbyes to the four women who look like they have no intention of going anywhere, and Evan gives me a big bear hug again. Tameka, Ray, Bryn, and I all say goodbye, and as I look back one last time, I swear he says, "Goodbye, Sweetie," and I am over the moon!

***

When we get into the elevator, we revel in what just happened. "Oh my gosh, that was so cool," I practically squeal.

Ray is smiling at me. "I think he really liked you."

"Really?" I ask, feeling giddy as my friends saw some sort of connection too.

"Yeah," Bryn says. "He was hugging you and kissing you."

"Just in a friendly way, though," I say. He's an older guy and my mind doesn't even go there. "It's weird. I feel like we had a connection, but an innocent one, like we knew each other in a past life or something." I try to explain how it felt to me. It almost felt like I knew him somehow, or at least was meant to meet him.

"Well, he didn't act that way around anyone else," Tameka says, and I feel a hint of jealousy in her tone.

I change the subject since this is making me a little uncomfortable. "Bryn!" I say as I playfully slap my sister on the shoulder. "You were so cool when that joint was passed around."

Bryn gives me a sideways glance. "I was like, is that marijuana? There's no way."

"Yeah, but you didn't freak out," I say. "Thanks for being so cool."

"Yeah, yeah," she says jokingly. "Can we go home now? I'm tired."

We laugh as the elevator door opens into the very quiet lobby. I look at my watch and see that it's after 3:30 a.m. "Oh my gosh, I didn't realize how late it was." As we walk to the car, we replay everything that happened, and I'm absolutely giddy with excitement, I don't know how I'll sleep. So far, this was the most exciting thing that has ever happened to me. As I look up into the clear, star-filled sky, I hope that someday I'll get to see Evan Dando again. After all, he promised.

Chapter 40

Sloane

I sleep late on Sunday, and I think Bryn did, too because she's in her pajamas when I shuffle into the family room with a bowl of cereal. I join her on the couch where she's watching the movie, *She's Having a Baby* for the umpteenth time. She loves movies with babies and I can't stand them. "Last night was amazing," I say to her. "Thanks again for being so cool." Sammy hops off the sofa and trots over to me for attention.

Bryn looks at me out of the sides of her eyes. "Yeah, you kept me out too late. I'm so tired."

I know she had fun going out and hanging out with us and is just giving me a hard time. "Me, too," I say as I stop petting Sammy and sit on the love seat where he joins me, "but you wanted to come along." I eat a spoonful of cereal, then say, " Wasn't Evan so nice? I couldn't believe it."

"Uh-huh," she says. "He was nice alright, and he was totally flirting with you."

I cock my head, my spoon hovering over my bowl. "No, he wasn't."

"Sure," she says with a laugh.

"He just seemed like a nice guy," I say as I take a bite of cereal.

"Uh-huh," Bryn says with innuendo in her response.

I toss a throw pillow at her. "It wasn't like that with me." I say. "Those girls who were in the room when we got there probably spent the night," I tell my sister as I think about last night. "Besides, I'm dating Ky, and I'm not that kind of girl, anyway. Plus, he's way older than me."

"Well, he was looking at you differently than everyone else." Bryn thinks a boy likes you if he's being nice to you, so that's where this is coming from.

I laugh, then finish my cereal. "Well, it was fun, anyway," I tell her as I stand and take my cereal bowl into the kitchen, rinse it, and put it in the dishwasher. When I'm back in the family room, I add, "I'll have to call Tameka and see what she and Ray thought." They spent the night at Tameka's house and I know her mom is happy to have her home since it's always been just the two of them.

After I shower and dress, I grab my journal and sit on my bed. I write down every detail about meeting Evan Dando. I still can't believe how nice he was, and that he invited us to hang out. And, he serenaded us! I write so fast that my hand cramps up. I'm trying to remember every detail so someday I can look back at this and recall what was officially the best night of my life so far. The phone rings as I'm writing and after a moment, I hear Bryn holler for me.

"Sloane! Lover boy is on the phone," Bryn calls up to me using her nickname for Ky.

I'm instantly mortified, hoping he hasn't heard her and rush to grab the phone beside my bed. "Hey!" I say as I pick up the phone.

"Hi, good lookin', how are you?" Ky's voice drips with his South Georgia accent, sending a wave of warmth through me.

I smile. "I'm good, how are you?" I ask as I lean back against the pillows on my bed.

Ky ignores me. "Lover boy, huh?" I can hear the smile in his voice.

I feel myself blush. "Oh my gosh, I was hoping you didn't hear that." Ky laughs through the phone. "It's what Bryn calls you, not me, so don't worry."

"I think it's pretty funny," Ky says, then proceeds to tell me about how boring it is in Thomasville and how much his job sucks. "I'm sorry you missed The Lemonheads show," he says.

"Me, too, but the coolest thing happened." I relay the entire story to Ky.

"Wow," Ky responds, but there's a tone in his voice I can't identify. "That's crazy. So, he was pretty nice?"

"So nice," I say, a bit too enthusiastically.

"Well, he's a rock star, and you're a beautiful girl..."

And there it is. I realize what he's thinking. "So, he can't just be a nice person?"

Ky huffs out a laugh. "He's a guy. A rock star. I don't think he was just being nice."

I bristle at this and sigh audibly. "Well, he was nice." I pause. "To all of us." I think back to last night and either I'm naïve, or everyone else is jumping to assumptions.

"Sloane?" I hear Ky say as my mind drifts.

"Yeah, sorry," I say. "Well, he didn't do anything weird. Besides I wasn't thinking of him that way because I have you." And he's a rock star who certainly has girls throwing themselves at him all the time. I'm not interested in that, and Ky should know I'm not that kind of girl.

Ky's tone changes noticeably when I say this. "I'm glad," he says sweetly. "How would I stand a chance against a rock star?"

"Oh, please, you don't need to worry about that," I reassure him.

"Good, because I got a bit worried when my girlfriend told me she went to a rock star's hotel room."

I can tell by his tone that he needs a bit more reassurance. "Oh my gosh, it wasn't like that at all." I laugh. "Tameka and Ray knew how bummed I was that I had to miss the show, and when I told them Evan gave out his hotel info on the radio, they suggested we go down there. You know I would never have gone there by myself, and I wouldn't have gone to try to hook up with him, right?"

Ky waits a beat, then says, "Yeah, I know." But I'm not sure I believe him and it makes me mad that he would think I would loosen my morals for a rock star.

I realize a change of subject would help us both. "I'm so excited that Spring Break is coming up. Do you think you'll be able to come see me for a couple of days?" I ask hopefully.

"I hope so, it would be so good to see you," he says, then adds, "but it all depends on work and when I'm scheduled."

My heart sinks a little because I've been thinking about how awesome it would be to hang out with him on the beach and watch the sunset in his arms. "I hope so, too," is all I can say.

"Don't be disappointed if I can't make it," Ky says. "Between work and school, it's tough, and I know prom is important to you."

I feel myself brighten a little. "It is," I say. "My mom and I are going dress shopping next weekend." I feel the excitement course through me. "I know you're always coming up here. I just figured if you could swing it, I'd be really close to your neck of the woods."

"I know," Ky says. "I'll try. You know I would love to come to the beach and wrap my arms around you."

Warmth runs through me when he says this. "I know," I say softly. "It's so hard not being in the same place."

"Yeah, it is," Ky says.

I really like Ky, and it's so cool having a boyfriend, even if he lives four hours away, but the distance is tough, and our conversations are getting kind of dull. Sometimes Ky just says stuff that's, well, I guess immature for his age. While he's only two years older than me, I think I have more interesting conversations with Kurt and Tyler. Heck, even Billy, although most of our conversations are joking and silly. I think I'm also still irritated that he seemed to question what I said about meeting Evan.

"Sloane?" I hear through the phone.

"Sorry, I'm here," I say, realizing that it was probably a shock to hear that I was in a rock star's hotel room last night. I guess that would intimidate the heck out of me if the roles were reversed. No, I know it would. "At least you'll be here for prom in May," I say. I start to get excited thinking about going to prom with Ky on my arm and hanging out with my friends.

"Do you," he pauses, "think we should get a hotel room for prom?"

I feel a lump form in my throat and my pulse quickens. "You know I'm not ready for that yet," I reply as my heart pounds. We've talked about this before and I told Ky that I would tell him when I was ready. I'm totally not ready.

The line is quiet for a moment. "Do you think you'll ever be ready?"

I huff out a laugh, "Um, yeah, someday, but I'm not ready now." I feel defensive immediately.

"I know you'll be ready someday, but I mean," he pauses, "do you think you'll be ready...with me?"

I'm totally caught off-guard. "Uh, yeah, of course," I say and hope I sound convincing because I'm not so sure I'm telling the truth.

Chapter 41

Sloane

At school on Monday, I can't wait to see Kurt and tell him all about meeting Evan Dando. Kurt is one of the few people I know who even knows The Lemonheads. I'm anxiously awaiting his arrival in AP French, and when he walks in the door, I almost jump out of my seat. "Hey!" I say as he slides his backpack off his shoulder and sets it on the desk as he sits in his chair. "You're never going to believe who I met this weekend."

Kurt looks at me through shaggy black bangs that almost touch his eyes. "Who?" he asks as he pulls out his French book and notebook.

"Evan Dando!" I practically squeal as my voice rises at least an octave.

Kurt's eyes grow wide and what I can see of his eyebrows disappear under his bangs. "Really? How'd that happen?"

I fill him in on the entire story, from not being able to go to the show to waiting around at the hotel and meeting Evan. "He was so nice," I tell him.

Kurt's mouth is agape. "That's amazing. I'm so glad he was cool."

"So cool," I say as my eyes go skyward, and I think about when he sang for us and hugged me. "One of the older ladies who was there took pictures, and I gave her my address so she can send them to me. I hope she does."

"That's awesome," Kurt says. "I hate that you missed the show because I know how excited you were to see them, but meeting Evan is a pretty cool consolation prize."

"Totally! I'm going to get to see them next month at the 99X festival at Stone Mountain."

"Oh, yeah. Isn't that the day of prom?" Kurt asks as he cocks his head.

I nod. "Yeah, I got tickets for Ky and me so we can go there before prom. We may have to leave early, but it starts at noon, so we should be fine."

"You're going to prom?" I hear an irritating voice of astonishment from across the room.

I look up and see Amber's annoying face. I squint my eyes at her, bothered by both her interruption and rudeness. "Yeah," I cut back and turn back to Kurt, but Amber's not done.

"Who asked *you* to prom?" I don't know if she said it this way, or if I heard it this way, but she says this as if I would be the last person on Earth anyone would ask to prom.

I glare over at her. "Uh, my boyfriend."

I turn back to Kurt. "What's her deal?" he asks, and I shake my head. My blood pressure is rising and I hate confrontation.

"I didn't know you had a boyfriend," she says. I can't believe she continues to press this. "Anyone I know?"

I totally do not want to be having this conversation right now. Or at all. "No, he's older than us and not from here." I turn back to Kurt. My heart is racing because I'm so uncomfortable and just want this conversation to end. I wish I could tell her where to stick it, but I just use avoidance and try to ignore her so she'll stop talking to me. Obviously, that's not working so well.

Amber snorts a laugh and turns to Ramsey. "Sounds like an imaginary boyfriend to me." She laughs but Ramsey does not.

"Amber, give her a break," Ramsey says.

Amber clearly isn't done yet and looks back at me. "Is he from Canada?"

Why must she tease me like this? "No-" I start, but am saved by Madame Carney walking through the door.

"*Bonjour!*" She sings as she shuts the door.

Kurt smiles at me and says so only I can hear, "Don't let her ruin your day. I'm so glad Evan was so nice. What a cool experience!"

I return his smile as I think about meeting Evan and how nice he was. People in this school may make me feel bad about myself, but a rock star just acted like I was cool, funny, and interesting. That's got to mean something, right? I will be so glad when I graduate and get out of this place.

***

When I get to marine bio, Billy *and* Tyler are already there, and I can't wait to tell them about my weekend. After I fill them in, Billy says, "So, what did Ky think of all that?"

I shrug. "He was okay. I mean, he was a bit suspicious, but that's just crazy." I laugh as I pull my book and notebook out of my backpack and toss it on the floor. "Like a rock star would want to get with me."

Billy gives me a look like I'm crazy. "What?" I ask genuinely curious. I look at Tyler whose smirk echoes Billy's look.

"How friendly was he?" Tyler asks.

I feel myself blush as I look down at my notebook and flip to the next blank page. "He was friendly to all of us," I explain. "I was there with my sister and two friends, and there were four other women in the room. He was just nice."

"Uh-huh," Billy says as he leans back in his chair with a satisfied grin.

"I'm an awkward, seventeen-year-old, high school student, kind of a tomboy, and he's a gorgeous twenty-something rock star who could have any girl he wants. I seriously doubt he even thought of me like that."

Tyler responds, "Or, you're not as awkward as you think." He looks at me, and I feel that flutter I shouldn't feel since I have Ky and Tyler has the sweetest girlfriend. Stupid raging hormones.

I laugh it off. "No, I'm pretty sure I am."

"Well, we all see ourselves differently than we really are," Tyler says. "Ky's into you, and he knows how guys are. I bet it really intimidated him that you went to see Evan and he was so nice to you."

I think about this. "Yeah, I guess you're right. I just...I guess I just don't think of myself that way, and well, I wasn't there to hook up with the guy. I just wanted to meet him. I'm just not that kind of girl, and Ky knows that, or at least he should."

"It's not you he's worried about," Billy says lightheartedly.

"Well, he doesn't have to worry," I say, "because I'm sure I'll never see the guy again. Besides, I'm only seventeen and don't think of him like that." Ugh, why does everything have to be about sex? Can't someone just be nice? Of course, I totally hope I see Evan again because he's an amazingly talented musician who fronts one of my favorite bands. I can't wait to actually see them live next month!

Chapter 42

Tyler

"Dude, I think you might have been right," I tell Brian as we walk downstairs to head outside for lunch.

"About what?" Brian asks before biting into an apple, unable to wait until we sit down to eat.

"Sloane. I think she likes artsy guys."

"Why? Did she show you a picture of that guy she's dating?" Brian asks around a mouthful of apple.

"No, but she and her friends and sister went to a rock star's hotel room over the weekend and met the guy."

Brian's eyes go wide. "Really? Who?"

"Evan Dando from The Lemonheads."

"Who?" Brian says as he shoulders the door open leading us outside.

"He's in an alternative band, long hair, and the kind of guy girls throw themselves at," I explain. "Basically, a talented musician who also looks like he could be walking the runway for Calvin Klein."

"So, she's like a groupie, then?" The look of shock on Brian's face is priceless.

I laugh. "Hardly. It was really sweet how innocent she was about it. She really did just go there to meet him. But this just proves that I'm not cool enough for her."

Brian slows his pace and stops on the pavement so we can talk before getting to the table where our crew is sitting. His voice is low. "So, things are still a little strained between you and Sara?"

I nod. "Yeah, she's just way more into partying with the popular crowd than I am." I toe at the pavement with my black and white Chuck Taylors. "I almost feel like she likes that I got her in with our crowd more than she likes me."

"Dang. For real?" Brian's shoulders slump ever so slightly.

"Yeah, it's gone from us going out on dates to her wanting to do all this group dating." I cross my arms over my chest. "I'm cool with that every now and then, but she wants to hang out with everyone all the time." I look at my friend. "Like at your party."

Brian's expression grows serious. "What she and Adam did at my party wasn't cool, but she had been drinking."

"I know." I sigh. "But she knew what she was doing. So did Adam." My voice is hard when I say that last part. "It's more than that, though. I really do think she likes the popular crowd more than she likes me. Our relationship may have run its course."

"That sucks, man," Brian says. "What are you going to do?"

I shrug. "We've talked about it, but it hasn't really changed. We're so close to the end of the year, I think we'll just do the whole Spring Break and prom thing, but I don't expect it to last much longer."

"Really?" Brian's head tilts to the side.

I nod. "Yeah. Besides even though she comes to most of the baseball games, I think she's there to socialize more than watch the game. And, she's been complaining about how much time I spend practicing. I think she thought I'd practice less for baseball."

"Doesn't she realize that baseball is your dream?"

I shrug. "I thought she did." I look over at our table and see that Sara is just chattering away with Ramsey, oblivious that I'm even out here.

"What if you just cut your losses and break it off now?"

"I've thought about it," I tell him as I rub the back of my neck. "But it's so close to prom, I'd hate to ruin that for her, for us."

"Well, you wouldn't have a problem finding another date," Brian says.

I shrug. "Maybe, but the only other girl I'd want to take is Sloane, and that's not gonna happen. Besides, Sara and I will have fun, plus she already bought her dress. I couldn't do that to her."

"Well buddy," Brian puts his hand on my shoulder. "I know you'll do the right thing. It's just too bad that Sloane is still dating that guy from South Georgia, otherwise, you could spend your last couple of months of school seeing if there's anything there."

I let out a loud sigh. "Tell me about it." I don't want to hurt Sara, but it feels like we both know this thing is temporary, that we're just going through the motions until graduation. As we walk over to our table, out of the corner of my eye, way down the sidewalk, I notice Sloane laughing at something her friend just said and my heart flutters at the sight.

Chapter 43

Sloane

My mom and I walk into Perimeter Mall to begin our hunt for the perfect prom dress. "I hope we can find something that fits well and is cute," I tell my mom as I fidget with my purse strap. I'm excited to finally get to go prom dress shopping with my mom, something I worried I might not get to do.

"Oh honey, we will," my mom says, her eyes shining with excitement. "If it takes all weekend, we'll find the perfect dress!"

I hope it doesn't take all weekend because shopping isn't my favorite thing in the world. Partly because I get sensory overload in the mall and partly because it's so hard to find clothes that fit me, especially dresses. As we walk through Rich's department store on our way to the juniors' section, I'm overcome with the strong scents of perfume. "Would you like to try Obsession by Calvin Klein?" A lady with big, curly hair and lots of makeup asks as she holds the bottle toward us.

"No, thanks," I smile as I try to avoid being sprayed as we walk by.

My mom is looking up at the signs, "This way," she says as I see the sign that says 'Juniors' pointing to the right.

When we walk into the juniors' section, the décor turns edgy and industrial as INXS's song 'New Sensation' blasts through the overhead speakers. We walk past the mannequins dressed in flannel shirts, jeans, and combat boots to the formal section.

"Okay," my mom says, "why don't you pick some dresses you like, and I'll pick some that I like, and you can try them on." Her expression is so excited, it's as if she's a kid on Christmas morning and the tree is surrounded by presents that need to be unwrapped.

I smile. "Okay, but no strapless dresses. I don't have anything to hold one up."

"Oh, sweetie, don't be silly. We can get you a padded strapless bra." She squeezes my elbow. "Something to help give you a little something up top."

"Mom," I groan as I feel my face flush. "I want to be comfortable, so let's just try to find something pretty that isn't strapless."

I slide dress after dress across the rack I'm looking at, the metal hangers screeching against the metal rods. "Why does everything have to have so many ruffles?" I ask my mom who's on the next rack over. I keep sifting through the dresses. "Or bows. I really don't want bows."

My mom looks at me then proceeds to put three dresses back onto the rack. "No ruffles, no bows. Okay. That's going to make it a little more difficult."

Once we each have an arm full of about five dresses each, we head to the fitting room. My mom sits on a bench by the three-way mirror as I go into the dressing room to try on the dresses. Of course, I start with one of my dresses, a simple black dress with spaghetti straps. When I slip it over my head and over my body, I expect to see a dress I love, except, I don't. It's just so plain.

I walk out to the mirror and stand on the platform in front of it. I can see my mom in the mirror seated behind me on a padded bench. "What do you think?"

I turn so she can see me from the front. My mom cocks her head. "It's pretty. It's just very plain."

I nod. "I agree. It doesn't do anything for me."

My mom shakes her head. "No, it doesn't. Try the black and white one I picked out."

When I go back to the dressing room, I pull the black and white dress out from the middle of the rack. When I see it fully, I realize the white at the top is a giant bow. "Mom, this has a giant bow across the top." I call out to her.

"I know, honey, but just try it on. It's cute."

I roll my eyes and put on the dress. "I look like a giant present." I call to her.

"Just come on out and let me see it."

As I trudge out to the mirror and stand on the platform, the giant bow looks even more overwhelming. I can see my mom trying to muffle a laugh behind me. I spin around and start cracking up with her. "I look ridiculous."

My mom cracks up even more to the point where she can't breathe, and I start doing the same. "Your frame is so tiny—" she says through laughter. "It really does make the bow look overwhelming."

"I think it's about to take over my body," I joke as I hop off the platform to try on a different dress.

I love these moments with my mom. When it's just the two of us, it's nice because I have her undivided attention. We have fun together and that's not always the case when my sisters are around. They are a lot more demanding of attention and I try not to rock the boat. I love it when my mom is so carefree and we share these silly, hilarious moments. When she starts laughing like that, it's totally contagious.

Next up is a teal dress that I had high hopes for, but the fabric is shiny and looks cheap. My mom agrees.

Next is one of her dresses, this one is magenta with a balloon skirt, and it's strapless. I walk out of the dressing room, holding up the top of the dress with my fingertips. "Now that one's cute," my mom says.

"I don't know, mom," I say with uncertainty as I turn from side to side in the mirror. "I'd have to have a really padded bra to hold this one up, and I'm not sure about the balloon skirt. Isn't it a little much?"

"It's the style, Sloane. I think it's really cute."

"Let me try on the two long ones I pulled," I tell her as I hop off the platform and scurry back to the dressing room. I put on the long navy dress, hopeful that it will be a contender, but it's not. While it's long, it's not 6-foot-tall-long. It hits at a weird length. I decide to try the emerald green one and much to my chagrin, it's the same, not long enough. I walk out to show my mom.

"The length is weird," I tell her.

She nods, "Yeah, and I don't like the halter straps on you."

"Really? But it's much more comfortable than the strapless one." I smooth my hand over the bodice as I look at the top of the dress.

"With your thin frame, the strapless just looks better. Those straps overwhelm you."

I sigh. "Okay, let's try Macy's."

***

Macy's turned out to be more of the same. "Let's go out through the upstairs," my mom suggests. "I think the Jessica McClintock store is upstairs. They should have some beautiful dresses."

When we walk out of Macy's, on the left is the Jessica McClintock store. It's all glass and light, showcasing the beautiful dresses. We talk to the sales associate and tell her what we're looking for. She pulls some dresses and gets me set-up in a fitting room. I look through the selection that she pulled and immediately put a pastel floral dress on the peg on the opposite side of the wall. Pastel florals are not me.

I try on a black dress with emerald green sleeves that are off the shoulder. While it's strapless, it's tighter than the ones at the department stores and fits better. It helps that we bought a padded strapless bra at Rich's to try on with these dresses.

"How's it going?" My mom asks from outside the fitting room. "Make sure to show them all to me, even if you don't like them."

"It's good, I'll be right out." While the black and green dress looks good from the front, there's a giant, and I mean super-sized, bow on the back. When I walk out, my mom's eyes light up.

"Ooh, that's so pretty!"

"It is at first," I say, then turn around. "Look at the size of this bow!"

My mom tries to suppress a laugh as the sales associate comes by. "What do you think?" she asks, hopefully.

"It's pretty, but I'm really not into bows, and this one," I turn to show her, "is mammoth."

The lady nods. "It does overwhelm your small frame. Try the teal one, it's pretty simple."

The teal dress is pretty, but it has poufy sleeves that are a bit much. My mom agrees and hands me a red damask dress with white lace across the top. It's strapless, like apparently every dress in the world, but I agree to give it a shot. I wouldn't normally go for lace, but it's a heavy lace that accents the arms and bodice and there's a pretty rhinestone in the center.

I step into the dress and am surprised that it actually looks pretty good. I hold it up so my mom can zip up the back then look myself over in the mirror. "Even though it's strapless, I think it's the best one I've tried on."

"I think so, too!" My mom is either giddy from her excitement about the dress or that this marathon prom dress hunt is coming to a close. "Sloane, it's elegant, just like you. Some of those other dresses were just too trendy, but this one is classic."

I'm flattered that my mom likes it so much and while I really didn't want a strapless dress, the joy on her face makes me want this dress. One she picked out and makes her happy. I smile, "Let's get it, then."

Even better than finding a dress for prom was shopping with my mom. Bryn usually tags along everywhere, but it was nice to have my mom to myself for a change. The dynamic is so different when it's just us; we have so much fun together.

After we pay for the dress, my mom says, "Let's grab dinner at Mick's. I think we both earned some of their Oreo cheesecake for dessert!"

My stomach growls at the suggestion. "Ooh, that sounds perfect." I turn to my mom. "Thanks so much for today, and for the dress. I had a lot of fun."

My mom's eyes go wide, "You had fun shopping? Wow, I should play the lottery!"

"Ha-ha," I reply as she hugs me around the shoulders.

"I had fun today, too, sweetheart. We should do this more often." She must see panic in my eyes because she says, "Not shopping, necessarily, but spending time just the two of us."

I smile. "I'd love that mom." I sure do have the most loving mom in the entire world.

Chapter 44

Sloane

April 1993

I've always gone on spring break with my family, but this year, I'm going with Maggie, Beth, and Annalise, and we've settled into the cool, air-conditioned condo. Beth and Annalise's moms are good friends, and are our chaperones, except they are staying in a different condo to give us some independence since it's our senior year.

After their moms leave us with a kitchen full of food for the week and strict instructions, Beth and Annalise scurry into the master bedroom which they are sharing. Moments later, they dash back into the family room holding bottles of liquor. "We packed a few special items!" Annalise practically squeals as she bounces from one foot to another.

I feel my eyes go wide. "How did you get that?"

"Older brothers have their perks," Annalise says with a smile.

Beth sets her bottle on the breakfast bar and dashes back into their room. When she comes back, she has two cases of beer. "Gotta get these into the fridge."

"Oh my gosh, how big is that suitcase?" Maggie asks.

Beth smiles wide as she opens the fridge and starts loading the cans into it. "Hopefully big enough that we don't have to ask anyone to buy us more."

Annalise joins her in the kitchen and locates the blender. "Margaritas or daiquiris?" she asks us, her eyes sparkling.

"Um, daiquiris?" I reply. Since I don't really drink, I'm not sure which would be best, but my mom has let me taste a strawberry daiquiri and it wasn't bad. I've heard stories about tequila, and they usually don't end well. That stuff can mess you up.

"I think I'll stick with water," Maggie says softly.

"Oh, no you don't!" Beth says as she puts the last can of beer in the fridge and shuts the door. "It's senior year spring break. We're gonna have some fun!"

I smile at Maggie and sense that she's uncomfortable. "Just have a couple of sips and see if you like it."

She seems to relax and says, "Okay, but you girls aren't going to get me drunk."

I walk over to the pantry. "Your moms were so nice to stock us up. We have more than enough food for a week." I turn to my friends. "I can make some cheese and crackers."

"Yes, please," Annalise says as she gets ice from the freezer. "And chips and salsa. I'm starving."

Once the drinks and snacks are ready, we take them out onto the balcony. I look at my watch after I take a seat. "It's four-thirty. What's the plan for tonight?"

"I'm so tired of driving," Annalise says, "can we just order a pizza?"

"Great idea," Beth says. "We can eat it on the beach."

"And watch the sunset," I add.

"Sounds good to me," Maggie says, then takes another sip of her strawberry daquiri. "This is really good."

"Just take it easy," I tell her. "You don't want that rum to hit you." She smiles at me like she's doing something she shouldn't do, but is enjoying it. I know she's out of her comfort zone, but I'm so glad she's having fun. As I watch the water glistening under the low afternoon sun, I can't help but think of Ky and how great it would be if he can make it here. I'd love to rest in his arms while watching the sunset.

"Sloaney, you've got goo-goo eyes," Annalise says. "Are you thinking about Ky?"

I smile as my cheeks heat up. "It's that obvious, huh?" My friends nod and giggle at me. I take a sip of my icy drink. "I'll understand if he can't get away from work, but it would be so amazing if he could come for even a day. He's just two hours away. That could totally be a day trip, right?"

"Oh yeah," Beth says. "I'm sure he'll make it happen. He could leave in the morning and be here before ten."

"And, if he can't stay the night, he could leave at ten and be back by midnight," Annalise says, then leans forward and grabs a cracker and a piece of cheese.

I don't want to get my hopes up, but they're right. He could totally make it happen.

"Does he work on the weekend?" Maggie asks.

I shrug. "It depends."

Annalise sits up and smacks her hand on the glass patio table making everything on it jump and rattle. "Girl, call that boy up and see if he's working this weekend. If not, see if he wants to come here tonight. Then he can leave tomorrow night and be back for work on Monday."

"I don't know," I hesitate. "He said he would try, and I don't want to call him right after I get to town." I think for a moment. "Besides, maybe he doesn't have the money for a hotel and just doesn't want to say anything."

"Oh my gosh, Sloane, he can totally stay here," Beth says.

"But your mom said-" she cuts me off.

"My mom isn't going to know," she replies. "Besides, you yourself said you're not ready to have sex with him, so it would be totally innocent."

I think about what her mom said about drinking and hormones. Plus, she very specifically just told us this would not be okay. "Maybe some of the guys would let him stay with them?" I suggest, knowing that Beth and Annalise would talk to their guy friends who are staying nearby.

Beth nods. "Yeah, I'm sure we can figure it out."

"You should call him," Maggie says before taking another sip of her drink. Her tongue sounds a little thick like the rum is already affecting her.

I pass her the plate of cheese and crackers. "Here, have some of these." We all start to giggle. "I suppose I could call him."

"Yes!" Annalise says. "Call the boy. I bet he'll be here in under two hours once he hears from you."

With that, I hop up and run to the kitchen to call Ky. I know I have a little liquid courage, but I also have butterflies in my belly because he could say no. I dial his number which I have memorized and look at my watch as it rings. It's just after five o'clock here.

"Hello?" a gruff Southern accent sounds from the other end.

"Hi, Mister Carter, this is Sloane. Is Ky available?" I ask his dad.

"Oh, hey, Sloane," Ky's dad says kindly. "I think he just got out of the shower. Hang on."

Why did he have to tell me that? Now I'm imagining Ky as he towels off. I shake my head. Beth's mom was right, drinking and teenage hormones *are* dangerous. I set my cup down so I stop drinking as I wait nervously.

"Hey, Ba--Beautiful," Ky says, correcting himself before he could get the word, babe, out of his mouth.

"Hey," I practically sing. "We got to Florida!"

"Awesome," he says, and his tone is one of amusement. "How many drinks have you had?" He laughs light-heartedly.

I giggle. "Like three-quarters of a daquiri," I reply as my insides flush with warmth. "It would be so amazing if you were here. In fact, my friends and I were talking and since you're just a couple hours away, do you think you could come down here tonight?" I don't let him answer yet. "We could spend all day together tomorrow. Maybe even catch the sunset together before you have to go back."

"I wish I could, but I've got, um, a family thing tonight."

"Oh," I'm struck by his lack of details of this family thing. "Do you think you could come after? It can't go that late, can it?"

"I don't know," he says. "Give me your number, and I'll call you, but I don't want you to wait around to hear from me. It's your first night of spring break. Go enjoy it."

I give him the number written on the little slip of paper underneath a skinny piece of plastic on the phone. "There's no answering machine, though."

"Okay," Ky says. "I mean, I really don't think I'll be able to make it tonight. It would be late if I could..."

I wait for him to finish, but he doesn't. This is silly, I think to myself. If he wants to see me, I'm closer than ever. "No worries. You go spend time with your family and let me know if you're able to switch shifts to come down here." I want to make my point, so I add, "We're closer than ever, so hopefully you can make it work."

"Me, too," Ky says softly.

I don't want him to say the 'L' word so I quickly say, "Awesome, well call me and let me know. We're going to head out and grab pizza and watch the sunset."

"Okay, bye."

"Bye," I say then place the phone firmly back in its cradle. I inhale sharply and will myself not to cry. It seems that this would be a perfect opportunity to see each other since we're so close. He never mentioned a family thing before, and I can't help but wonder if he's telling me the whole story. Maybe I'm just letting my imagination get the best of me, or maybe he's not as interested in me as I thought he was.

Chapter 45

Sloane

Our first full day at the beach wasn't the beautiful beach day we had hoped for. Instead of warm Florida sunshine, we got cool cloud cover. However, we were determined to layout by the pool, even if we did keep covering ourselves with our towels to keep warm. After we showered, however, Maggie and I were in for a rude awakening. I look at my red face and body in the foggy mirror. How the heck did this happen? I think to myself. I dress and walk through the bedroom I'm sharing with Maggie and into the family room. "Oh my gosh, y'all, look at me!" My skin is burned and tight. I look at Maggie whose skin is just as red, if not more so.

"I know," Maggie says sullenly. "I had no idea we would get this much sun on a cloudy day." She shifts on the sofa and winces at the pain.

"I have aloe," Annalise says as she hops up and runs into the room she is sharing with Beth. Annalise is a beautiful shade of bronze, clearly not affected by the sun like me and Maggie. She arrives with aloe in hand and offers it to me. I sit next to Maggie, and we share the bottle, applying it liberally to our arms, legs, and face.

"I can't believe we were so stupid," I say to my friends. "Our first day, and we're burnt to a crisp."

"I know," Maggie laments. "This is not fun."

Beth hollers from the kitchen, "I'll make strawberry daquiris. That'll make you feel better."

"I've got ibuprofen in the room," I tell Maggie. "I'll get us some." As I stand, the skin on my legs feels so tight and uncomfortable.

***

After eating too much fried food at a tourist restaurant on the beach, we head back down to The Summit, the condo where most of our class is staying or hangs out. We had a pretty good time there last night. As we walk down the moonlit beach, I joke, "At least it's dark so people won't see just how sunburned we are."

This elicits a chuckle out of Maggie which I'm glad for because she seems more uncomfortable than I am. "At least the ibuprofen helped with the pain a little," she says.

When we get to the crowded beach, Beth says, "I'm going to find some beer."

"Hang on," Annalise says, "I'll go with you." The two best friends dash off.

"It's sweet how concerned they've been," I say to Maggie as I watch groups of kids drinking, playing hackey sack, and some couples making out. I try not to think of Ky when I see the couples enjoying this beautiful night together.

"I know," Maggie says as we gingerly take a seat in the sand. "I just hope we bounce back quickly. I can't believe we got so sunburned on our first day."

"Hey!" a girl's voice squeals from behind me. Before I know it, I'm being bear-hugged from behind and wince in pain.

I shriek as my tender skin burns even more at the touch.

"Oh my gosh, oh my gosh. I'm so sorry!" Sara's worried face appears in front of mine. Her hand goes up to her mouth. "Ouch," she says as she takes in my redness.

"Yeah," I say with a smile. "We now know that you can indeed get a sunburn when the sun's not out." I quip.

"It's not that bad," Sara says, giving me a sympathetic smile.

"It's because it's dark," Maggie says. "It's worse than it looks right now."

"I'm so sorry," Sara says, then points to an area where a bunch of kids are sitting in a group. "We're hanging out over there. Y'all should join us."

I can't make out anyone she's with, but I'm guessing Tyler is there, and if he's there, I'm sure other football players are there and that means cheerleaders, too which makes me nervous. "Okay," I reply. "We're just waiting on Annalise and Beth." I secretly hope we can avoid that group, but just as I have that thought, Annalise and Beth appear with four cans of beer.

"What are you waiting for?" Annalise asks. "We're back!" Beth hands me a beer and Annalise hands one to Maggie.

Sara hops up, still smiling. "There's a group of us hanging out over there." She points to the gathering of kids again. "Come hang out with us."

Before I can protest, Beth says, "Awesome, let's go!"

Maggie and I stand and follow Sara, Beth, and Annalise. "I honestly don't know that I'm up for this," I say quietly to Maggie as I dust sand off my backside.

"I know," my fellow introverted friend says. "I don't even think I want this." She raises her can of beer.

"I can't tell who's there, but I bet there are jocks and cheerleaders," I practically groan. "I just feel so out of place around those people. Like I don't belong."

"Me, too. At least you'll have someone to look at," she says playfully.

"Stop," I joke. "He's with Sara, and I'm with Ky." I think about Ky and really hope he was being honest with me yesterday. "But I do enjoy talking with him. It's not just music, either. We have interesting conversations."

As we approach the group, the first face I see is Tyler's and I feel the tiniest fluttering in my belly. Sara plops into his lap, and his smile grows wide. I'm standing there not knowing where to sit, feeling awkward like I usually do when Maggie tugs lightly on my shirt sleeve. I follow her, Beth, and Annalise around the left side of the group. The same way Sara went. Beth and Annalise recognize a couple of the quirky, yet semi-popular boys from our school and sit next to them. Maggie then sits next to Annalise and that leaves me between Maggie and Tyler, with Sara in his lap. "Oh, this is awkward," I whisper to Maggie, making her chuckle.

"Sloaner!" Tyler says, a little too loud for my liking, making heads turn. Thankfully, I don't see Amber's face in the crowd.

Even though I have an easy time talking to Tyler in marine bio, I don't know what to say or how to act right now. I look at him with sweet Sara in his lap and smile. "Hey Tyler, heard any good music lately?" As soon as I say it, I'm mortified. Who says that? Why did I say that? Why am I so awkward?

Thankfully, Tyler just laughs and says, "Actually, no." He waves his hand at the group around us. "I love these guys, but dang, their taste in music is bad."

Now it's my turn to laugh, and I immediately relax my shoulders. "Would you rather listen to their music or Billy's?"

Tyler's smile grows across his face. "Definitely Billy's. You know I've got some country music in my blood."

I hear someone gasp across from us, and I turn to look. Staring at me with her mouth agape is none other than Amber Gates who has just walked up. "Oh my gosh, what happened to you two?" She says bursting out in laughter, making her friends laugh along with her.

I roll my eyes and sigh. "Oh, look, Amber's here. Yay." I deadpan under my breath which makes Tyler stifle a laugh.

Amber's tone becomes one of annoyance as I ignore her question. She's in her group. This is her domain, and she is going to make sure to make the most of it. "Seriously," she cuts as her face looks like she's just smelled rotting fish, "did y'all go to a tanning bed and stay in it too long?" She laughs at her own snide remark as she plops down onto the sand and looks at her friends who laugh with her. "You know you're supposed to build up your time in those. It looks like you should have started with five minutes."

I look at Maggie who seems to be shrinking within herself, and this makes me mad. "Tanning beds? Seriously?" I scoff a laugh because she has my blood boiling, and it's one thing to come after me, but it's another to come after my friend. "No, this was from the real sun." I have no idea what to say to her, and I'm sure an amazing comeback will come to me in an hour.

"Oh my gosh, I know," says a friendly voice from someone I hadn't seen sitting around us. I look to my left and see Ramsey from French class. "It was so cloudy and cool today. I didn't wear sunscreen and got so burned."

I exhale with relief and smile at Ramsey then steal a glance at Amber who is clearly disappointed that her game has been cut short. "Same," I say to Ramsey. "Lesson learned." I look at her bronze skin with a touch of pink and say, "You're lucky yours is already tan." I motion to myself. "This will be red for days." I pop open the beer I've been holding and take a long swig then grimace.

Tyler looks at me and says, "Not your favorite?"

I shake my head and feel my mouth turn downward. "Nope." I hold my beer out to him and Sara. "Do either of you want this?"

Sara has moved from Tyler's lap to his other side. She smiles and holds up her own beer. "I'm good, thanks!"

Tyler downs his beer then holds out his hand. "I'm ready for a new one. I can never let a beer go to waste, even if it is The Beast." I hand him my cheap beer that I guess people call 'The Beast,' and he takes a long gulp, then grimaces. "Yeah, it's pretty bad, but it's still beer." He gives me that mega-watt smile that lights up his whole face, and I feel my cheeks burn. At least no one can tell I'm blushing when I am already so sunburned.

Chapter 46

Sloane

On our last night of Spring Break, we once again walk down to The Summit to hang out with the large crowds of high schoolers, many of which are our classmates. "I'm so sorry Ky couldn't make it here," Maggie says as we sit watching the sun inch further down the horizon while Beth and Annalise are off somewhere together.

"Me, too," I say as the glorious coastal breeze blows my hair back. "I get that he has work, and I'm just so excited that he's coming to prom." My friends told me I need to trust Ky, so I put my disappointment about not seeing him this week behind me. After all, I've had a great time with Maggie, Beth, and Annalise, and thanks to them, I've mingled with other classmates who I never thought would be interested in hanging out with me.

I think about going to my first school dance ever and feel a rush of excitement. "While it kind of stinks that no one has ever asked me to a dance, I'm glad Ky said yes when I asked him. I can't wait to do the limo, dinner with you, Beth, Annalise, and your dates, prom pictures...It's going to be so much fun!"

Maggie's eyes light up, and the golden sun looks so pretty on her face which is almost not pink anymore...almost. "I know. We're going to have a blast. I'm so excited we connected this year." She gets a pensive expression. "I love that you are reserved like I am and not a big partier. It's so hard to find girlfriends who are like me." She puts her arm around my shoulder. "Thanks for being such a good friend."

"Aww, Mags!" I say as I hug her back. "I'm so glad we became friends, too. And I feel the same way. Girlfriends can be hard, and I've lost some because I'm just not going to be half drunk, chasing boys. It's just not who I am, and I'm so glad I've found a kindred spirit." I give her a gentle squeeze. Maggie and I did partake in some drinking, but not much. Personally, I don't like the feeling of not being in control. Plus, I'm a worrier and have been called "mom" once or twice by Beth and Annalise. Since those two like to party, I feel like I need to watch over them.

We sit in silence as we watch the remaining sliver of the sun disappear below the horizon. The sky still glows with pinks and oranges. My skin feels sticky with humidity and salty air, but I feel so peaceful right now. I think about how I so wanted to be sitting here in Ky's arms, cuddling with the boy who makes me feel special and desired, a feeling that I've never felt from another boy, ever. While it would have been so cool to have him here, even for a day, I'm grateful that I have a friend by my side who appreciates me and understands me.

"Hey girlies!" Maggie and I turn around to see Beth and Annalise tromping through the sand toward us, beers in hand. They plop down beside us giggling. "We found out about a bonfire down the beach. Do you wanna go?" Beth says.

"Sure," I say and look at Maggie.

"Yeah, that sounds like fun," Maggie nods.

"Awesome," Annalise says. "We'll meet some new people, it'll be great."

"Cool," I say. "It'll be good to get away from the Dunwoody crowd for a night."

We head down the beach just past The Summit, and there's a huge crowd of kids at the bonfire. "Remember," I say to my friends, "don't accept a drink in a plastic cup from a stranger, only something sealed like a can of beer."

"Okay, Mom!" Annalise jokes.

"She's right," Maggie says, "we don't want to get roofied."

Beth and Annalise's expressions grow sober as they look around at the crowd of kids we don't know. "Yeah, you're right. We don't know any of these people. Good call." Beth says.

Music is pumping from a stereo somewhere in the crowd. When Annalise recognizes the song, she grabs our hands and starts dancing. Of course, we all start dancing with her as the chorus begins to TLC's "What About Your Friends." This is normally not my kind of music, nor do I dance in public, but I don't know any of these people, and I'm having fun with my friends on the beach. I can get lost in the crowd, and that's what I prefer. I look at Maggie who is smiling, and I'm glad she's feeling relaxed, too.

The four of us are in our own world when I realize that random guys have come up and started dancing around us. Nothing threatening, just guys dancing, and I think about how funny it is because we don't get this kind of attention from guys at our own school. I say to Maggie, "I think my theory is right." She gives me a questioning glance. "That at our own school, we're classified from middle school and stuck into groups." I nod to the cute boys dancing with us. "These guys are interested in us because they don't know us. They must find us cute and fun, something that doesn't happen back home."

Maggie looks around, and I can see the wheels spinning in her head. A smile spreads across her face. "You're right!" She pauses before excitement fills her eyes making them sparkle in the firelight, "I can't wait for college."

"Me neither." Her excitement is contagious, and I think about all the possibilities of a fresh start in a place where no one knows me. I think about Ky and how he was definitely attracted to me when he first saw me. "It's going to be amazing," I tell her and grab her hand, twirling her around.

When Maggie spins back and faces me, her eyes are wide. "Do you see that cute boy dancing behind me? He's so hot."

I can't help but smile. "Go dance with him." I nod to Beth and Annalise who are dancing together, but a pair of guys are trying to dance with them. "Just keep an eye on them."

Maggie nods. I know she will look after them and she hasn't had a drink all day. I turn and head toward the water since my friends are having a blast dancing. Even though Ky couldn't come down here, I respect him and am not going to get jiggy with some random dude. Dancing in a group with my girlfriends is one thing, but now that these guys are here, this is a good time for me to bow out and sit in the sand and soak in the beautiful water for one last night. I walk away from the group, closer to where the waves crash on the sand. The dark, inky sky is clear tonight and stars begin to dot the sky. I feel a pang of loneliness as I think of Ky and wish he were here. I've longed for a relationship for so long and while I'm so grateful to have one, it would have been so different to have a boyfriend from my school. To hold hands with in the halls, to go to dances together, to cuddle with under the stars at the beach on spring break. I'm lost in my thoughts when I hear a laugh that I recognize, and my stomach clenches anxiously. I turn toward the sound and see Amber Gates with two guys just down the beach. "Ugh," I think to myself, "I guess we weren't the only Dunwoody kids to find out about the bonfire."

As I watch Amber drink from her plastic cup, I can see the boys seem to be holding her up. I sit up straighter. "What's going on?" I think to myself, now on high alert. It looks like one of the guys is groping her, and I feel so unsettled. This doesn't feel right. Instinct takes over, and I hop off the sand and jog down the beach. When I approach the trio, I realize these boys aren't from Dunwoody and Amber looks like she doesn't know what's going on.

Chapter 47

Sloane

"There you are," I say to Amber. I look at the two guys. "Thanks for taking care of her, I've got it from here." I grab Amber around the shoulders and pull her from their clutches, steering her back toward The Summit. Thankfully, the boys appear to be caught off guard and aren't following us, yet, but I'm too scared to look back. Unfortunately, Amber is like dead weight and even though she's a foot shorter than me, her tiny, athletic body feels like dragging an anchor down the beach, made harder by our height difference.

"Wha's happ-ning?" Amber slurs. "I'm so...tired." She moves to take another sip out of her cup, and I smack it out of her hand. "What'd choo do tha' for?"

I don't think she knows who I am right now, and I'm glad about it. I'm trudging down the beach in a sweat, and I see the lights of The Summit up ahead, but at the beach, everything looks closer than it really is. Amber is getting heavier and heavier, and she's getting to the point where she can't put one foot in front of the other. I'm certain that those boys put something in her drink because the way she's getting worse is not typical of someone who is just drunk. I don't want to turn back to see if they are following us, so I say a silent prayer for protection.

The wind blows Amber's long hair across my face, and through it, I see a tall, dark figure walking our way. We're still in the dark, remote area on the other side of The Summit. I can't see well with Amber's hair whipping my face, but am determined to trudge on past this person coming our way. As the dark figure is steps away, Amber's hair falls from my face and relief washes over me. "Tyler!" I scream over the crashing waves.

The dark figure stops just feet from us. "Sloane?" He jogs toward us, his face contorted in confusion. "Amber?" She moans in response as Tyler hurries over to her right side and relieves the weight, then scoops her up. He looks at me with fearful eyes. "What happened?"

I shake my head as we start walking faster now that I'm not weighed down by my nemesis. "I don't know. I was at the bonfire and went down to the water for a bit. I saw her with two guys that aren't from our school, and she looked like she was in trouble. I pretended like she was with me and that I had been looking for her and just took off with her. It was like fight or flight. I just started walking back this way." I explain. "I think they put something in her drink."

"Dang," Tyler says. "She's lucky you were there."

I shudder just thinking about what they were going to do to her and inhale a deep breath. "I didn't see any other kids from Dunwoody there, but there were tons of people. I just assumed she's staying here," I explain as we approach the giant condo complex, "but obviously I have no idea."

"She is," Tyler says as we make our way from the sand onto the pool deck, "but I have no idea which room she's in." He stops. "Can you check her pockets and see if she has a key?"

I nod, and he sets her feet on the ground, his forearms under her armpits to support her. Amber's head is drooping, and I can tell she's fully out of it now. "Amber? I'm just going to check your pockets, okay?" No response. I fish my hand into her left pocket, but it's empty. I move to her right pocket and feel a key on a ring. I pull it out, and the large plastic keychain for The Summit is attached. "Looks like room 1206," I hold up the keychain so Tyler can see.

"Can you come up there with me?" he asks. "Help me open the door and get her into bed?"

"Of course, "I reply as we head to the doors for the lobby.

When we get to room 1206, I put the key in the lock and open the door. "It sounds like the TV is on," I whisper to Tyler. I can't walk into a condo where I'm not staying without announcing myself, so I call out, "Hello?"

We walk in and I recognize Amber's mom walking toward us from the family room. "Oh my gosh, what happened?" Her mom rushes over to see her daughter.

"We think someone put something in her drink," Tyler says. "Where's her bed?"

Amber's mom scurries to a bedroom and we follow her. Tyler sets Amber on the bed, her mom immediately at her side. Tyler wipes his brow as he stands. "Sloane saw her with two guys she didn't recognize and Amber was slurring her speech and out of it, so she got her out of there. I saw them when they were halfway back here."

Amber's mom turns to me, her eyes search my face reflecting both concern and relief. "Oh, Sloane, thank you so much. I haven't seen you since Brownies in third grade. Amber is so lucky to have a friend like you." Then, she focuses back on her daughter, checking her vitals.

I feel my eyes go wide at the word 'friend' but smile. "Us girls have to look out for each other." I explain, "She had a plastic cup in her hand, and two guys were groping her. I grabbed her and got her out of there, but I have no idea what might have been in her drink."

Amber's mom looks back at me and clutches her chest, then shakes her head. "She is so lucky you were there. I'm a nurse, so I know what to do."

I had forgotten that Amber's mom was a nurse. Brownies and third grade seem so long ago. Things were different back then. Kids were pretty much nice to each other in those days before puberty, hormones, and the caste system of middle and high school. I smile, "That's right. We'll get going, unless you need us."

"No, I've got what I need, thanks you two," Mrs. Gates says, then turns back to her daughter.

When we leave Amber's room and head to the elevator, Tyler says, "You look like you could use some water."

"Yeah, I could," I say as I wipe my forehead. "I definitely got a workout lugging her down the beach."

"Are you staying here?" Tyler pushes the down arrow for the elevator.

I shake my head. "No, we're down at Edgewater."

The elevator doors open and once inside, Tyler pushes the button for the seventh floor. "Let's go to my condo," he says as the elevator doors start to close. "I'll get you some water."

When we arrive at Tyler's condo, we walk into the small kitchen. He opens the fridge, grabs a jug of water, then opens a cabinet and gets two glasses out. He pours a glass, hands it to me, and I chug down the ice-cold water. "Ahh," I say when I come up for air. "Thanks, I needed that."

Tyler smiles as he sets the jug on the counter then does the same, drinking half his glass in one long gulp. "That was really nice of you to help Amber," he says, then wipes his mouth with the back of his hand. "Especially since she was so rude to you the other night."

I huff out a laugh. "What?" Tyler asks.

"Amber Gates has been rude to me for half my life, if not longer," I explain. "Like her mom said, we used to be in Brownies together, but after, like, fourth grade, she became a mean girl and has something against me."

Tyler's eyes go wide. "Wow, then it's even cooler what you did for her."

"She may be a total witch, but she doesn't deserve what those guys were doing to her. No girl does." I feel anxious just thinking about it, and my voice cracks. I can't help it, but tears stream down my face as the adrenaline of the event wears off. I wave my hand in front of me. "I'm sorry, it was just so sc-scary." I'm trying to stop crying, but the enormity of what happened is washing over me as I finally have time to process it.

Tyler wraps his arms around me and hugs me. "You're a really good person, Sloane." I hug him back and cry into his shoulder as I let out the stress of this evening. There is nothing romantic about this hug, no electricity or heart-pumping feelings, just gratitude and comfort. I settle myself and take a deep breath then release the hug and wipe my face. "I'm sorry, that was a lot. I didn't mean to break down in front of you."

Tyler smiles down at me. "It's okay. I can't imagine how scary that was for you." He walks over to the sink and grabs a handful of paper towels then runs them under the water and hands them to me.

I take the towels and wipe the tears off my face. "Thank you for helping me. I don't think I would have made it much further without your help." I say with a smile, then think about where he was going. "Were you heading to the bonfire?"

Tyler nods and I notice a muscle in his jaw clench. "Yeah, Sara went out with her friends." He runs a hand through his hair, then briefly drops his gaze to the floor, then looks back up. "Some of the guys were going to the bonfire, so I thought I'd check it out."

"Shoot," I say, "Your last night here and I—"

Tyler holds up a hand stopping me. "You did the right thing and helped someone in need, and I happened to come along at the right time." He smiles ever so slightly.

I grab his forearm and my chest constricts with worry. "Wait. Is there any chance Sara and her friends went there, too?

Tyler starts to shrug as I release his arm, then realizes the same thing I just did. "Crap!" He looks at me, his eyes now filled with worry.

"Before we went down there, I gave my friends my paranoid mom reminder about accepting drinks in open containers. But, would Sara and her friends know to be careful? Heck, we need to get back there to warn any other girls are there."

Tyler heads to the door. "You're right; let's go."

***

As Tyler and I jog onto the beach just in front of The Summit, we see a group of kids running down the beach toward us. "Look!" I point down the beach where blue lights are flashing.

Tyler stops a kid running by us by grabbing his arm. "Hey! What's going on down there?"

A boy about our age with red cheeks and sandy blond hair stops and Tyler releases his hold. "Cops busted the bonfire, man." He jogs past us and up to the pool deck behind us.

"Shoot!" I say. "I hope our friends got out of there."

We start jogging toward the bonfire. "We have to find out," Tyler says.

About twenty yards down the beach, I spot my friends. "Maggie!" I shout, then wave my arms.

Maggie, Beth, and Annalise jog toward us. "Oh my gosh, that was crazy," Annalise says between winded breaths and laughter.

"Did you see Sara there?" Tyler asks as worry shines in his eyes.

Annalise nods. "Yeah, she was there. She should be right behind us."

"Thanks," Tyler says then waves at us and jogs down the beach to find his girlfriend.

"Oh my gosh, what happened?" I ask my friends.

"The cops showed up and everyone scattered," Beth says a little less breathless than Annalise. "I think the real question is, what were you doing down here with Tyler Finlay?"

I roll my eyes. "Definitely not what you think." I fill them in on what happened with Amber and how Tyler helped me, though I don't divulge her identity. "We were just heading back to warn y'all and any girls who were there."

Annalise play-punches me in the arm. "Mama Sloane was right. Thanks for reminding us to be careful."

Maggie is more serious. "Is the girl going to be okay? That had to be so scary."

I nod. "Her mom is taking care of her. And, yeah, it was super scary. I think I'm ready for spring break to be over."

Beth puts her arm around me. "I agree, let's take this party back to our place and start planning for prom."

I smile as we trudge through the thick, sugary sand toward our condo. "Sounds perfect."

Chapter 48

Tyler

I spot Sara, Ramsey, Kara, Adam, Josh, and Tim running down the beach hand-in-hand. "Sara!" I run to her and notice Adam release his grasp on her hand, a look of nervousness in his eyes.

"Hey!" Sara releases Ramsey's hand and gives me a quick hug. Her eyes are glassy and she has a huge smile on her face. "Oh my gosh, that was so crazy. The bonfire got busted and we all had to scatter!"

"Are y'all okay?" I search their faces.

"Yeah, we're fine," Ramsey says and Kara nods. Adam, Josh, and Tim nod and look at me with concern in their eyes.

"Why? What's going on?" Sara asks.

I run my hand through my hair as I consider how to tell them what Sloane saw at the beach. "Apparently, a girl who was at the bonfire had her drink spiked. That's why I was headed that way. To warn you." I grab Sara's hands. "You didn't accept a drink from anyone, did you?"

Sara shakes her head. I look at Ramsey and Kara who do the same. "We had these guys to protect us," Sara says as she puts her arm around Adam's shoulders and hooks a thumb at Tim and Josh.

I feel my eyes narrow and Adam moves toward me and out of my girlfriend's grasp. "It's all good, man." He pats my shoulder. "Come on, let's get out of here."

I can't tell if Adam is interested in Sara or not, but either way, I'm glad she, Ramsey, and Kara were with them because being with those guys might have kept them safe. I'm not going to make a scene in front of everyone and am just so relieved that Sara is safe.

I take her hand as our group heads back toward our condo. I let our friends continue walking and stop so I can talk to Sara.

"What are you doing?" Sara asks as she looks ahead to where our friends are going.

Her brown curls are dancing in the gulf breeze. "I'm so glad you're okay." I tuck a strand of hair behind her ear and look into her eyes which go from confused to happy.

"Of course, I'm okay, silly." She jokingly punches my arm. "Now, let's go. It's our last night of spring break and I'm not done partying!" Sara tugs me down the beach and starts jogging toward our friends. "Hey guys, wait up!"

I begrudgingly jog with Sara, disappointed that she didn't so much as kiss me, or even hug me for that matter. She punched my arm like we're buddies. That's when I realize that maybe that's where we are now. Friends. Buddies. Pals.

Chapter 49

Sloane

April 1993

Spring break marked the downhill point in our senior year, and the halls are abuzz as those in my graduating class look forward to all the festivities that come along with our last quarter of school. My skin is almost back to normal as I plop into my chair in French class the Monday after spring break. Next up is prom and I am so excited!

Kurt is right behind me, and I can tell he has gossip for me today. His face holds some kind of secret. "Hey!" I smile brightly. "What's up? You look like the cat that ate the canary."

Kurt's eyes are serious, and this makes my pulse race. "Sloane," Kurt whispers, "there's a rumor going around that you and Tyler Finlay got together over spring break."

"What?" I say a little too loudly and feel my eyes bulge in their sockets. "No way. Maybe in my dreams."

"Seriously," Kurt says, "apparently someone saw you leaving his room Saturday night."

I exhale and lean back in my chair. "Oh, that? No, that was nothing." Kurt's eyes search mine, and I don't want to spread gossip about Amber and what happened to her, but I also want my friend to know why I was seen leaving Tyler's room that night. I lean in and explain to him what happened, leaving Amber's name out of it to protect her.

Kurt's face washes with relief. "I knew you wouldn't do something like that," he says almost triumphantly. "Man, kids in this school have got to get a life."

Amber saunters into the room, and I give her a soft smile but am dumbfounded when she looks right at me and makes a face as if she's just smelled something foul. She then proceeds to roll her eyes and sits in her seat, turning her face away from me and toward the front of the room.

Kurt sees it too and looks at me, "What's her deal?"

"I guess it's just Amber being Amber," I say quietly to him as I shake my head. I can't believe she would still be so rude to me after what I did for her on the beach that night. Graduation simply can't get here fast enough.

***

By the time marine bio rolls around, the rumor about Tyler and me has permeated the entire school, and I'm so mad, I could spit nails. I have a boyfriend. He has a girlfriend. I would never do that, and we were doing something nice for someone. I feel mad, sad, and irritated all at once. I make my way to class and hope to see Tyler and Sara in the hallway since she usually walks with him to class, but I don't. I toss my backpack down as Billy says, "Hey Sloaner-"

I cut him off. "Sorry, Billy. Be right back." I march out to the hallway and wait for Tyler and Sara. Kids pass me, left and right, but there's no sign of either of them. Occasionally, kids pass by me and whisper to each other, and I feel my face grow hot. I want to cry, but I also want to scream. The bell rings, and I go inside and slump down in my chair.

"What's the matter Sloaner?" Billy asks.

"Come on, hurry up, Romeo," Coach K says, and I look up to see Tyler rushing into class.

When he sees me, there's the slightest pause in his steps, but he continues forward and sits in his seat next to me. "We need to talk."

"Yeah, I know," I whisper. "I cannot believe what people are saying."

"Me neither," Tyler says as he pulls out his book and notebook. "It's insane."

Okay, that kind of hurt, but I try to brush it off. "How's Sara?"

"Pissed," he whispers.

Coach K gives us a look, and I don't want to draw any more attention to us, so I keep my mouth shut and my head down. While I try to focus on my book and taking notes, all I can think about is how to make this right. I've known Sara since the sixth grade, and I hope she knows the kind of person I am. I decide that the only way to fix this is to talk to Sara, if she'll hear me out.

***

After class, Tyler tells me that Sara isn't talking to him, but suggests that I come to the table that they sit at for lunch outside. Of course, I know which table this is, and of course, it's in the middle of everything and everyone. Maggie and I walk outside together, and nervous butterflies fill my stomach as I look out at the picnic tables where the cheerleaders, football players, and their popular friends eat lunch. It's far from the little piece of shady sidewalk where my friends and I eat lunch. I inhale deeply, trying to still my nerves.

"I hate confrontation," I say to Maggie.

"Me, too," she says softly. After a beat, she adds, "Do you want me to come with you?"

I know Maggie is only offering to be polite. I turn to her, "No, thanks." She looks more nervous than I feel. "I'll join y'all in a few." I take in another deep inhale, then exhale slowly as I see Tyler walk up to the group and sit next to Sara who promptly turns her back and talks to the girls on her right. "This is ridiculous," I say to myself and march over as my heart feels like it's going to beat out of my chest. Obviously, my body is much better at flight versus fight.

I walk up to Sara's right side and smile. "Hey, can we talk for a second?"

Sara opens her mouth and is about to say something when Amber sits across from her. "I don't think she has anything to say to you, Sloane." She says my name as if it tastes like a bitter pill.

I feel my eyebrows raise and notice Tyler shifting out of the corner of my eye. I can't believe I'm not dropping dead of a heart attack right here, right now. I'm the worst at confrontation and feel my eyes prick with tears. Like a scared dog, I'm using avoidance, wishing I had the courage to stand up to Amber.

"Sara can think for herself, Amber," Tyler says. "You, for one, know this rumor isn't true." I look at Tyler whose fierce gaze is focused on Amber. I've never seen him look angry like this.

I look back to Sara. "Please?" I plead. "It's not what you think." I look at Amber. "At all."

Sara looks from me to Amber, whose mouth hangs open as if she's stunned and can't speak, then back at me. "Okay," she says as she stands up. She glares at Tyler, "Come on."

Tyler stands up, and I swear he looks like a puppy who realizes he's no longer in trouble for chewing on a shoe. Relief washes over him, and he looks anxious to be heard.

We follow Sara to the pine trees where no one sits at lunch. She stops and crosses her arms over her chest and looks at me. "Tyler has told me what he says happened, and I want to hear if your story matches."

"Sara, the reason I was seen leaving Tyler's condo the night of the bonfire was because he offered me some water after he saw me helping a girl who had been drugged at the bonfire." I search her face, seeing if she believes me. "I was at the bonfire with Maggie, Beth, and Annalise, and they were all dancing with guys." I shift uncomfortably as I say, "I felt out of place and didn't want to be disrespectful to my boyfriend, so I went to sit down by the water and just watch the waves. I heard A-," I stop myself as I still don't want to say who the girl was. "I heard a girl who was being groped by two guys, so I sprang into action. I grabbed her and started heading toward The Summit because I had to get her out of there." As I'm telling the story, I turn to Tyler. "Wait, didn't you tell her all of this Saturday night after it happened?"

Tyler says, "I told her a girl had been drugged with a spiked drink, but I didn't go into all the details." He looks at Sara, and I can't help but feel like there's something going on between them that I don't understand. "The bonfire had just been busted and all."

Sara nods for me to continue. "So, I was dragging this girl down the beach when I saw Tyler. He grabbed her and carried her back to The Summit because he knew she was staying there." I search Sara's eyes.

Sara turns to look at Tyler. "How did you know that?" she snaps.

Tyler looks at me, and I nod. "The girl goes to Dunwoody."

Sara's eyes open wide. "Is she in our class?"

Tyler and I exchange glances again, and I say, "Yes, we agreed not to say anything to protect her privacy."

Sara's eyes soften and so does her tone. "So, what happened?"

I continue. "I searched her pockets and found a key with her room number on it. Tyler carried her while I opened the door to her unit. Her mom was there, watching TV. We got her settled into her bed and let her mom take it from there. Tyler asked if I was thirsty, which I was, so we went to his condo and grabbed some water. Once the adrenaline wore off and I realized what had just happened, I broke down crying. Tyler gave me a hug— totally non-romantic, and we walked back toward the bonfire. He wasn't sure if you would be there, but wanted to make sure that if you were, you'd be safe. And, of course, I wanted to alert my friends about what had happened. That's when we saw kids running and police lights. We saw my friends, and they told us you were right behind them, so Tyler dashed off to find you. That's the last time I saw him since marine bio today." I look at Sara as she processes all of this, then I add, "And, if it makes you feel better, I was pining away for Ky the whole time I was at the beach and talked to him every night on the phone." I smile and this causes her to smile, too.

"That's the same story Tyler told me," she says. "Except he also said he gave you some wet paper towels to wipe your face with." Sara offers Tyler a slight smile and relief floods through my body.

I laugh. "Yes, he did do that. I'm pretty sure I freaked him out by breaking down." I think about the whole scene which still unsettles me and won't leave my memory. "It was just so scary because if I hadn't grabbed her..." I shudder. "It would have been bad."

Sara nods her head and says, "I'm so glad you were there for her." She gives me a giant bear hug, squeezing me tightly. When she releases me, she turns to Tyler. "Sorry I doubted you."

Tyler smiles tightly at Sara. "Thanks." As Sara turns, his gaze meets mine and his smile turns soft and feels genuine. He stuffs his hands into his pockets as he turns to head back to their table. "I wonder who started this rumor anyway?"

The three of us start walking out of the little pine forest with Sara in the middle. She says, "I don't know who saw you guys, but Amber's been telling anyone who will listen."

I stop dead in my tracks, and so does Tyler. His eyes meet mine. "What?"

Sara stops, too, nodding her head. "Yeah, she's been telling people." She looks between me and Tyler. "Why would she do that?"

I look at Tyler and shake my head in disbelief. I can't believe Amber did this to us after what we did for her, but I decide to take the high road. "Amber has had it out for me for a while, and I have no idea why," I say.

"Well, I'm going to have a word with her," Sara says as she picks up her pace.

"Yeah, me too," Tyler says as he follows Sara.

"Good luck," I say to them. "I've had enough of her for the rest of my life." They laugh as I wave then turn and make my way over to my friends on the shady sidewalk. I will keep what happened to Amber a secret because I won't let someone like Amber Gates drag me down to her level. "Prom, then graduation," I say to myself. I think I will be the happiest person in my class when we throw our graduation caps into the air in June.

Chapter 50

Sloane

A week after the spring break rumor was nipped in the bud, all was forgotten, and all eyes focused on prom. While I felt bummed that Ky couldn't come visit me on spring break, that sadness didn't last long as he would be coming up for prom, and I couldn't wait to show him off!

At lunch, Maggie, Annalise, Beth, and I discuss our plans for prom. "My mom ordered the limo," Beth says as she cracks open her diet Coke. "So, that's all set!"

"And I made dinner reservations at the Pleasant Pheasant," Annalise says then pops a grape into her mouth.

I can't contain the smile on my face and the excitement coursing through my veins. "I'm so excited," I tell my friends as I sit up straight, bouncing a little in my seat. "I'm so glad I finally have someone to go to a dance with. Senior prom no less."

"I can't believe no one has ever asked you to a dance," Beth says as she sets her soda can down. "Guys here are so lame."

"Precisely why we had to look elsewhere," Annalise says as she hooks a thumb at Beth. Steve's friend is taking Annalise, and I know we'll have a fun group.

"All of us," I say as it dawns on me as I look at Maggie. "Your date goes to St Christopher's."

Maggie smiles. "Who would have thought the guy that opened the door for us at Jesse's party would end up in my class at church?"

"Have you two moved past the friendship level, then?" Annalise asks as she wiggles her eyebrows.

Maggie looks down at her sandwich as her cheeks turn pink. "Not quite, but I feel like we might be moving in that direction." She looks at us with a huge smile.

"Maggie! Stop holding back from us," Beth says as she grabs one of Annalise's grapes and tosses it at Maggie making us all crack up.

"I'm excited to meet Ky." Maggie looks at me trying to get the attention off herself. "I wish he could have visited on spring break."

"I know, I was so bummed," I say as I grab my juice box and sit back in my seat. "But, at least he can come for prom." I smile then take a sip of cranapple juice. "I hope y'all like him. He's a sweet guy."

"Of course, we'll like him," Annalise says as she plucks another grape off the bunch in front of her. "We're gonna have a blast at prom!"

"Y'all are going to prom together?" a voice says behind me, and I recognize it right away. Is Amber being nice to me now after what happened on spring break?

I'm about to turn around, but see Annalise squint her eyes at Amber. "Uh, yeah..."

"Even Sloane?" her voice cuts with insult as my excitement turns to anxiety.

Before I can say a word, Beth says, "Yeah, Amber. Sloane's boyfriend is coming to town for it. What's it to you?"

Amber scoffs. "The old out-of-town boyfriend story," she laughs derisively. "I'll believe it when I see it."

I can't help myself and whip around in my chair. "It's not a story Amber. My boyfriend lives in Thomasville." I can feel myself shaking.

Amber flips her black hair over her shoulder. "Right," she says, "because boys want to date flat-chested girls who are tall enough to be on the boys' basketball team." She laughs at her cruel joke.

My mouth drops open, and I have no words as Annalise pops up from her seat ready to lay into Amber, but it's too late. Amber saunters off as if she is God's gift to humanity. Tears burn behind my eyes, but I will myself not to cry.

"That witch!" Annalise says as she sits down heavily, her eyes wide, unblinking. She leans forward and grabs my hand. "Sloane, you know none of that is true."

I inhale deeply then exhale a long breath of air and blink tightly. "It probably is," I say as I toss my bag of Doritos on the table and reach for my napkin. I dab at my eyes. "I still can't believe Amber is treating me this way after-" I stop myself.

"After what?" Beth asks, as her brow knits with concern.

I sigh, trying to think of a quick explanation. "Uh, after all these years." I drink the rest of my juice sucking the air out of the juice box then toss it on the table. "I was in Brownies with her. Ever since middle school, she's been so awful. She's probably right about guys. Ky's probably only with me for one reason and once he realizes he's not going to get it, he'll probably be gone."

Maggie puts an arm around me and squeezes my shoulder. "Ky likes you, loves you, even. Besides, she just has something against you. I have no idea why, but that's on her not you."

Annalise crumples up the bag that contained her grapes, popping the last one into her mouth. "If Ky was just with you for sex, he wouldn't still be with you," she says around her grape. "It sounds like he really likes you for you."

"Yeah," Beth says leaning forward. "You'll show her when you show up to prom with a gorgeous guy on your arm." She wiggles her eyebrows making me laugh. "I've seen the pictures of you two, he's hot."

Now I'm laughing. "Thanks, guys," I say as the tension starts to leave my body, and a small smile forms on my mouth. "It will be pretty cool to prove her wrong."

"Yes!" Annalise says and holds a hand up to give me five. I smile bigger and slap her hand. "Prom just got even more exciting. I can't wait to see Amber's face when you show up with Ky." She rubs her hands together and has a glimmer in her eyes.

"Y'all are the best," I say as I pick up my bag of Doritos. "I'm so glad I got lunch period with you this year." I grab a chip and take a bite as Maggie gives my shoulder another hug. I'm so grateful to have found three girls who are kind, fun, and just as ready to get out of this stupid school as I am. I just wish I had found them before senior year.

Chapter 51

Sloane

May 1993

Prom is just ten days away, and I lay on my bed working on my homework. Maggie, Beth, Annalise, and I have plans this weekend to do each other's hair and makeup to see what looks best, and I can't wait to finish out the week. Just two more school days. As I work on a trig problem, the phone rings. Normally, I would assume it's another real estate agent calling for my mom, but she and my dad are at an event downtown for my dad's work. Since Bryn gets nervous answering the phone sometimes, I hop up as it rings a second time and grab it.

"Hello?" I say into the receiver.

"Hey," Ky's voice sounds through the earpiece.

"Hey!" I say as the butterflies start fluttering in my belly. I lay back against the pillows on my headboard, smiling. "This is a nice surprise."

"Yeah," he says. "How are you?"

"I'm great," I say, "especially since I get to talk to you on a weeknight. How was work?" I can tell by his voice that it must have been a tiring day.

"You know, it was work. What are you up to?"

He doesn't sound happy, so I figure I'll try to make him feel better. "Just working on homework and counting down the days 'til I see you. I can't wait for prom." The butterflies are fully awake, and I feel my pulse quicken as I continue. "Everything is set. The limo is booked, and we have reservations at a delicious restaurant close to the hotel where prom will be. It's going to be amazing, and my friends can't wait to meet you!" My adrenaline must be pumping because I can't stop talking. "You're going to love them and their dates."

"Sloane-" Ky starts.

"Oh," I interrupt, "and I have our tickets to the Metro Mount concert. The Lemonheads are headlining, but since it's a daytime show, we should have plenty of time to see them, then go back to my house to get ready for prom."

"Sloane," Ky says again, his voice firm.

"Yeah?" I ask, my voice quiet as my throat tightens with concern.

"Uh," he pauses. "Um--I'm not going to be able to take you to your prom."

All the happiness and joy that filled my body seconds ago has been sucked out of me, replaced by complete and utter shock and devastation. "What? Why?" For a split second, I think he's joking.

"My car is acting up, and I don't think it's safe to drive all the way up there."

I feel like a quarterback who has just been hit from his blindside. "Can't you borrow your mom's car? I've been looking so forward to this. The plans have all been made..."

"My mom needs her car, so I can't borrow it. I'm sorry." While he sounds sorry, I can't wrap my head around this.

"So that's it? You're not going to even try to find a way to get here?" My voice cracks as tears flood out of my eyes.

"I don't know what else to say, I just can't come. Sorry."

"Sorry?" I yell into the phone as tears and snot leak from my face. My sadness quickly turns to anger. "You're sorry? Do you know how long I've been looking forward to this? I've planned everything with my friends, who are expecting me to pay for part of the limo, by the way." I can't stop my tirade. "Ten days before prom, and you're just going to stand me up?" I can't help it, I'm so mad, so sad, so disappointed, and if I don't start taking deep breaths, I'm afraid I'll start hyperventilating.

"What do you want me to do?" Ky asks, irritation clear in his tone, as if I'm being unreasonable.

"Oh, I don't know, maybe be a man of your word. Find a way. Borrow a car?" My heart is breaking with every word.

"Look, this is out of my control," he says defensively.

"No, Ky, if you loved me as much as you say you do and if you really wanted to be here, you would find a way."

"Well, I'm sorry, I can't," is all he says to me.

I don't say anything at first, the silence on the line deafening. "That's it?"

"Yeah, I guess so," he replies after a beat.

"Wow, alright," I say making my irritation and disappointment clear. I swallow hard. "Bye." I slam down the phone without waiting for a response and fling myself down on my bed, sobbing into my pillow. I've never experienced this kind of heartbreak. I feel as if my heart has been ripped in two, the sadness bleeding out into my veins and arteries, consuming my entire being.

Chapter 52

Sloane

At school the next day, I have to tell everyone about prom, all without crying. I can tell that Kurt, Billy, and Tyler feel bad for me but don't really know what to say. I'm glad for it because I don't want to talk about it anyway. I called Maggie after I pulled myself together last night, only to fall to pieces again telling her I couldn't go to prom with them. Since it's a beautiful, sunny day, we meet outside for lunch, and I get there early to pick a spot farther down the sidewalk so we can have some privacy.

When Beth and Annalise see me, it's everything I can do not to cry. They frown and alternately hug me. "We're so sorry," Beth says. "Do you want to talk about it?"

I shrug my shoulders. "There's not much to say. He told me his car has issues, and he can't come," I say despondently.

Maggie chimes in since she knows the story. "He said he can't borrow his mom's car because she needs it." She looks at me with sympathetic eyes which causes me to start crying. "Oh, I'm sorry, Sloane." She hugs me as I compose myself.

After a minute, I pull back and wipe my eyes with a napkin. "You know what's even worse?" I ask my friends as my voice cracks.

"What?" Annalise asks.

I sniffle. "Amber is going to think I really did make Ky up."

Annalise rolls her eyes and sighs. "Ugh, she's miserable. Don't worry, we'll back you up."

"Yeah," Beth adds, "you were clearly talking to him every single night on spring break." She jokes and this makes me laugh a little.

"I promise I was talking to Ky and not my mom," I joke back.

"Oh, we know," Annalise says, "we overheard a few things."

I blush. "Stupid Ky. I just feel like he didn't try hard, you know?" I look at my friends who nod. "I would get it if something major had happened, like a death in the family, but his car?"

"I can't believe he turned out to be such a jerk," Annalise says. "If anything, it sounded like he liked you more than maybe you liked him."

I inhale deeply. "That's what I thought, too. I told him that if he loved me as much as he said he did that he would find a way. I should have known when he couldn't come visit me when I was only two hours away at the beach that something was up." As I say this, something dawns on me. I look at my friends. "When we were first talking about prom, he asked if we should get a hotel room downtown. I told him I wasn't ready for that."

"What did he say?" Beth asks.

"He asked if I'd ever be ready for that and when I told him, of course, he asked if I'd ever be ready for that with him." I search their eyes for their reaction.

All three sets of eyes go wide. "What did you say?" Annalise asks.

"I told him I just wasn't ready now. He knew that. I was up front about that all this time," I explain.

"Well, if that's the reason why he stood you up *ten days* before prom, then he doesn't deserve you," Annalise says as anger surrounds her words.

Beth nods. "She's right." She thinks for a moment, then says, "Did you have that conversation before spring break?"

I turn my eyes skyward as I think back, then nod. "I think so." My shoulders slouch, and I let out a sigh. "How could I be so stupid?" I feel tears stinging behind my eyes.

Maggie looks at me with uncertainty in her eyes. "Are you going to ask him about it, or just go your separate ways?"

"I don't know," I say. "I want to believe his excuse, but the fact that he just didn't seem to try to find a way really hurts. It was just like, 'Sorry, I just can't make it,' like it wasn't a big deal." I think for a moment as I pick up a stray piece of pine straw off the sidewalk. I look at my friend. "I bet it was because he wanted what I wasn't ready to give him." Everyone is quiet, and I think about it, then sigh again. "You know what? I don't care. He's shown his true colors and if he can't respect me and what I'm comfortable with, he doesn't deserve me."

"Damn straight," Annalise gives me an encouraging smile.

"My dad told me that when God closes a door, He opens a window." I fidget with the pine straw, wrapping it around my index finger. "I don't know what could make this situation better, but maybe it's my sign that Ky isn't right for me." I'm trying so hard to be positive.

"I just wish he hadn't messed up your prom plans," Beth says. "He should have told you sooner if it's not about the car."

"Yeah," Maggie says, "he should have given you the chance to go with someone else instead of telling you right before prom."

I sigh. "At least I have The Lemonheads concert that day. I'll see if Tameka can come into town and go with me. That'll take my mind off the fact that I will have gone through middle school and high school without ever going to a dance." My shoulders slump, and I feel like the biggest loser. What little optimism I had has faded. I'm the loser who won't even get to go to her senior prom. Pity party, party of one...

Chapter 53

Tyler

I stay after baseball practice to get some time in the batting cage and to work off some stress. Coach can tell I'm off my game and I don't dare tell him it's girl trouble. Sara and I have been bickering and I don't think either of us is looking forward to prom anymore. Why did I think it was a good idea to stick this out when it's clear our relationship has run its course? I should have let Sara go after Spring Break and let her find a prom date she would be happy with, but I didn't think things would get this bad. I whiff at the third ball in a row and set the end of my bat down, the handle resting against my legs. I readjust my batting gloves and inhale deeply, trying to let all my stress leave with my exhale.

Coach K walks up to me and crosses his arms over his chest. "Somethin' bothering you, son?"

"I'm just in my own head, I guess," I lie. I mean, I am in my own head, but I don't elaborate.

"Try to clear your mind and just be in this moment. See the ball. And, relax, you look wound-up." Coach walks back behind the screen and gets ready to pitch some more.

"If only it were that easy," I think to myself. I grab my bat, get in my batting stance, and try to clear my head, but I don't think it's working.

To top it all off, Sloane told Billy and me about Ky backing out on prom and it felt like my blood was going to boil over. Swing and a miss. I haven't ever seen Sloane so sad and despondent, and I have to say, it made me want to find the guy and punch him in the face. She was so excited to go to her first school dance and this tool totally ruined it for her. I make contact, but it's a bad hit. Maybe if I pretend like the ball is Ky? I've never seen him before, but I don't need to. I can let my aggression out on the ball.

"Just focus" Coach says. "And relax your shoulders, they're up to your ears!"

I breathe in and out again and feel my shoulders relax. I visualize hitting the crap out of Ky, I mean the ball, and I do. A ding sounds off my aluminum bat and Coach reflexively ducks.

"That's more like it!" Coach is grinning from ear to ear. "Whatever you did, keep doing it."

I feel more settled, and he throws another one. Ding! The force of the hit reverberates through my hands, up my wrists and forearms. This feels better.

"There you go!" Coach hollers with encouragement. He throws some more and I'm consistently making contact. I'm in the zone. After ten solid hits in a row, Coach comes toward me again. "Stay out of your head," he says as he looks at me earnestly. "Whatever's going on up there," he taps my forehead, "leave it off the field, okay?"

"Yes, sir." I nod. "Thank you."

"You got it, Finlay." He smacks my hip with his glove. "Come on, let's end on a positive." He starts picking up balls and I help him, then grab my duffle bag, take off my gloves, and pack everything up.

As we walk to the storage shed, I say, "Thanks for taking the time with me, Coach, I appreciate it." I hand him the bucket of balls I'm carrying and he stows it inside, then locks up and we walk up the hill toward the parking lot.

"Of course," he says. "Anything you want to talk about?"

"Nah."

"Everything okay at home?" Concern washes over his eyes.

"Oh, yeah. Everything's great at home. Promise." I smile at him genuinely.

"Grades are okay?"

"Yes, sir," I nod. I guess this is what he's supposed to do to make sure I'm okay and am on track to graduate.

"Girl trouble?"

Dang, how the heck does he know? I look at the ground and my cleats make a shuffling sound on the asphalt. I look up and feel my mouth twist to the side.

Coach puts a hand on my shoulder. "Look, you are young and high school relationships usually don't pan out. You've got a bright future ahead of you and if you want to go pro, I believe you can, but you'll have to limit the distractions."

I nod. "Yes, sir."

"You didn't get anyone pregnant, did you?"

Oh my gosh, I can't believe he just asked me this. I feel my cheeks burn as I let out a nervous laugh. "No sir, definitely not."

"Good. Keep it that way," he says as he pats my shoulder. "Whatever's troubling you will pass. Just be a good guy, okay?"

"Always," I say with a smile and feel relief wash over me. "Thanks, Coach." He salutes me as he starts walking to his car and I head to mine.

As I throw my stuff into the passenger seat of my truck, I realize why I feel so relieved after talking to Coach. I need to focus on baseball and graduating. I'll talk to Sara after prom and I think she'll be relieved, too. As for Sloane, I just hope she's okay. I would jump at the chance to ask her, but I'm committed to Sara until we go our separate ways. And, there's no way I would do to her what Ky did to Sloane. Maybe someone will take Sloane to her prom, she deserves so much better.

Chapter 54

Sloane

I go through the next eight days in a funk. I don't care how I look, and I even made the most melancholy mixed tape because happy music just isn't what I want to hear right now. I also don't want to hear about prom. I just want to get the heck out of this school and leave all this behind. Thankfully, Tameka came home from college to go see The Lemonheads at the Metro Mount festival with me, and I know we'll have a blast. I try not to think about prom as we drive to Stone Mountain together.

"How about we go to the Mick's for dinner tonight?" Tameka suggests as I park my car.

"Ooh, good idea," I say, already thinking about their delicious Oreo cheesecake for dessert.

"Then, maybe we'll go see Benny and Joon again," she says referring to the Johnny Depp movie that I saw when it came out last month. "I know Johnny Depp will make you happy." She giggles as she wiggles her eyebrows at me, making me laugh.

"Or maybe we'll just go to Blockbuster and rent a bunch of his movies," I say as we get out of the car, then grab our blanket and cooler out of the trunk.

"Whatever you want to do," she says as we head across the parking lot to the field where the stage is set up.

I smile. "Thank you so much for coming home this weekend and hanging out with me."

Tameka smiles wide. "Of course. We're going to have so much fun. Maybe we'll get to talk to Evan again."

"That would be awesome." We find a spot for our blanket and get situated. We arrived late so when the crowd thins out in between bands, we move our set-up closer to the front. Once we're seated again, I see people hanging out by the lake off to the side of the stage. "Is that Evan?"

Tameka pops up and looks. "Yeah! Let's go say hi."

When we make our way to Evan, I recognize the girls we met at his hotel. As we approach, Evan sees us and his face lights up. "Hey!"

"Hi," Tameka and I say, and I feel the butterflies start to flutter. Is it possible that he is better looking than he was when we met him?

"Sloane and Tameka, right?" Evan says.

I can feel myself beaming, "Yeah, you remembered."

"Of course," Evan says. "You remember Nikki and Ashley." He nods at the redhead and blonde seated with him on the grass, and I notice they have backstage passes hanging from their necks.

"Yeah, hi," I say, still smiling.

"We're so excited for your show," Tameka says.

"Yeah, cool," Evan says. "I'm glad you could come out," His eyes are fixed on me. "Especially since you had to miss the last show."

"I can't wait," I tell him.

"That last show was *amazing*," Ashley says as she tosses her blonde hair over her shoulder. "You really missed a good one." She looks at me as if to try to make me feel bad about missing it.

I smile tightly. "I'm sure we did." I mean, what else am I supposed to say to her?

"I'm glad y'all made it to this one," Nikki says sweetly, her gorgeous red curls vibrant in the sunlight. "It's gonna be great!"

"I think you'll like the setlist," Evan says as he winks at me causing my heart to flutter.

"I know I will," I say then worry that I sound like an idiot. I feel awkward on a good day and here's this gorgeous rock star talking to me and making my brain forget how to work. It doesn't help that there are two gorgeous girls sitting with him who are way cooler than me.

"Does that mean 'Bit Part' is on the setlist?" Tameka asks referring to her favorite song.

Evan smiles at her. "You'll just have to wait and see." He stands up. "I've gotta go talk to my band." His eyes fall on me again. "It's good to see you."

"Yeah, you, too," I reply softly as my voice decides to ebb, as if caught off-guard by his stunning beauty. I clear my throat. "Have a great show."

"Thanks," he smiles, and I worry I will quickly become a puddle in the grass. He turns to Nikki and Ashley. "See you in a few."

Ashley beams at Evan. "See ya!" As he walks away, she grabs the lanyard around her neck and holds it up. "We've got backstage passes."

"Cool," I say.

"It's so great seeing you two again," Nikki says to us, and we chat mostly with her for a bit.

"This is fun and all, but we've gotta get backstage," Ashley says as she stands up and holds out a hand for Nikki.

"It was so good seeing you," Nikki says. "Bye!" She waves as Ashley pulls her other hand toward the backstage area.

"Well, it was cool we got to see Evan again," Tameka says.

"Yeah, it was." I plop myself onto the grass. "I wish we had backstage passes."

Tameka sits down next to me. "Do you want to hang out here and see if they come back?"

"Sure, I'm really only here to see them anyway," I tell her as Gene Loves Jezebel takes to the stage. We end up staying there the whole time and when we see Evan run onto the stage, we hop up and run over to our blanket.

When we get there, Tameka looks at me and says, "Let's try to get up front."

We leave our blanket and cooler and make our way to the front where it's standing room only. Somehow, we get all the way to the barricade and are right up front to watch my favorite band. Evan's presence is magnetic on stage and off. The band sounds amazing, and in no time, I'm lost in the jangly sounds of his guitar and his soulful and smooth voice. About midway through the set, the band plays 'Being Around,' and the third song was 'Mrs. Robinson,' the two songs I told Evan I liked. They also play 'Bit Part' and I'm so happy because Tameka lights up when she hears it and sings her little heart out. Prom is not even a thought in my mind as I'm lost in the music and energy of the crowd.

Chapter 55

Sloane

By the time the show is over, Tameka and I are exhausted. It's hot, it's humid, and while The Lemonheads aren't really music to mosh to, people were doing just that. We head back to our blanket and cooler which are untouched and gather them. "Do you want to go back and hang out by the lake?" I ask Tameka as I watch the crowd moving en masse to the exit.

"Sure," she says as we head toward the lake. "We can hang out until the crowd thins out and maybe we'll see Evan again."

I smile. "You're reading my mind."

We stash our cooler and blanket under a bush and climb on top of large rocks and face the small lake. "That was such a great show," I say to Tameka.

"It was. I'm so glad I could come with you."

"Me, too," I say and am reminded that I'm not going home with my boyfriend to get ready for prom but will be hanging out with her tonight. I try to look on the bright side. "Even though I'm not going to my prom, I've had a great day. Thanks for coming to town for me." I lean over and bump my shoulder against hers.

"You bet," Tameka says as she bumps me back. "I'm sorry you're not going to your prom tonight."

"It's okay—" I'm interrupted by seeing Evan and the girls walking across the lawn. "Let's go." I hop off the rocks, and we head toward them.

Evan sees us, and his eyes light up. "Hey!"

"Hi," I say, a little breathless from hustling over to them. "The show was amazing."

"Yeah, you liked it?" He asks as he looks at me, sincerely interested in what I have to say. As we're walking, other people I don't recognize join us. They all have backstage passes, so I assume they are with the band.

"Yeah, it was so great. I was supposed to go to my prom tonight but couldn't, and it totally made up for it."

Evan stops and looks at me, causing me to stop walking, too. "When's your prom?"

Either he didn't hear me, or he's making sure he heard me right. "Tonight."

"Really?" he asks and cocks his head.

I don't know what comes over me, but the way he's looking at me and the way he just asked me that causes me to be bold, like Kurt suggested so many months ago. "You wanna go?"

"That would be cool," he says, his voice slow and easy. He continues walking and so do the rest of us.

Did he just say yes? Did this gorgeous rock star just say he would go to my prom with me? My heart starts to flutter.

"I don't know, Ev," a young man with fair skin and dark brown hair says. "You're supposed to go see INXS tonight."

My eyes are wide as I let out a breath I didn't know I was holding.

"Yeah," Ashley says as she grabs his arm and rubs his bicep, "you don't want to miss INXS."

We approach a barricade, and I realize this is the end of the line for Tameka and me because this appears to be the backstage area. There are trailers set-up for all the bands, and we're the only people in the group without passes. As the group walks through, a heavyset man with a shiny and sweaty bald head holds up a hand stopping me.

"They're with us," Nikki says as she flashes her beautiful smile at him.

The man nods and my heart leaps for joy as Tameka and I follow the group to The Lemonheads' trailer. I swear I have a hop in my step!

Inside the trailer, we meet Nic and Dave, Evan's bandmates who are just as friendly as Evan. I can't believe we're sitting here right now. We chat for a while, and Tameka strikes up a conversation with one of the members of the Judy Bats, another band on the bill. As I'm talking with everyone, I notice Evan looking at me and I wonder if he really will go to my prom with me. I smile at him, and he returns it with a smile of his own.

"Alright, we've got to get going," the young guy from before says. I found out that his name is Tod, and he is from the record label.

I stand up, and Evan does the same. "It was great seeing you again," he says and pulls me into a hug.

"Do you really have to go see INXS tonight?" I ask as he releases his hug. "I'd love to take you to my prom." I smile, giving it one more shot, deciding to take this bold thing all the way to the end.

He looks behind him to where Tod is standing in the back of the RV. "Hang on." He walks down the narrow hallway and goes to talk to him.

As I wait, I catch Ashley giving me a disapproving look, but I ignore her and talk to Dave about INXS. "So, what's the deal with the INXS show?" I ask.

He waves a hand at me. "Oh, we're on the same label, and they want us to go see them tonight."

"That's cool," I say. "I love them. I think I wore out my copy of Kick."

"Yeah, that's such a great album," he says before taking a sip out of his beer bottle.

Evan walks up to me and is smiling. "It's cool, I can go with you."

I feel my eyes double in size. "Really?"

Evan's eyes mimic mine, and his eyebrows arch up. "Yeah!" he nods. "Can you pick me up at my hotel, though?"

"Of course!" I say. "I'll just run home, clean up, and get dressed." My whole body feels like it's tingling with excited energy. My adrenaline is pumping.

"Cool. I'll try to find something nice to wear." He smiles. "Oh, here," he turns to the counter and grabs a pen and scrap of paper. "Write down your number so we have it just in case."

I scribble down my number and hand him the paper and pen then he tells me where to pick him up. "Okay, oh my gosh, this is amazing, thank you!" I give him a bear hug and wave goodbye to everyone as Tameka and I head out. I cannot believe this is happening. I'm about to go to prom after all, with a rock star on my arm!

Chapter 56

Sloane

Tameka and I race home and find my house empty. My mom and Bryn must be at the mall or running errands and my dad is at the lake this weekend. I shower as fast as I've ever showered, there's not even time to wash and dry my hair. When I get out of the shower, I hear the phone ring and pop my head out of the bathroom. "It's Evan," Tameka says as she holds the phone against her chest, covering the mouthpiece with her hand.

Holy cow, I can't believe Evan Dando is calling my house! I walk into my bedroom, and Tameka hands me the phone. "Hey," I say into the receiver.

"Hi," Evan says. "I don't think I'm going to be able to go..."

My heart drops into my stomach at these words. I have not come this far to get dumped for my prom a second time. "What do you mean? Why not?"

"Well, we can't find anything for me to wear. We couldn't rent a suit in time or anything."

I breathe a sigh of relief. "Oh, don't worry about that. You don't need to dress up." I am this close to taking Evan freaking Dando to my prom. I am not going to let this opportunity pass me by. Be bold, seize the day, life is short, take the bull by the horns, and all that stuff. This is the boldest I've ever been in my entire life. Who am I right now?

"Are you sure? Do you think they'll let us in?"

"Oh, they will let us in," I say, imagining myself busting past anyone who tries to stop me and Evan Dando from going to this dang dance. "I will make sure of it." I can tell he's hesitant, and I really don't want him to worry about what he's wearing. "Listen, I'll be in my dress, so one of us will be dressed up. It seriously won't be an issue."

"Okay, cool," Evan says, and I can hear the smile in his voice. "As long as you're sure, and you wear your dress."

"Absolutely," I tell him. "I can't wait to see you! We'll be there in about an hour."

With that, we hang up, and I get dressed, smooth out my hair with the blow dryer, and put on a bit of make-up. I honestly don't have time to fuss with anything right now.

"I can't believe you're ditching me tonight after I came all the way back from school to hang out with you," Tameka says, and I nearly drop the make-up brush in my hand.

She's standing in the doorway watching me get ready, and I can't tell if she's actually serious. "You're joking, right?"

She shakes her head. "No, I mean, I came home to hang out with you, and now you're going out."

I feel my eyes practically bulging out of my skull. "Tameka, you understand that I have the opportunity to not only go to my prom, but to go with Evan Dando. It's not like I decided I just didn't want to watch Johnny Depp movies with you all night. Heck, it's not like I decided I want to go to prom by myself." I can't believe she's doing this right now. My pulse is racing. She has to understand that, as my friend, she should be so happy for me, not thinking about the fact that she now has to spend a few hours by herself.

"Will you at least drop me off at Tech so I can hang out with my friend there?" She says as she crosses her arms across her chest, referring to the university in downtown Atlanta.

Is she seriously pouting? I take a breath. "Of course, I'll drop you off. No problem." I feel like a parent dealing with a petulant child, giving in to whatever she wants so I don't have to argue with her. There's no time for arguing, I've gotta leave as soon as possible, so I can make it to my darn prom. I force a smile still not believing that she can't see how selfish she's sounding right now. "You know I'm so grateful you came to town to see the show with me, right?"

"Yeah, of course," she says. "I'm going to go call my friend."

"Cool," I say as I put on a neutral eye shadow. "I'll be ready in about ten minutes."

***

Tameka was unable to get in touch with her friend, but makes me stop by a different friend's house on the way to see if he's there. I love her and am so glad she came back home to be with me, but she is starting to get on my nerves. I'm already late to prom and now I'm late to pick up Evan. Of course, said friend isn't home, so we go to Evan's hotel together where she will try calling the first friend again. When we get to Evan's hotel room and he answers the door, his smile melts me. "Hey," he says and as he sees Tameka behind me, his eyebrows arch in surprise.

"Hey," I say. "Tameka came with me because we're going to drop her off at a friend's on the way," I explain.

"Oh, cool." He opens the door and motions for us to come inside. "You look really nice."

"Thanks," I say and feel myself blush as I smooth a hand on the front of my red Jessica McClintock dress, hoping it's not sliding down my flat frame. "You look great, too."

This causes Evan to chuckle, and he has the cutest, goofiest chuckle. "It's the same thing I wore on stage today. I hope that's okay." He dips his head forward as he says this, like he feels bad. He's wearing dark green jeans, a T-shirt under a black sweater, and black Beatles-style boots. He looks perfect to me.

"Of course, it's okay. You look great." I noticed it was what he wore on stage, and I don't care one bit. He could be wearing jeans full of holes and a ratty sweatshirt, and I wouldn't care.

Tameka and I walk to the far side of the room where there are chairs in front of a large window. "Can I use your phone to call my friend?" she asks.

"Yeah, sure," Evan says. "I'm gonna finish getting ready."

As Evan busies himself in the bathroom, I have a thought as I watch Tameka waiting for her friend to pick up the phone. "Oh my gosh," I whisper, "I have to call my mom. I forgot to leave a note."

Tameka nods and after a couple of seconds, hangs up the phone. "He's not answering."

My heart sinks a little as I realize that this may be a three-person date because I can't just leave Tameka downtown by herself. I don't have time to worry about it, though, because I have to call my mom. I dial my home phone number, and my mom picks up on the first ring. "Hey!" I say into the phone.

"Hi! Are you going to prom?" My mom asks, and I can hear the confusion in her voice. She knows I would never go to prom by myself.

"Yeah," I say and proceed to tell her who I'm taking to my prom.

"Sloane, remember, he's a man, not a boy." My mom says as if this is the most scandalous thing in the world. "You don't even know him."

"Mom, you don't have to worry. Nothing weird is going to happen." I assure her, and I mean it. While Evan is practically a god among men, I'm seventeen and still a virgin. I'm not ready for that and not looking to hook up with anyone, especially a rock star who could have any woman he wants. Women much more beautiful and voluptuous than scrawny old me. "Besides," I add quietly, "Tameka is with me. I was going to drop her off at a friend's, but she couldn't get in touch with him."

"Okay," my mom says, and her voice sounds more relaxed. "Please just be careful."

"I will," I promise her, and I mean it. "Can my curfew be a little later tonight?" I might be pushing my luck because my curfew is normally midnight, but this is certainly a special occasion.

I hear my mom sigh through the phone. "Okay, your curfew can be one a.m., but promise me you'll be careful."

A smile immediately grows across my face, "Thanks, mom! I appreciate it." I lower my voice again, "And don't worry, I'm not going to do anything stupid." It's funny that my mom is worrying because I'm probably the last girl on Earth who would do what she's worried about.

I hang up with my mom just as Evan comes out of the bathroom. "Are you ready to go?" he asks.

"Yep," I smile. Heck, I don't think I've stopped smiling since we got here. "Uh, Tameka couldn't get in touch with her friend, so she's going to ride with us and hang out in the lobby while we're in the dance." I feel like such a heel having my friend tagging along, but what am I supposed to do at this point?

"Okay," Evan says and doesn't seem bothered by it.

Now that we're on our way to the prom, I can't believe this is actually happening!

Chapter 57

Sloane

We arrive at the ballroom on the second floor of the Hyatt Regency Hotel, and who do I immediately see? None other than Dave, my first kiss and the boy who compared girls to shoes. Standing with Dave is Tracy, a sweet girl whose parents were clients of my mom's. "Hey," I say to Tracy and Dave. "This is Evan."

Evan holds up a hand in a wave. "Hi."

I am not sure if Dave and Tracy know who Evan is, but he is so gorgeous and has such star quality, even if you don't recognize him, you know he's someone, and he's definitely not a high school senior. "Hi," Tracy says, and I imagine that my face looks just as happy and sparkly when I look at Evan as hers does right now.

I explain to them that Evan is worried they won't let us in with him dressed how he is and Dave says, "Here, take my jacket." He slips off his tuxedo jacket and hands it to Evan.

"Are you sure?" Evan asks as he takes the black jacket.

"Yeah, we'll come in behind you, and I'll get it from you." Dave is smiling and eager to help.

"Thanks," I say as Evan slides his arms into the jacket, then takes my hand. "Ready?" I ask him. He nods, and we stride toward the ballroom doors with purpose. Of course, no one even stops us, not even to take my money for the tickets I haven't paid for. It's so late that no one is manning the doors anymore. I look up at him and smile brightly, "See? I told you I'd get us in."

He chuckles, and his mouth turns up into a smile. He gives my hand a squeeze as we head into the ballroom.

***

As we walk into the room, I'm surprised at what I see. I guess I had built up the idea of prom so much and watched enough teen movies to expect it to be an extravagantly decorated affair. It's not. There's a hand-painted banner of the Atlanta skyline behind the DJ and a few bunches of balloons scattered around, but that's it. There's really nothing special about it, except for the date on my arm. I turn to look for Tracy and Dave, and Evan turns with me. I see them heading our way and wave. "Thanks so much," I tell Dave as Evan releases my hand and slides the jacket off.

"You bet," Dave says with a wink.

"Yeah, thanks, man," Evan says as he hands Dave's jacket back to him. He takes my hand again. "Let's go dance!"

I wave at Tracy and Dave, "Bye!"

As we near the dance floor, I see Kurt and Shelly. "Ooh, we have to say hi to my friend, Kurt. He's a big fan-," I stop myself. "Oh, if that's okay?"

Evan smiles at me, "Sure, yeah."

Kurt's back is to me, and I tap him on the shoulder. He spins around and at first looks shocked to see me, then blurts out, "Holy crap, it's Evan Dando!"

I can't help but laugh. I turn to Evan. "This is my good friend Kurt and his girlfriend, Shelly."

Evan holds out his hand, first to Shelly, then to Kurt. "Hey, nice to meet you."

"Oh my gosh, it's great meeting you." Kurt shakes Evan's hand with such enthusiasm, I'm afraid he might yank his arm right out of socket. Once he lets go, he looks at me. "How did you two..." he points to me then Evan.

"She told me her date backed out and asked if I wanted to come," Evan says as if it's no big deal.

I don't think Kurt's mouth has closed since we walked up. It's just hanging open in awe. "I had to make sure to introduce you," I tell him. "But we just got here so we're gonna go dance."

"Uh, yeah, you kids have fun," Kurt jokes as Evan grabs my hand again. "Nice meeting you."

"You, too," Evan says with a wave, then leads me to the dance floor.

I spot Tyler and Sara across the room. I'm about to tell Evan that I want to introduce him to one last person, but I realize that Tyler and Sara look serious, like perhaps they are arguing. Tyler's stature is rigid and his arms are folded across his chest as Sara talks with her hands. Yeah, we're not going to interrupt whatever is going on over there.

I'm generally a self-conscious person in front of groups of people, especially when it comes to dancing, but as we reach the dance floor, I feel like Evan and I are the only people in this hotel ballroom. It helps that Prince's 'Raspberry Beret' is playing because I love this song. I haven't stopped smiling since I picked up Evan, and I love seeing that he's smiling, too. We move to the quick beat, hopping and shaking without a care in the world. When Prince's song comes to an end, the DJ fades it out and the recognizable notes of Eric Clapton's guitar plucking fill the room. 'Tears in Heaven' begins playing, and while it's a terribly sad song, I'm thrilled that it's a slow song, partly because I'm not the best fast dancer, but also because I want to slow dance with the most handsome guy at prom.

As Evan takes my right hand in his left, I rest my left hand on his shoulder. Heat runs through me as my nerves and awkwardness start to get the best of me. I silently pray that my deodorant holds up. I think the last time I danced with a boy was at my cousin's wedding two years ago and that boy wasn't a gorgeous rock star.

Evan seems to notice my nerves and smiles sweetly, "This is kind of a weird song to play at a prom, huh?"

My nerves immediately disappear as I laugh. "Yeah, I was thinking the same thing."

Evan pulls me closer, and I rest my chin on his shoulder. I'm lost in the moment and just before the song ends, my gaze is pulled to the lobby beyond the ballroom doors.

"Oh, my gosh! My mom is here." I see my mom and Bryn scanning the crowd. I can't believe it.

"Really?" Evan says as he turns to look. "Cool, I'd love to meet her."

Could he be any sweeter? "Yeah?" I ask.

"Totally," he says as he takes my hand and leads me toward the doors.

Evan Dando just might be the nicest person I've ever met.

Chapter 58

Sloane

When we walk out of the dimly lit ballroom, the corridor feels so bright and busy. There are people milling about, probably because they have been here a lot longer than we have. My mom sees us, and I smile. "Hi! What are y'all doing down here?"

"I didn't want to disturb you, but I also wanted to make sure I got some pictures," my mom holds up one of the many cameras we have in the house on account of my dad being a regional manager for a major camera company.

If one could die of embarrassment, I'm surprised there is still breath in my lungs. However, Evan seems sincerely happy to meet my mom, so my embarrassment quickly fades.

My mom extends her hand to Evan, "I'm Louise," then gestures to Bryn, "and I guess you've already met Bryn."

"Yeah, hi!" Evan says as he shakes my mom's hand and flashes Bryn a beautiful smile then says to her, "Good to see you again."

"You, too," Bryn says. Even though she's nervous around men who she doesn't know well and people in general, I can tell by the happiness on her face that Evan has the same effect on her that he does the rest of us.

"Is it okay if I get a couple of pictures?" my mom asks Evan.

"Sure, yeah, of course," Evan says as he nods his head. I love his slightly goofy countenance, it reminds me of a golden retriever, happy, sweet, and eager to please.

"Are you sure that's okay?" I ask quietly.

"Absolutely," he says as he squeezes my hand that he's still holding.

We pose for my mom, and thankfully, she really only does take a couple of pictures. "Oh, there's Miranda." I look at Evan, "She's my best friend from childhood and the one who introduced me to your music. Can we get a picture with her?"

"Yeah, cool," he says, and we walk over to where Miranda is talking to Tameka.

After I do the introductions, and my mom snaps a couple of pictures, she says, "Are you two going to get a professional picture?"

Not wanting to put Evan out, I'm about to say no when he says, "Yeah, we should do that." He looks genuinely excited to take a professional prom picture with me.

Thank you, mom! I never would have asked Evan to do that, so my mom turning up is definitely a good thing.

Miranda is on the prom committee and explains, "There are two backgrounds, and there's a long line for the good background." She points to the line I didn't even realize was there, and when I finally look around, I notice that all eyes are on us. Even if they don't recognize my date, Evan is definitely someone who stands out. "And the bad background is over there. It's mostly for large group pictures."

I look at the line, "That could take forever," I look at Evan, "let's go look at the 'bad background' and see what it looks like."

"Good idea," he says, and now we have a small entourage composed of my mom, Bryn, Tameka, and Miranda, following us to the photo area.

When we walk into the room, I see a small group of people by the "bad background" which is solid blue with fake dogwood trees situated atop a piece of green astroturf and ferns at the base of each tree. "Well, that's not bad," I say.

Miranda points to the "good background." "That's the background the long line is for."

I take in the background which is a really cheesy airbrushed nighttime scene in shades of gray and purple with a full moon glowing in the starry sky. "That's the 'good background?'"

"Yeah," Miranda says.

I turn to Evan, "I think that's pretty ugly, don't you?"

He nods his head. "Yeah, the 'bad background' is way better."

This makes me laugh. "The bad background it is, then!"

When we walk over to the short line, we see Tracy and Dave again. "Hey guys!" I say as we approach them. "Is this the line?"

Tracy says, "We've already taken our picture. I don't think anyone is waiting ahead of you."

"Oh, even better!"

Dave says, "Evan, do you want to borrow my jacket again?"

"Oh, yeah, that would be cool," Evan says.

Dave slips off his jacket and then says, "Here, you can have my vest, tie, and cummerbund, too." He tilts his chin up and starts unfastening his clip-on bow tie.

"Great, man, thanks," Evan says, and I can tell that he's sincerely appreciative of this gesture.

"No problem," Dave says as he takes off each piece.

Evan takes off his sweater, revealing his white T-shirt which I now see has a faded design on it. "Here, I'll hold that," my mom says and holds her hand out for Evan's sweater.

Dave helps Evan with the bow tie and cummerbund, then Evan slips the vest over his shoulders, and finally, puts the black jacket on. He looks at me, "How do I look?"

"Great!" I smile, "but you looked great to begin with so..." While Dave isn't as tall as Evan, he's only a couple inches shorter, so the jacket fits him pretty well.

"But now I'll look all proper for the picture." He smiles as he holds the jacket lapels in his hands and raises his chin, giving me a dignified look.

Could he be any cuter and sweeter? See what I mean about the golden retriever comparison? He really is going above and beyond for me, and I wonder if he'll ever know just how much this night means to me.

"Are y'all ready?" I look up and see the photographer looking our way.

"Yep, all set," I reply, and Evan and I step in front of the camera.

"Stand right in the center of the trees," the photographer says as he motions with his hand for us to move to our left. "There, perfect."

"Fix my hair how you want it," Evan says.

I look at that gorgeous brown mane of hair and wonder how anyone could make it look any better. I pat down some stray frizzy pieces. "There, it looks good." I look across the room and notice that everyone waiting for their picture at the "good background" is watching us, and dead center is none other than Amber Gates looking like she just sucked on a lemon.

Evan slides his left arm around my waist and pulls me close. I instinctively put my right arm around his lower back. His right hand goes to my left waist, and I place my left hand on his forearm as the photographer looks up, "Okay, so you'll..." he realizes we're already posing for him. "Great, yeah, you know what you're doing." I imagine with all the press Evan has had recently, including several magazine covers, he must look like a natural to a photographer who has had to direct awkward teens posing all night. He steps back behind the camera as Evan pulls me even closer, so that the sides of our faces are touching. I am so glad my mom came down here, because I can't wait to see how this picture turns out!

Chapter 59

Sloane

We head back into the ballroom after giving Dave half his tux back and saying goodbye to my mom and Bryn. Of course, it's a fast song, but Evan is so enthusiastic about dancing that it must be rubbing off on me and I don't feel half as awkward as I normally would. He's flailing his arms in such an exaggerated way, I say, "You look like a cheerleader!"

He laughs and starts imitating a cheerleader on the dance floor. Of course, he manages to make that look adorable and cool all at the same time. When the song ends, he says, "Do you want to get some punch?"

"Yeah, I am pretty thirsty."

Evan takes my hand, and we go to the food and beverage stations. "Oh, no. No punch." He lifts up the ladle in the empty punch bowl.

I look around. "Well, there's fruit."

"And these things," he says as he picks up some sort of finger food wrapped in pastry then takes a bite.

"How is it?"

He shakes his head and says, "Not very good."

His disappointed expression makes me giggle as I go for the cantaloupe, and Evan joins me. "This isn't bad."

"It's really good," he says as he moves from the cantaloupe to a large piece of watermelon. He takes a bite, "Ooh, this is better." He feeds me a piece of watermelon, and as he does so, a seed falls to the floor and I hop back so it doesn't land on my dress. Evan chuckles that adorable, goofy chuckle. "That would make a great dance." He starts imitating my backwards hop while he holds his large watermelon slice in one hand.

I take another bite of cantaloupe, then say, "Yeah, that watermelon is much better. Maybe it's because I'm thirsty."

"Here," Evan offers me another bite of watermelon.

"So good," I say through a juicy mouthful.

I see Maggie, Beth, and Annalise heading our way with their dates and wave to them. "Hey!" I say as they join us.

"We were so excited to see you two here," Beth says, and I notice my three friends also have the same blissful expression Tracy had as they look at Evan.

"Evan, these are my friends, Maggie, Beth, and Annalise, and their dates."

"Nice to meet you," Evan says with a wave of his left hand, the half-eaten watermelon slice in his right hand.

"We can't wait to hear this whole story on Monday," Annalise says with a smile as she waves her hand between me and Evan.

"Yeah," Maggie smiles sweetly. "Thanks for bringing Sloane to her prom."

We chat for a bit, then my friends wave and head back to the dance floor.

"They seem nice," Evan says then takes another bite of watermelon.

"They are. I was supposed to do the whole limo, restaurant, prom thing with them, but my boyfriend canceled on me ten days ago."

Evan regards me with confusion. "Really?"

I nod. "But I don't want to talk about that because this night is way better than it would have been with him."

Evan laughs. "I'm glad." He offers me another bite of watermelon which I accept.

I look at Evan and smile. "What do you think? Are you ready to blow this popsicle stand?"

Evan laughs. "Sure, yeah. This has been fun. I've had a really great time."

My heart clenches with gratitude upon hearing this. "I'm so glad," I say and can't contain my smile. "Thanks so much for coming with me." I can't believe he's so nice and kind. And, I think he really did have a good time taking me to my prom.

As we make our way out of the doors, we notice two huge bunches of balloons that I had somehow not paid attention to before. Evan takes my hand, and we bust through them then burst into giggles.

"I really do hope you had fun," I say.

"I totally did. Thank you for asking me to come with you." He gives my hand a squeeze, and he looks genuinely happy.

We keep walking and see Tameka wave at us. It's the person standing next to her who makes my heart flutter.

I can't contain my smile. "Hey." My smile is returned. "Tyler, this is Evan."

Evan is still holding my right hand with his left and extends his right hand. "Hi, nice to meet you."

I didn't think Tyler could look any hotter, but here he is, standing in front of me in a tuxedo. "Thanks for bringing Sloane tonight, that's really cool of you."

"Yeah," I smile up at Evan, "I'm so grateful for him."

"How could she not have a date to her prom?" Evan says to Tyler. "I had to set the universe right." He smiles at me and I'm overcome by his kindness and generosity.

"My dad was right," I say to them, "When God closes a door, He opens a window." I never thought I'd look back at Ky standing me up for prom as a good thing, but boy, this turned out better than I could have ever dreamed. Evan squeezes my hand, and I'm on cloud nine.

***

Tameka and I take Evan back to his hotel, and I'm so glad I brought a change of clothes because I'm much comfier in the jeans and T-shirt I changed into before we left prom. Evan picks up his guitar and plays 'Being Around' and 'My Drug Buddy.' I always love watching performers' hands when they play guitar and am mesmerized by Evan's playing and singing. I should learn to play guitar, I think to myself.

We chat for a bit, and he tells us about life on the road and some of his favorite places to visit in the U.S. "I do like Atlanta," he says. "You have really cool skyscrapers here."

The phone rings, and he leans back on his bed and picks it up. "Hello?" There's a pause as someone talks. "Oh, okay. Yeah, sure, come on up." He hangs up and is facing us again. "It's the two girls from earlier. They're coming up."

"Oh, cool," I say and glance at Tameka who rolls her eyes, and I have to stifle a laugh. Nikki is so cool, but Ashley is kind of rude. I don't really want to hang out with her. She'll probably just trivialize my prom, and this night has been so good.

There's a knock at the door, and Evan sets his guitar down to go answer it. I whisper to Tameka, "Do you want to get going?"

"Yeah," she nods. She's still in her jean shorts and T-shirt from the concert and I'm sure she's ready to go home.

Nikki and Ashley walk into the room and take a seat on Evan's bed since Tameka and I are in the two chairs in front of the windows. "Hey," Nikki says. Her eyes shine bright and she smiles wide. "How was prom?"

I return her smile. "It was so great." Since I don't want to open the door to Ashley's rudeness, I say, "How was INXS?"

"They were amazing!" Nikki gushes.

Ashley looks at Evan who is still standing. "You really missed a great show."

Evan looks at me, "Nah, I didn't. We had a great time. I'll have plenty of opportunities to see INXS in concert again. Sloane only gets one prom, and we had a blast."

My heart swells as I smile at him. "We did."

Tameka stands up, "Well, we should get going."

I stand, too, "Yeah," I agree, even though I don't want this night to end.

"I'll walk you out," Evan says to me.

As I follow him, Nikki says, "Tameka, did you go to prom with them?" I'm so grateful that Nikki strikes up a conversation with Tameka so I can say goodbye to Evan alone. I wonder if she did that on purpose?

I hear Tameka explaining why she ended up with us all night as Evan and I go out into the hallway. I smile up at him. "I had so much fun. Thank you for taking me to my prom."

Evan smiles softly. "I had fun, too. Thanks for inviting me." He pulls a slip of paper out of his pocket. "Here's my address. Keep in touch."

I look at the paper and smile at him again. "I will, thanks."

Evan gives me a big hug and then kisses me on my cheek. I know I will never forget this day and I hope I'll get to see him again someday.

***

When I get home, I go straight to my parent's bedroom where my mom is watching television and tell her all about our night. My dad is out of town, and my mom tells me the story of her night.

"Bryn and I got home from shopping, and she saw your dress bag and shoe box out. She came downstairs and told me that she thought you went to prom." She smiles at me. "I knew you wouldn't go by yourself."

I shake my head. "No way, that would have been lame. I'm sorry I didn't leave a note. I was rushing to get ready and get down there. I totally forgot."

My mom smiles at me. "It's okay. I'm glad you called." She gives me a puzzled look. "Why did Tameka go with you?"

I groan. "Oh my gosh, I was so embarrassed!" I explain to her Tameka's plan to hang out with friends that didn't pan out.

"Do you think she just wanted to tag along and be part of this night?" my mom asks genuinely.

I think about it and shrug. "Maybe. I hadn't thought about it, but I could see her doing that. When there were no friends to take her to, I had to bring her with us. I hope Evan didn't think I was totally lame."

My mom smiles sweetly. "I thought about telling her to come home with Bryn and I, but I didn't want to overstep."

"Oh, man, you totally should have! I didn't even think about that." I fling myself back on her bed. "Oh well." I lean onto my side and prop my head on my left hand. "She definitely made for a good chaperone," I half-joke.

"That was my second thought," my mom admits with a twinkle in her eye.

"Well, it was a perfect night," I say as I sit up again. "At first I was embarrassed to see you and Bryn, but I'm so glad you came and took pictures. I never would have asked Evan to pose for the official prom picture, so thanks for that."

"See, your old mom is pretty smart," my very youthful and beautiful mom says.

"Evan was excited to meet you, too," I add.

"I'm glad he took you, honey. You deserve it."

"Thanks, mom." I give her a hug and hop off her bed. "I'm going to go write all this down so I don't forget it." I'm so energized, I don't know how I'll go to sleep, but I practically skip to my room to write down everything I can remember about this magical night.

Chapter 60

Sloane

When I get to school on Monday, I can't wait to fill Kurt in on everything, and I suspect that's the reason he's there earlier than me for a change. "Hey!" I smile when I see his eager expression.

"Oh my gosh, you have to tell me how the heck you got Evan Dando to come to prom!"

I chuckle as I sit in my seat, dropping my backpack to the floor. I fill Kurt in on everything, and he is hanging on my every word. When I'm done, he sits back in his chair and runs his hand through his dark hair. "Too bad about Tameka tagging along."

"I was embarrassed at first because I didn't want Evan to think I was scared to be with him alone, but he was cool about it," I say as I open my backpack and fish out my French book and notebook. "My mom said she thought about taking her home, but didn't say anything." I pause, then laugh, "I think my mom was worried Evan might try something if I was by myself."

Kurt gets a pained look on his face. "Yeah, about that..." I cock my head to the side, trying to figure out what he means. I look at him and narrow my eyes as he leans in and quietly says, "Amber is telling people that you slept with him and that's why he went to prom with you."

I lean back in surprise. My eyes involuntarily open as far as they can. "What?!" I say a little too loud, then lean toward him again. "I did *not* sleep with Evan. I haven't slept with *anyone*!" I practically hiss.

"I didn't think you would have," Kurt says with sympathetic eyes.

"How would *she* even know anyway? It's not like we're friends, or I would have confided in her." My blood boils, and my heart races. "Besides, just because she would do something like that, doesn't mean I would." I'm so angry. I feel like I could spit nails. "That's probably the reason I've never been asked to a dance, because I *don't* do that!" I cannot believe this. I have an amazing thing happen to me, and this popular cheerleader is trying to soil a perfectly sweet night.

"I'm sorry to upset you," Kurt says, "but I thought you'd want to know."

"No, I do, thank you," I assure him. "I really appreciate your friendship." Just then Amber walks into the room, and I can't even look at her, so I busy myself by doodling in my notebook.

"Bonjour classe!" Madame Carney says as she walks into the room and shuts the door behind her as the bell rings. She walks to the front of the room. Her face alight with a smile. *"J'espère que vous avez passé un excellent week-end!"* I wonder if Madame Carney knows how excellent my weekend was, but I don't have to wonder for long because she adds, *"Sloane, parlez-nous de votre week-end."* She looks so giddy as she tells me to tell the class about my weekend.

I start off speaking French, but mercifully, she says, *"C'est bon,"* she waves her hand. *"En anglais."* Thank God, I can tell the story in English.

I give the very abbreviated version of this rather long story and pointedly look at Amber when I say, "Apparently there are some rumors spreading about how I got Evan to go to prom with me, but he was a complete gentleman."

Amber shifts uncomfortably in her chair. The old me would have left it at that, but I've had about all I can take, so I decide to be bold again. "Amber, I would really appreciate it if you would stop telling people that I slept with my prom date, because that couldn't be further from the truth. It may be hard for you to believe, but sometimes people are just good and want to do something nice for someone else with no strings attached."

Amber's face turns red, and her mouth is agape. I catch Ramsey out of my right eye, and she gives me a big smile and a wink. I smile and lean back, finally taking a breath as I see Kurt's proud face immediately to my right.

Madame Carney pretends like she didn't hear that last part. "That's so wonderful, Sloane! You deserve that. You are such a good person, and I'm so glad Evan was able to take you to your prom."

Take that, stupid Amber Gates. Sometimes, nice girls finish first!

Chapter 61

Sloane

When I get home from school, I'm still on cloud nine and feel like I've told my prom story a hundred times. I'm working on homework in my dad's office when the phone rings. "Hi sweetie," my mom says as she walks into the office.

"Hey," I say. "I didn't realize you were home."

"I just got in," my mom says, and she's smiling. "I can't wait to hear how it went at school, but the phone's for you. It's a man named James from Atlantic Records."

"Really?" I say as I sit up straight in my dad's office chair. "That's The Lemonheads' record label!"

"I figured," she winks. "Pick up, see what he wants."

My mom closes the door behind her as I pick up the phone. "Hello?"

"Hey Sloane, this is James from Atlantic Records."

"Hi, how are you?"

"Great! I heard about your amazing prom date with Evan and just wanted to get the full story," James says through the phone.

I tell the story for the 101st time today, and of course, include that Evan was a gentleman, hoping everyone understands what I mean by that. It may sound silly, but that's important to me.

"That's so cool," James says. "Evan's a good guy. Do you have any pictures you could send me?"

"Yeah, my mom took a few that we should get developed soon, and we took a professional prom picture which I should get in a week or so, I think." I have no idea how long those pictures take to come back since I've never been to a dance.

"That's great, I'll send you a FedEx envelope so you can send me what you've got."

"Okay, sounds good."

"The press might be interested in this. Is it okay if we give your number to people who want to do a story?"

"Of course," I reply. Gosh, this is all happening so fast. I wonder who might want to do a story on this?

"Great! I'll be in touch and look forward to getting those pictures."

"You bet, thanks," I say before hanging up the phone. My mind starts turning with all the possibilities of what may happen next, and then I think of Evan. I hope he will be okay with me talking to press and sending our pictures to his record label. I have no way to get in touch with him to ask him, other than the address he sent me to a post office box. Since he's on tour, there's no telling when he'll see a letter.

My mom knocks softly, then opens the door. "Hey! He sounded nice. What did he have to say?" The light glimmers in her excited blue eyes.

"Yeah, he was nice. He just wanted to hear the prom story and asked if I could send pictures to him. He's going to send a FedEx envelope. He also said that the press might be interested in the story, so we may get some calls."

"Wow!" My mom says, her eyes still sparkling, and I can tell she's holding something behind her back.

I lean to my right, trying to peek around her. "What do you have?"

My mom whips her hand out, and she's holding a black envelope with Wolf Camera written across the front. "You got the pictures developed?" I hop up, so excited to see them.

She hands me the envelope. "Don't tell your dad that I got these developed before we finished the roll." She winks at me. "And, I paid more for the next day prints because I couldn't wait any longer."

It's cute to see how excited my mom is. I open the envelope and flip through the pictures and my heart speeds up. "Oh my gosh, these are so good!" There are two of me and Evan that look really good, two of me and Evan with Miranda and Tameka, and a couple of candid shots when we were helping Evan get Dave's tux jacket and everything on. I look at my mom as excitement courses through my veins. I give her a bear hug. "Thank you! These are great! I'm so glad you came down there and brought a camera."

"See, I'm pretty smart, huh?"

"You're the best!" I tell her and mean it. I think she's relieved to see me so happy after I was so sad that Ky backed out right before prom, and she knows that high school hasn't been easy for me.

"Don't stare at those too long," my mom says as she heads toward the door. "You've got to get that homework done."

"I won't," I say as I feel my cheeks burn.

"Oh," my mom turns back. "How could I forget? The newspaper called today for a quote." She points to the answering machine. "They left a message and said they would call back. They didn't leave a number."

"Oh, wow, okay," I say, and I can't believe so many people are interested in this story. "Thanks, mom."

My mom turns back to the door, and as I hear the soft click of the door close behind her, I sit back in the chair and look through the pictures. I know the grin on my face must be goofy, but I don't care. Evan and I look good together, and I still can't believe I took him to my prom!

I'm finishing up my homework for the evening and look at the clock. It's six o'clock, and as if my stomach knows, it growls. As I'm stuffing my books into my backpack, the phone rings, and I pick it up. "Hello?"

"Hi, can I speak with Sloane?" A woman's voice says through the phone.

"This is she."

"Hey, Sloane, this is Alex from Sassy Magazine. I heard about your prom story from James over at Atlantic and wanted to see if you had a few moments to chat."

Oh my gosh, Sassy Magazine! Sassy is the cool girl's magazine which eschews all the fluff and vanity, talks about real issues, and, of course, covers cool music. It's well-known that they are fans of Evan Dando. "Hi, uh, yeah I have time to chat." I hope dinner isn't quite ready.

"Great! So, you must tell me, how in the world did you get Evan Dando to go to your prom?"

For the 102nd time today, I tell the story. I'd gotten it down to an abbreviated version even though there are so many details.

"Wow, that's so cool!" Alex gushes. "You are so bold. I love it! Our readers are going to swoon over this story. You know they love Evan as much as we do."

I smile. "Yeah, he's pretty great, and he was a complete gentleman. I couldn't have asked for a better prom date."

"I love hearing that. Well, I'll let you get going. We'll probably run this in the September issue as we work a few months ahead. I'll let you know when it's scheduled to run."

"That's awesome, thanks so much!"

Alex and I say goodbye, and I steal one more glance at the pictures my mom took. How did a dreamy rock star agree to go to prom with me? I feel like I'm the main character in a John Hughes movie.

Chapter 62

Sloane

A week after the dance, I think I've finally come down from my prom high, but it's about to ramp back up. When I get to school, I find out the prom pictures are ready and in the cafeteria. I look at my watch. I have plenty of time, and if I don't get my pictures before the day starts, I'm going to have to wait until lunch period, and I can't wait a moment longer! I've got to see how this picture turned out.

When I walk into the cafeteria, there are students going in and out. Pictures are at various tables alphabetically by last name. I walk to the furthest table and search through the photos briefly before finding mine. "Oh my gosh," I say quietly. My jaw drops open, and I look at the 8x10 picture of Evan and me through the plastic sleeve.

"Nice lookin' couple," I hear the familiar voice behind my shoulder.

I turn around and see Billy, and my smile grows. "Isn't this the best?" I can't contain my excitement as I show him my picture.

"That guy is a total pro," Billy says. "Look how he's standing all cool and look at that face. The man knows how to pose."

"This has to be the sexiest prom photo ever," I reply.

"Now, don't speak so fast there, Sloaner," Billy jokes. "You haven't seen mine yet." He holds up his plastic sleeve containing his pictures.

I look at Billy's picture with his date. His flat-top haircut covered by his black cowboy hat, ruddy cheeks, and proud smile make me happy. "This is true. Evan does have some competition," I joke back. "Must be all those covers of GQ you've been on."

I make Billy laugh hard at this. He pats his little belly. "Yeah, right!"

We head toward the exit and into the main hallway near the front doors. "What's up, you two?" Billy and I turn as Tyler joins us, and even though he has the sweetest girlfriend, and I just took a rock star to my prom, the butterflies flutter at the sight of that wicked little grin of his. He sidles up to me. His shoulder touches mine which causes a spark of electricity to run through me and looks at my prom picture. "Look at that man," he says as he points to Evan. "Even I will admit he looks hot."

I look up at him, and he has a look on his face that I can't quite decipher. "Have you gotten your pictures yet?"

Tyler shifts uncomfortably, his jaw clenches ever so slightly, as he tugs on his backpack straps. "Nah, I'll leave that to Sara." I think back to when I saw them at prom, something I had completely forgotten about, and wonder if everything's okay between them.

"Hers may be great, but you can't beat this." Billy holds his plastic sleeve in front of Tyler.

Tyler cocks his head and nods. "That's pretty fresh, man. I love the black hat and boots."

"Why thank you, kind sir," Billy says with an Old West accent and mimes straightening his non-existent tie.

"The slickest dude at prom," Tyler says, and I can't help but think he's not 100% into this conversation.

Billy and I laugh audibly at this, and Billy says, "Well, I wouldn't go that far." He holds his hands up in front of him. "I'm just really happy for our little Sloaner-loner. Her first ever high school dance, and she shoots for the moon."

Tyler smiles slightly then his face grows serious. "Yeah, I was pretty upset when you told us about Ky. I couldn't believe he did that to you. We knew you were so excited for prom."

"I thought for sure you guys would think that I made him up, just like Amber teased me about," I look down at my picture. "But, boy, did this work out for the best." My smile returns in full, but I swear Tyler's smile seems forced.

"No way, Sloaner," Billy says as the three of us start walking down the hallway. "We know you wouldn't do that."

"Yeah," Tyler agrees, "Ky obviously doesn't know a good thing when he's got it." He jokingly punches me in the shoulder as the bell rings and the smile he gives me makes my stomach tumble over itself. Tyler looks at Billy. "See you at the game today?" He says as he breaks off from us, walking the other direction.

"I'll be there!" Billy says. "Wouldn't miss it."

Tyler gives him a salute then turns and walks away.

"What's so special about today's game?" I ask Billy.

Billy eyes me suspiciously then says, "If I tell you, you can't say a word to anyone."

I feel my eyes go wide as I nod my head. "Promise, I won't say anything."

"A scout from the Braves is going to be at the game today."

Now my eyes feel like they are popping out of my skull. "What? That's amazing!"

"It is, but you've gotta keep this between us."

"Of course," I nod. "But, how did you find out about it?"

"I went back to class to ask Coach K a question and walked in on him discussing it with Tyler." Billy looks as if he's just had a thought. "You should come to the game today and help me cheer them on. The scout will be looking at several players, I'm sure. I think they'd appreciate the support."

I smile. "I'd love that. I haven't been to a game in a while and went to practically all the home games last year. I'll come find you."

As I head to French class, I think about watching Tyler play today, then think about what he said before he left, that Ky didn't know a good thing when he had it. I can't help but wonder if it took a rock star taking me to prom to show my fellow classmates that I am, in fact, a catch. For the first time in all my years here, I walk to class with my shoulders back and head held high.

Chapter 63

Tyler

"The stands are getting full," Brian ducks into the dugout, a smile wide across his face.

"That's awesome, hopefully that'll give the scout a good first impression, but we need to be on our game today." I tighten the laces on my glove. I stand and walk onto the field, scanning the crowd on the metal bleachers.

Brian walks back out and stands next to me. "Which one do you think he is?"

I shrug. "I don't know. He may not even be here yet." Just then, I see Sara, Amber, and Lori walk toward the bleachers, scanning them for a seat and feel my jaw tighten.

Brian squeezes my shoulder. "Come on, let's do some stretching."

I follow Brian back into the dugout where we each put a foot on the bench to stretch our legs.

"You were right about that guy Sloane took to prom," Brian says and I know he's trying to keep my mind off the magnitude of today's game. "Dude does look like he could be a model." When I don't say anything, he adds, "It was nice of him to take her after her boyfriend backed out on her."

"It totally was," I switch legs. While Brian got my mind off of stressing about the scout, now I'm thinking about Sloane and her hot rock star prom date.

"I know you were otherwise engaged that night," Brian says, "but you should have seen Amber and Lori's faces when she showed up with him. I need to check my footage to see if I caught it on camera. It was priceless."

This makes me chuckle. "Serves them right. I hope you did catch it. I'd love to see it." I pull my leg off the bench and start stretching my shoulders. "When do you think you'll have all the editing done?"

Brian grins. "Probably a couple of weeks after graduation. It's been too busy lately." He stands and twists from side to side, loosening his torso. "I'll definitely get it done before we head off to Southern."

"You better. That gives you all summer," I joke.

"Alright," Coach K joins us in the dugout with his ever-present clipboard. "I can't believe it's the last game of the season. While we didn't make it to the playoffs, we've had a great season. I've seen so much growth and this is a young team. I know we'll be even stronger next year." Coach looks at where I'm sitting with my fellow seniors, Brian, Andre, and Travis. "We've got some incredible seniors on this team, so I want you all to play for them. Send them off with a W." Coach walks to the middle of the dugout. "I want you to play today's game like any other. Yes, we have a scout here, but don't let that get into your heads. While he might be here to watch a certain player or players, he's going to be watching all of you. Do your best for yourselves and for your teammates. We shine brightest when we shine together. Got it?"

"Yes, Coach!" We shout.

"Okay. I'm done being sappy. Go out there and have fun. It's just a game. Play with the exuberance of a child, and the skill of a varsity baseball player."

***

Brian's arm is on fire today and he is in the zone. He's already struck out five guys and we're in the top of the fifth. As for me, I've had a double and a walk. Plus, I've caught everything that has come my way in the outfield, which hasn't been much due to Brian's pitching. We're winning 3-0 because our guys have been getting hit after hit. No homers yet, but it's like we're all in the zone.

Brian struck out the first batter this inning, and the second grounded out. The third batter for the Raiders has a full count, 3 balls and 2 strikes. Brian winds up and his sixth pitch just misses and the batter makes contact. I hear the ping and follow the ball which is headed my way. It bounces into the outfield just short of me. I catch the ball and see that the batter is trying for a double and throw to second from centerfield. My throw is dead-on and Josh catches it just before the runner slides. Josh tags the runner out and we jog into the dugout.

"Thanks, my man," Brian says as he smacks my butt with his glove.

"I couldn't believe he went for second," I say.

"He got greedy," Josh says. "We've got them on the ropes and they're getting desperate."

"The score is still close," Coach says. "Keep it up! Keep it up!" He looks at Brian. "How are you feeling, Applequist?"

"Good, Coach," Brian says with confidence. "My arm feels great."

"Alright," Coach says. "Keep it warm." He pats Brian's arm and heads back to his spot on the other end of the dugout.

I sit next to Brian since we're at the bottom of the order and I likely won't hit until the next inning. "You're making a great showing," I say as I toss sunflower seeds into my mouth.

Brian grabs the bag of seeds, then does the same. "You, too, man. That scout has to like what he's seeing."

"Yeah, but I want to show him my power, knock one out of the park."

Brian nods. "Then do it." He smiles at me with challenge in his eyes.

I accept the challenge. "Alright, I will." I grin back at him and while I watch Josh walk up to the plate, I do what I've read that Michael Jordan does, visualize myself hitting a home run. I close my eyes and see myself squaring up. I focus on the ball watching it as if it's in slow-motion. I kick my front leg up as it approaches and swing. I feel the hit reverberate through my hands and wrists and see the ball fly high and fast, over the centerfield wall. I see myself rounding the bases and pumping my fist in the air as I round third and head home to cross the plate.

As it turns out, I don't get to bat until the sixth inning and this is my last chance to show my power since it would take a total breakdown of the game for my number to come up again in the order. Robbie popped out and Andre is up to bat. As he stands in the batter's box, I put rosin on my bat, then take some swings to loosen up. I look up in the stands and I see Sloane chatting with Billy. She's back and it makes my heart flutter. She hasn't been to a game in a while and I can't stop the grin that forms on my face.

I turn back to the field and adjust my batting gloves, then focus back on my swing. I go through my visualization exercise again as Andre gets another ball. He's a patient hitter and I love being behind him in the order. I feed off his energy. I'd be surprised if he doesn't go pro. The ding of the ball hitting Andre's bat brings my focus back to the field. Our fans cheer as Andre gets a single. I walk to the batter's box and dig my cleats into the red dirt. "Come on, Tyler!" I hear from the stands.

I adjust my stance so it feels just right and tap my bat on the plate. I bring my bat up to my shoulder and it wiggles as I anticipate the first pitch. I see the ball, just as I did in my exercise, but it drops low so I lay off it. Ball one. As the pitcher watches his catcher's signals, I adjust my stance, tap home plate, then bring my bat up in anticipation of the next pitch. The pitcher winds up and I focus on the ball. I see it clearly and it's heading right down the middle. Just as I start to swing, it curves to the outside, but I'm able to make contact, fouling it off behind me. I turn and watch as the ball arcs high, then lands on the grassy hill beside the bleachers.

The crowd cheers me on as I square up for the next pitch. The pitcher shakes his head twice, then nods once. My bat wiggles by my shoulder. The pitcher winds up and I focus on the ball. It's dead center again, a little lower than last time, right where I like it. I swing and hear the ping, but don't feel a thing in my hands or wrists. I watch as the ball arcs high over the field and drop my bat, running to first. Andre is already on the way to third and is being waved home. As I round first, the centerfielder has run out of room and hits the chain link fence. I watch as my ball sails through the air and out of the park. The crowd goes wild, because let's face it, everyone loves a homer, and I pump my fist as my foot hits second base. I jog to third and look into the stands. Our crowd is on their feet and I spot Billy and Sloane cheering causing my smile to grow wider. When I hit home, Andre gives me five, so does Travis who's up next.

"Nice job, Finlay!" Coach smacks my backside as I enter the dugout.

I can't help my smile. "Thanks, Coach." I head to the end of the dugout and sit next to Brian.

"Well done, my man." Brian gives me five as I sit next to him and take off my batting gloves. Andre has grabbed himself a water and hands one to me, too. "Thanks," I tell him. "And, thanks for the RBI, too."

"Any time, bro. Thanks for bringing me home." He messes my hair up with his hand then sits next to me. "I think we've made a good show for that scout."

"I agree." I down the water, crumple up the paper cup and toss it on the ground. "Wouldn't it be cool if we all made it into the league?"

"Oh, man, that would be amazing," Andre says.

As I gaze out onto the bright green field, I visualize myself playing in the big leagues. The field is so much larger, the stands huge, the crowds massive. There are so many ways to get there and I'm determined to do it. I can't imagine doing anything else.

***

Brian stays in for the top of the seventh and is working on what we hope is his last batter. The count is two balls, one strike, two outs with a runner at first. Brian winds up and delivers a pitch on the outside of the plate. Their batter swings and makes contact. The ball flies toward right field and Andre uses his speed to run to the ball that wasn't hit deep. Andre dives for the ball and makes the catch. We win our last game of the season!

"Woo!" I scream as I run toward Andre. He's on his feet now and gives me a huge hug then starts running toward the pitcher's mound. The rest of us follow Andre and in no time, we're a mass of bodies surrounding Brian. We celebrate for a moment, then head to the dugout where our coaches congratulate us.

"Great game, guys," Coach K says. "Every single one of you did your jobs today. I'm so proud of you. I know our seniors are proud, too."

He looks at Brian. "Incredible job, Applequist. A complete game and shutout, you did good."

"Thanks, Coach," Brian says with pride in his eyes.

"I know we didn't make it to the playoffs this year," Coach continues, "but we've had a great season and this team is still young. All of you have improved this year and you've supported each other unlike any other team I've coached. Our seniors are all going to great programs, and we have built a really strong foundation for next year. Enjoy this win and we'll celebrate at our banquet on Saturday."

We start gathering our gear. "Man, you pitched so well today," I tell Brian.

"Thanks. That homer of yours was pretty sweet, too." Brian says with a grin. "I knew you could do it."

We walk out onto the field and make our way to the stands where people are still milling around. Coach is talking to a man with salt and pepper hair, wearing a navy polo shirt. "Think that's the scout?" Brian asks.

I nod. "Probably." My stomach turns with nerves.

"Great game, Finlay!"

I look up into the stands and see Billy grinning at me. Sloane is standing next to him. She holds up a thumb and excitement is written all over her pretty face. I can't contain my smile and wave at them.

"Finlay, Applequist," Coach calls from our left. I look and Andre is with Coach and the man in the navy polo.

Brian and I walk over to Coach. "Tyler, Brian, meet Mister Hazelton. He's a scout for Atlanta."

"Call me Dwight," the man says as he shakes my hand, then Brian's. He looks younger up close. "Nice game today." He looks at Brian. "You've got quite an arm. How's it feeling?"

"Great, sir," Brian says. "Thank you."

Dwight turns to me. "I enjoyed watching you hit, Finlay. You're patient and powerful."

"Thank you, sir. Coach and I worked on my swing this year."

"Whatever you're doing, keep it up," Dwight says.

We talk to Coach and Dwight for a bit before the scout says his goodbyes. I think about what might happen next, with baseball and with the one thing I'd like to do but am not sure I have the confidence to do.

Chapter 64

Sloane

"I can't believe we're actually willingly going to hang out with kids from our school now that we're outta there." I say to Maggie as I open the passenger door on her brother's 1985 Mustang and take a seat next to her. "We graduated today. We don't need to hang out with these people anymore!" I joke.

Maggie smiles at me. "I know, but it's tradition." She pulls out of my driveway, and we head off to a park on the outskirts of town where graduating seniors from our school, and a couple of private schools celebrate the end of high school together.

"Did your brother tell you what we should expect at this party?" I ask Maggie as nerves fill my stomach.

"Nothing crazy," she tells me as she watches the road in front of us. "Mostly just drinking and hanging out. I think they invite some of the juniors and make them do stupid stuff, as like, a hazing ritual or something." She waves her hand like it's no big deal. "We're so good at being wallflowers, I'm sure no one will even know we're there."

I laugh at her. "The people-watching should be fun." I notice Maggie can't stop smiling. "What's up?" I ask her as we make our way the short distance to the park. "You look...so happy."

"Scott and I have kind of started dating," Maggie says about her "we're-just-friends-from-church" prom date.

"Oh my gosh, that's amazing!" I squeal. "When did this start?"

"We went out for coffee after prom and have been talking on the phone a lot." She looks at me sheepishly, then back at the road. "We went to dinner last Saturday night."

"What? Why didn't you tell me?" I'm so happy seeing her this happy.

"I wanted to make sure it was really happening, you know?" She glances at me again and bites her lip. "Also, I know you're still dealing with all the Ky stuff."

"Oh, please!" I wave her off. "Prom ended perfectly, and Ky...well, I'm over that. He acts like he still wants to be together, but I'm getting ready to go off to college. I still can't figure out if he was telling the truth about prom or not. Besides, just because I don't have someone in my life doesn't mean you can't tell me all about your new beau."

Maggie is full-on blushing now as she pulls into the dirt parking lot and parks between two cars. "Thanks, Sloane." She shifts the car into park, then gives me a hug. "Come on, let's go see what this senior party is all about."

"Wait," I grab her forearm. "Is Scott going to be here?"

Maggie nods, and I realize why she wanted to come here so badly. "Yeah," she admits, and my heart is so happy for her.

I'm more than happy to accompany Maggie, but a thought dawns on me, and I stop in my tracks. "Shoot, I'm going to be the third wheel."

"No you're not," Maggie says as she grabs my hand and pulls me forward. "Everyone will be here, including Beth and Annalise. We'll all hang out together!"

I trudge behind her and hope she's right. "See, this is why it would have been so cool to have a boyfriend who actually went to my school or lived in my area code for that matter." When we get to the clearing by the lake, there are people everywhere, and quite a few people are already making out around the lake. "How do people just do that right out in the open with everyone watching?" I ask Maggie.

"I have no idea," she says as she scans the area, presumably for Scott as I search for Beth and Annalise.

The sun has set, so it's hard to see faces. "Is that Beth?" I ask as I see the back of a girl who is seated and kissing a boy with light-colored hair.

Maggie looks, "I don't know..." the girl stands and turns so we can see the side of her face. "No. Wait, is that-?"

My eyes go wide, and my mouth involuntarily drops open. "Sara?" I'm dumbfounded. "That's totally not Tyler she's kissing."

Maggie shakes her head, and she looks as surprised as I am. "No, that's Adam Turner, I think."

"Ho-lee crap," is all I can say.

"I wonder what happened?" Maggie says, then turns to me, her eyes lighting up. "I guess Tyler Finlay is now fair game!"

"Oh no," I shake my head. "I'm not going to be a rebound girl. You know that's totally what that would be."

"Well," Maggie smiles, "then be his friend and see where things go."

"Mags! Sloane!" We turn to see Beth and Annalise jogging toward us.

"Can you believe we're finally done," Beth hollers and raises the plastic cup in her hand.

"It feels amazing, doesn't it?" I reply.

"And we're all off to Georgia in the Fall," Annalise says referring to the state school where I swear at least half our class will be attending and where I decided to attend as well even though I really can't tell you why.

Maggie smiles nervously. "I'm so glad y'all will be there. I'm going to be so homesick."

"Not me," I say. "I can't wait to get there. I'm excited to start fresh, you know? To go where no one has already labeled you like a library book and stuck you on a shelf where you don't want to be." I'm excited merely thinking about it. "I just hope we don't run into half of these people all the time."

"I know," Annalise agrees. "We won't though. There are going to be so many cool people in Athens!"

"I can't wait for all the awesome concerts. So many cool bands go through Athens," I tell my friends.

"Hey guys, I'll catch up with you in a few," Maggie says as her eyes finally land on Scott. She practically skips over to him, and my heart swells for her.

"Are they-?" Annalise asks as her jaw is now hanging open.

I smile and nod, "Yep! I just found out. She's so happy."

"That's awesome," Annalise says, and Beth nods in agreement. "Good for her!"

"Come, on," Beth says to us. "Let's go over to the keg."

Of course, the keg is where most kids are congregating, and I wait on the perimeter while Beth and Annalise get a refill. Even though Maggie is driving, this party could get busted, and I'd rather be sober.

"Sloaner!" I hear behind me.

I turn, smiling because I know I'm going to see my marine bio buddy with the flat-top and cowboy boots. "Hill-Billy!" I exclaim, giving him a hug. When I step back, I look at his shirt. "Okay, so who are you wearing tonight?"

Billy pulls at his shirt. "The one and only."

I squint at his shirt in the dark. "What does that say? George Street?"

Billy looks crestfallen. "Sloaner, are you serious? It's George Strait! The King of Country!"

I grin at him. "Of course!" I say but really have no clue, and we both know it. "It's just so dark," I joke.

"Hey, did you hear about Tyler and Sara?" Billy asks me with a conspiratorial tone.

I cock my head, narrow my eyes, and grin. "Hill-Billy, when did you become a gossip?"

Billy's naturally pink face turns red. "I guess because I've had a couple of these." He holds up his plastic cup.

"Well, since you asked," I say quietly. "We saw Sara kissing Adam Turner when we got here, and you could have knocked me over with a feather. But, I have no idea what happened. Do you?"

Billy leans in, and I can smell the beer on his breath. "Word on the street is that they've been on-again off-again since before spring break."

"What?" I can't believe this.

"Yeah, crazy, huh?" Billy asks. "Apparently they officially broke up a few weeks after Spring Break, but still went to prom together since everyone else basically had dates. I think they tried to go as friends, but when I saw them that night, they didn't look too friendly."

"Oh, man, that sucks." I feel bad for Tyler as I think about how heartbreaking that must have been. While I had the night of my life, he was probably pretty miserable. I think back to seeing him and Sara and they had looked like they were arguing.

"She wasn't the right girl for him anyway," Billy takes a long sip out of his plastic cup.

I cock my head and look at him through narrowed eyes. "Why not?"

A sheepish grin creeps up Billy's face. "Because she's not you."

I practically recoil with surprise, "Wh-what?" I laugh nervously.

Billy has a knowing look on his face. "I've sat and watched you two all year, Sloaner. You're perfect for each other."

Now you could knock me over with something lighter than a feather. I feel my cheeks get hot, and I try to laugh it off. "Billy, that's just crazy."

"No, it's not," I freeze as Tyler's voice says these words somewhere behind me.

I turn around and the beautiful boy with the grin that melts me is standing there, and the butterflies start to take flight. I turn back to Billy who smiles and bows at me as he spins his first two fingers in the air. "I bid you adieu," he says, and I'm glad he chose to make me laugh at a time like this because the butterflies are wreaking havoc inside my stomach now.

Chapter 65

Sloane

Billy leaves us, and I turn to Tyler, absolutely stunned. "Hey," I manage to say just above a whisper.

He smiles. I melt. "Hey." His eyes light up, and this warms my insides. I always think Tyler looks good and tonight is no exception. He's wearing jeans, a white T-shirt, and black Chuck Taylor sneakers and he takes my breath away. There is just something about a guy in a white T-shirt and jeans.

"Tyler!" I hear from behind me. I recognize the voice immediately and want to scream. I turn and see Amber walking toward us.

I guess it's because we've graduated and I don't care anymore, but I don't hold back. "Amber, now is not a good time." I almost don't recognize the stern tone coming out of my mouth. It sounds like I'm talking to a child. "I'm done with all your bullying."

A mix of surprise and concern washes over Amber's face and her eyes soften. "I'm so sorry. This will just take a minute."

"We really are in the middle of something," Tyler says firmly but way nicer than me.

"I wanted to talk to both of you," Amber's eyes are pleading as she searches our faces. "I want to apologize." She looks at me. "And thank you both for what you did for me on spring break."

I feel my eyes go wide and I look at Tyler whose mouth has dropped open, though I'm sure he's not nearly as shocked as I am. I'm stunned speechless.

Amber continues. "Thank you so much for getting me home that night." She looks down at her fidgeting hands, then back up at us. "And for not telling people that it was me."

Tyler and I share a glance. "Of course," I manage to say. "No one deserves that."

"It was Sloane who got you away from the guys and down the beach. I happened to walk by at the right time."

Amber's eyes grow wide, and, are those tears? Amber blinks back her tears as her wet eyes look at me with sincere regret. "Sloane, I am so sorry. After how mean I've been to you. I can't believe you would want to help me."

I feel my shoulders soften. "I wouldn't want to see that happen to anyone, Amber." I pause. "But, why have you given me such a hard time throughout high school? I've known you since first grade."

Amber bows her head and fidgets with her fingers some more. She looks at me and shrugs. "I guess I was intimidated by you."

I scoff. "What? Why?"

"I don't know. You're pretty, athletic, you always did so well at Field Day," she jokes and reminds me how competitive I was during Field Day. "And, you are just so nice to everyone. I guess, I just felt bad around you because...I'm not that nice."

To say that I'm in shock is an understatement. "Wow. Um, well, that's just how I am."

"I know, and I think I really envied that." Amber looks at me hopefully. "Will you accept my apology?"

I inhale a deep breath. "Of course, but Amber, you have to know how miserable you made me. Especially this year. That's not cool."

Amber nods solemnly. "I know. I truly am sorry...and grateful for you." She looks at Tyler. "Both of you."

Tyler smiles slightly. "Of course," he says softly. She looks between the two of us. "I'll, um, leave you alone now." She smiles sincerely. "Thanks again."

We watch Amber walk away, then I turn to Tyler. "Well, that was...pleasantly surprising."

Tyler huffs out a laugh. "Seriously." He turns to me. "That's cool she finally apologized."

"Yeah," I nod. "It's about time." This makes Tyler laugh for real. "I'm sorry to hear about you and Sara," I say sincerely.

Tyler looks at the ground and toes at the dirt with his sneaker. "Yeah, it probably should have happened sooner. Things weren't going that great for a while, and I think we both felt like we had to make it work, to do all those senior year milestones together, you know?"

I exhale a laugh. "Well, I don't really know, but, yes, I can understand." I look around at the people milling about around us.

Tyler notices. "Wanna go somewhere more private?"

I nod. Tyler reaches out his hand, and I take it. Oh my gosh, how can holding a hand spark so much energy inside of me? I can't believe I'm holding Tyler Finlay's hand!

Chapter 66

Sloane

Tyler guides me through the woods to a small creek. "There's a bench over here." He walks me over to a bench that has been cut out of a log and faces the creek.

"This is beautiful. I didn't even know this was here."

Tyler reaches into his back pocket and pulls something out. "Here," he hands me a small rectangular box, "I made you a mix tape."

I take the cassette tape and flip it over to read the song list, but all I see are blank lines. "Wait, you didn't list the songs?"

Tyler shakes his head and there's a glimmer in his eyes. "Nope, it's a surprise this way."

"I love surprises." I smile and see writing on the side. "Songs for Sloane." My smile grows and I look at Tyler's handsome face. "Thank you so much." I squeeze his hand.

"You're welcome." He sits down, and I follow. Tyler angles his body toward me. "I wish I had the guts that you have." He runs his free hand through his hair as I look at him with a puzzled expression. "I've liked you for a long time, but boy was my timing off."

I tilt my head and my eyes grow wide as I gaze up into those beautiful dark eyes, stunned at this information. "What do you mean?"

He releases my hand and rubs his palms on his jeans. I miss his touch instantly. "I really liked getting to know you in marine bio and when we were at that party at the beginning of the year, I was going to ask you if you had a date to the Snowball dance." He pauses. "Because I wanted to go with you."

I cannot believe it. My left hand goes to my chest and I let out a breath that relaxes my shoulders. "Is that what you were going to ask me when I ran into you in the hallway?" I smile at the memory of walking straight into his bare chest.

He nods, and his eyes widen with expectation. He looks so vulnerable; I can almost imagine him as a child. I'm speechless, so he continues. "After we were interrupted, I didn't see you again. Sara played beer pong with us, and we had a lot of fun. I wasn't sure if you were into me. I guess I just got mixed signals from you." He ducks his chin, then looks back at me, giving me a nervous smile. "If I had waited, would you have asked me?"

I can't believe it. I close my eyes as I nod my head over and over, then look back into those handsome eyes. "Yes," I smile. "Remember when I saw you before football practice?"

Tyler's shoulders visibly relax and he nods. "When your friend came screaming for you?" A slow smiles spreads across his face.

"Yeah," I tuck my hair behind my ear. "Kurt knew I was going to ask you. In fact, I was going to ask you in class but that was the missing tarantula day." Tyler's chin tilts up as he looks skyward, then nods. "And Coach K held you after class. I was determined to ask you that day and went to find you before football practice. I had no idea Sara had already asked you in between marine bio and the end of the school day. Kurt found out and saved me from embarrassment."

Tyler shakes his head as he looks at his lap. "Dang tarantula." He looks at me and his Sloane-melting grin appears. "That means you would have asked me before Sara did. I can't believe it." Another pause as his eyes search the sky. "If Kurt hadn't stopped you, I would have at least known you were interested."

"I never thought about that. I was just so glad I didn't embarrass myself." My pulse is beginning to race as I realize that Tyler has liked me all along. "And as for the mixed signals," I add, "I was so nervous around you and I'm generally awkward so..."

"Then Sara and I started dating—"

I add, "And then I met Ky at the concert—"

"Then you took Evan-freaking-Dando to prom," he says, smiling, then he rubs a hand on the back of his neck. "I thought for sure I didn't have a chance after that." He shifts on the bench and looks down at it. "I didn't think I would be cool enough for you, especially after you showed up to prom with Evan."

I laugh as I look down at my lap, then back at Tyler with a smile. "Evan is awesome and so kind and fun, but he's a rock star, and I'm a high school senior. He's living in a whole different world than I am." I pause. "I want to be with someone my age, who I have great conversations with, who loves good music...and who lives within an hour of me."

I swear I can see relief in his eyes now. "Man, it's crazy how one thing could have changed everything." He runs his hand through his hair again.

I think it all through, and he's right. "Just like how I never would have met Evan if I didn't have to stay home with my sister instead of going to his concert. With us, it all started with Amber and Lori in the hallway at Jesse's party," I say. "Dang, Amber made this year so hard for me," I quip, hoping to lighten the moment. "Even when I didn't realize it, she foiled things from the start." I smile softly at him.

"Stupid Amber." Tyler grins which of course, melts me. "You looked so cute in that Pantera shirt."

I feel myself blush and laugh. "Right," I say then look at him and his expression is serious. His eyes make me decide to continue being bold. "If you only knew how much I liked you...Since the first day of school when you dropped your flannel, then sat next to me in marine bio."

He grins again, and this time, it's a smile of pure happiness. "Is it too late to try?"

The butterflies are back and warmth spreads through me. "I want to say yes, but—" Am I really telling Tyler Finlay no? "We're both coming off of break ups and going to different colleges in a few months." Why is my brain being so rational right now? Tyler inhales sharply, and I reach for his hand, my body reacts with a flood of warmth. "I just don't want us to be each other's rebound, you know? Or make it harder once we go off to school." I can't believe I'm saying this to him because I want this so bad.

He dips his head, and I don't like it when his smile goes away. "For what it's worth, you wouldn't be my rebound...because I've liked you all along. I've thought a lot about it and, subconsciously, I think that's why things didn't work out with Sara and me."

I squeeze his hand. "For what it's worth, your smile still made me giddy when I was with Ky. And, he wasn't nearly as interesting to talk to as you are." There it is, the grin is back.

"Yes!" He pumps his fist with his free hand and makes me laugh. I'm glad for the levity.

We're quiet for a moment and I think about seizing the day and all that. I give his hand a squeeze. "You know what?" His eyes shine with hope. "We'd be stupid not to try." Oh my gosh, that grin is back in full force, and I must be seconds away from turning into a puddle and flowing into the creek.

"Really?"

I nod and now I'm smiling wide, too. "I don't want to be forty years old wondering what-if, you know?" He nods, then I add, "We just need to have a plan for college because I don't think I can take another long-distance relationship."

"What are you thinking?" he asks as he rubs his thumb on the back of my hand, sending shivers through my entire body.

I mull it over. "Well, if things go well this summer, and we go our separate ways..." I hate even thinking about it. "I don't want to worry about all the girls that are going to be hitting on you." I search his face and his eyes are serious. "I can't believe I'm even saying this, but we might have to take a break when we go off to school and just...see what happens."

He nods, "The whole, if you love something, set it free-thing?"

"Yeah, I think it's just better if we go into it that way. I mean it'll be hard either way because we know we're not going to the same school." I realize that Tyler will be in South Georgia, just like Ky, and try not to dwell on that fact.

"Yeah it will, because I'll have to think about all the guys throwing themselves at you. Not to mention all those cool musicians in Athens."

I laugh. "Yeah, right," I say as I look at my lap then back at Tyler.

His smile fades. "I mean it. It's going to be hard for both of us." His eyes grow serious, and it's like he can see into my soul. That connection I've felt since the first day of school is so strong, like there's a magnetic force pulling us together. I feel like the Millennium Falcon trapped in the Death Star's tractor beam. Except Tyler is the opposite of the Death Star. His face inches toward mine. "Can I kiss you?" he says softly.

My body is humming with energy, and I smile. "Yes, please. I've kinda been waiting for this moment all year." I giggle as he cups my cheek and leans into me. When Tyler Finlay's lips meet mine, it's like nothing I've ever felt before. Electricity zings through my body and makes me feel like I've entered another dimension. It's like I've just entered hyper speed. I no longer hear the sounds of the forest; the tree frogs, the crickets, or the babbling stream. It's as if all my senses have dulled while my sense of touch is heightened. Tyler kisses me softly at first and in unison, our kiss becomes more urgent, filled with passion and longing. We're both breathless as we pull away from each other and neither of us can help the smiles on our faces.

"Dang," Tyler says with that grin and his eyes sparkle.

"That was a pretty good start, huh?" I feel myself blush and make that grin of his grow which makes me happy.

Tyler leans toward me and rests his forehead against mine. "This is going to be a great summer." His grin turns devilish and makes me squirm.

I wrap my hand around the back of his neck and kiss him some more.

The End

Evan + Megan
DHS Prom - 1993

Author's Note

Thank you so much for reading Nice Girls Finish First! I so appreciate your interest in this book and my story and hope you loved it. If you did, I would be so grateful for your review on Amazon or Goodreads! Reader reviews are the biggest compliment authors can receive and it will help other readers find stories they'll enjoy. Plus, it helps get this book in front of others giving it all that SEO juice and algorithm love. ;)

If you'd like to read an excerpt from Sloane and Tyler's summer, go to MeganWargula.com to sign up for my mailing list. I promise I won't inundate you with emails. Plus, I'll share never before seen pics my mom took at prom along with articles from some of the music trade magazine that wrote about our prom story.

If you're like me, whenever you read something based on a true story, you probably wonder how much is truth and how much is fiction. The story of meeting Evan Dando and then taking him to my prom is all true! Of course, I don't remember every detail of every conversation, but I wrote those chapters and scenes to my best recollection and with the help of a journal I kept. Thank goodness I journaled about that experience and saved the pages!

I wrote Sloane as myself (mostly) and I was very shy and quiet, uncomfortable in my own skin a lot of the time. I am also thin and six-feet tall and was never asked to a dance at my school. Ever. I did meet a boy from South Georgia at a Dinosaur Jr. concert, and we did date long distance.

I asked him to go to my prom with me and yes, he did indeed back out ten days before prom. I was crushed and heartbroken. My friend came home from college to go to The Lemonheads concert on the day of my prom and everything leading up to prom is as it happened. I wrote all that down so I wouldn't forget it and it's a great testament to journaling. There are a lot of details I would have forgotten or gotten wrong if I hadn't kept a journal.

What's so cool about this story is how many things had to happen to get me to asking Evan to my prom. If my sister hadn't pitched a fit and my parents had let me go to The Lemonheads show when they went out of town, I wouldn't have gone to Evan's hotel with my friends and this story wouldn't have been written. Life is crazy that way and I don't believe in coincidences. The night my long-distance boyfriend backed out of going to prom with me, my dad told me, "When God closes a door, He opens a window." You can imagine that my seventeen-year-old self couldn't see the silver lining, but boy, did I see it later! God's hand is everywhere in this story, even getting me to write it into this book!

Several music trade magazines ran the story of the prom, and I did get that call from Sassy Magazine. Sassy was the "cool girls" magazine using more realistic models and writing articles with more substance than typical teen magazines. They were also huge fans of Evan!

As for the fiction...I was not bullied, thank God, but a popular cheerleader did spread a rumor that the only reason Evan took me to my prom was because I slept with him. It made me so mad because while she may or may not have been that type of girl, I certainly was not. I did get to say something indirectly to her in class, but I was nowhere near as bold and direct as Sloane was. I had to give Sloane the confidence that I wish I had back then. The spring break incident with Amber is total fiction and the real-life Amber never apologized for the rumor, but in the story, I wanted Amber to have redemption.

I'm sure you are wondering about beautiful Tyler. There was a boy that I had a massive crush on, and he did sit next to me in class. He was tall and handsome and played football, just like Tyler. We bonded over music after he wore a Smashing Pumpkins shirt to class one day, but he ended up dating a really sweet girl who I am still in touch with to this day. Like Sloane, I was so glad he picked a nice girl who wasn't popular. That was uncharacteristic of most football players, and I liked that about him. He seemed to walk to the beat of his own drum, and I wanted to give Tyler that quality, too. Incidentally, I married a man a lot like Tyler – a football player who had a mohawk, great taste in music (he saw Nirvana before they blew up), and wasn't into cliques. I didn't know him back then, but I think he and the real Tyler would have gotten along great.

When I started writing this book, I was excited to write about my amazing prom story, but what I didn't realize was how much I would learn about myself through this process. I looked back at seventeen-year-old me and was so sad for her because she was scared of most everything. If you are a teen yourself, or an adult for that matter, please don't let fear hold you back. Take chances and be bold, because failure is a great way to learn and following your heart is key to your happiness. I'm still reminding myself of that to this day!

I'd love to hear from you, so be sure to sign up for my mailing list and if you have questions about what else in the book was fact or fiction, please reach out!

Acknowledgments

God, thank you for opening that window and putting it on my heart to share this story with the world. Of course, this story would not have been possible if not for the kind, sweet, and talented Evan Dando. The prom story is our story, and I am so grateful that you gave me your blessing not only to write it, but to use your name and The Lemonheads name. I don't think you will ever know how impactful your kindness was to me and the confidence it gave me. I tell people all the time that it's the nicest thing anyone outside my family has ever done for me, and I mean it. You made me feel seen after a lifetime of feeling invisible, and you were such a gentleman. Thank you forever.

To my husband, Michael, for listening to me read the story aloud to make sure it flowed and for making sure all my football and baseball references were accurate. Your support of me and my dreams is the best gift in the world. Mom and Dad, thank you for your steadfast support in all I do, and for going out of town and telling me I couldn't go to that concert! Courtney, thank you for pitching a fit and for being totally cool in that hotel room. ;) Joy and Catherine, thank you for always being the very first to read my books, give your input, and find my typos and mistakes. I appreciate it more than you know! Christine, Natalie, Ramsey, and Natalie G. (yes, there are two!), thank you for reading my first final draft, giving your feedback, and helping me make this story even better. Antonia, thank you for your support, kindness, and for passing along all my messages! :) Sharon, thank you for telling me to pick up that copy of It's a *Shame About Ray* in Turtles, or was it Tower Records? And, thank you for introducing me to a lot of great bands. I'm forever grateful for that and your friendship. Bobbette, thank you for being my sidekick way back when and going to all those great shows with me! Ray, thank you for your encouragement when I told you I was going to write this story, it meant so much. David, thank you for explaining to me how baseball recruiting and college offers go. This helped as I formulated my plan for the next books in the series. Tod, thank you for helping me get Evan to my prom and your friendship! Barnes and Leslie, thank you for your interest in this story and for having me on the Morning X. A huge thank you to 99X! When you flipped to alternative, you set me on a path of music discovery that I still cherish to this day. Music went from, really, no part of my life, to a huge part of it and I am so grateful for that. You pioneered alternative radio and not only made a big impact on bands, but on listeners. I'm glad you're back!

Dansby and Strider, thank you for bringing us joy every single day and for healing our hearts. Now, if you would just learn not to bark at everything outside, you could be sitting with me while I write this!

Finally, to my readers, you make me feel like my work matters. Thank you! You keep me writing and make me smile every time I sell a book, read a review, see a recommendation, or read a comment on a post. You are the ink to my pen. Every. Single. One of You. I am truly honored that you took the chance on this story and spent your hard-earned money on it. From the bottom of my heart, thank you so much!

About the Author

Megan Wargula is a native of Atlanta, Georgia and is passionate about kindness, dogs, music, and making the world a better place. From an early age, *The Golden Rule,* "Do unto others as you would have them do unto you," was instilled in her and is a guiding principle not only in her books, but in her life.

After writing the Riley Carson Series, middle-grade mysteries with an animal welfare twist, Megan decided it was time to incorporate the true story of Evan Dando from The Lemonheads taking her to her prom into a sweet young adult romance. It's such a great story, it had to be told! Everyone says it is straight out of a movie, so hopefully you'll see Nice Girls Finish First on the big screen someday.

In addition to writing novels, Megan loves hiking with her husband, Michael, and their dogs, designing gifts for dog lovers through her business, Hound and Thistle, and co-hosting a podcast with Michael called Dog Nerd Show. Megan and Michael are currently documenting their home build in the North Georgia Mountains at Thistledown Home.